THE AWAKENING

THE WITCH HUNTER SAGA - BOOK FOUR

NICOLE R. TAYLOR

PROLOGUE

Coraline expected the air to smell of death, as a witch was able to sense these things, but it radiated with earthy grass and rain.

She pulled her coat closed and shivered. It wasn't particularly cold, but the air was unsteady and full of mist. Maximus stood beside her, the warmth of his body comforting. Taking her hand, he squeezed.

Why Max still moonlighted as a priest—considering the things he'd seen—was beyond her. His hold over his faith was admirable, as was his devotion to her, considering she was a witch. A few hundred years ago, his brothers would've burned her alive.

They stood by their rental car, looking across the field at their destination, trying to decide the best course of action. Ireland really was a spectacular country, but Coraline couldn't focus on that. Bigger things required her attention.

Brú na Bóinne was a tomb. It was protected by

Ireland's National Trust and closed to visitors—as if that would stop them. Coraline couldn't make them invisible to anyone watching, but she could render them negligible.

On the outside it looked like a large, unnatural hill, but underneath lay a warren of tunnels and chambers. It really was an impressive sight; the ancient structure built by people long dead. Did they know what was hidden below? What about the people who studied it now? Of course, they didn't. The place crawled with power—concealments, traps, wards—and now that she focused on the tomb, the air seemed to crackle with them.

The grey sky and heavy air didn't do much to cheer Coraline up, knowing what they could possibly face inside. If it wasn't the original witch, then who was it? The vampire Zac had told them the last Roman founder, Regulus, had hinted it was something else. The thought of the unknown scared her.

"Come on, Corrie," Maximus said. "The sooner we're in, the sooner we're out."

"I know."

"Think about the nice hot meal we'll have tonight when we find nothing inside."

"Max..." she began, but he pulled her across the road and into the field. Dropping the spell over them, she had no choice but to follow. He was right, after all.

There was no one around this time of morning. They were up even before the birds. As they approached the entrance, the air electrified with the tang of power.

"Do you feel that?" she asked Maximus, knowing he couldn't as he was human.

"It feels strange here," he said, surprising her. "Like a creepy old house that's full of ghosts."

He wasn't far off. Archaeologists would've removed many of the bones within, but their energy would remain. Perhaps that was what he was picking up on.

Breaking the lock on the modern door at the entrance was easy. Maximus pushed it open and shone a torch into the blackness within, revealing a narrow tunnel burrowing into the artificial hill. Every so often an opening presented itself—a round hole of black against the white light of the torch.

Reluctantly, Coraline followed him.

"Where do we look?" he asked in a whisper.

"Below," she replied. "Alisandra's grimoire spoke of tunnels beneath the surface." She didn't know why she spoke of it as Alisandra's grimoire still. The Hunter, Aeriaya, had torn the matriarch to pieces, and the book was now in the hybrid's possession.

All Coraline had to do to find the entrance to the sub-terrain was follow the wards. They had a strange tang to them, almost metallic. Definitely not cast by a normal witch or even one of the Coven. Perhaps it was pure Celestine magic?

Soon, hidden at the rear, she found the entrance inside a small chamber. It was nothing more than a narrow opening with a staircase that led down. It was set in plain sight, but anyone without a sense of power could only see a blank wall.

"Here," she said, leading Maximus by the hand.

He was used to it by now, so he didn't flinch when he passed through the ward. Walking through solid walls was a normal everyday occurrence when she was around.

As they wound their way farther and farther underground, the air became frosty as they passed through layers of clay and bedrock. When they finally reached the bottom, it wasn't exactly what they were expecting.

"What the..." Max breathed.

The tunnel opened out into a small chamber, lined with smooth rock, like someone had melted it into shape. Two tunnels opened on either side and they looked to be just the same.

Coraline heaved in a breath, her lungs filling with stale, earthy air. "Tuatha."

"Who?"

"You know the old stories of Ireland, Max," she explained, keeping her voice low. "The Tuatha de Danann were a race of Fae—creatures of power like the Celestines. They built this place."

"What do they have to do with the original witch?"

She looked at him pointedly. "*Everything.*"

The question of which tunnel they should take, left or right, was abruptly answered for them when

Coraline felt a dull boom shift the air. Her gaze snapped to the left as a sick feeling of dread sunk in her stomach.

"Corrie?"

"You felt that?" she asked, not taking her eyes off the dark opening.

"Yeah."

"C'mon," she said, swallowing her fear and walked headfirst into the darkness.

After a short while, the tunnel emerged into a natural cavern. Stalactites hung from the ceiling and reflected off the rock walls in all directions, the slow drip of water the only sound that echoed back to them. As her gaze raked over the floor, she put a hand up to stop Max behind her.

A man stood at the opposite end of the cavern.

His back was to them, but she could see he was dressed in strange clothing. Not modern at all, his shirt looked handwoven and dyed in a myriad of blues. He was tall, lean, muscled, and stood so still, it was as if he was made of marble. Coraline would've thought he was elegant and magical... if it wasn't for the dead body he was standing over.

It could only mean one thing...

Coraline didn't have to see his face to understand what he was.

Hybrid.

They'd failed and the Coven had won. The ritual had completed after all.

She placed a finger over her lips and Max nodded. Somehow, she knew the man had already sensed their arrival. Her heart thumped a million miles an hour and her spell couldn't cover that. Besides, the hybrid stood so still because he was listening to them.

She took a slow step back towards the tunnel and, as if to confirm her fear, the man's head snapped up. Their only option now was to run.

Max pushed her in front of him and they ran headlong down the tunnel, back towards the staircase. If they could get back through the wards, maybe it would be enough to slow him down. They were there to keep him in, they had to be.

Max screamed and Coraline skidded to a halt. She turned, the torch lighting up the tunnel behind her. The hybrid had him on the ground, mauling his neck like a rabid animal.

"*Run*," Max gurgled through a mouthful of blood and she dropped the torch in horror.

She stumbled forwards blindly, too terrified to call on her power for light, the horrible growling of the hybrid echoing after her. Deep down, Coraline knew she wouldn't get out. Deep down, she knew this was the end.

She had enough time to type a text and send it to Zac before she felt the vampire behind her. Whirling around, she called on her power, her hand coming to rest on the hybrid's heaving chest, but nothing happened.

His manic laughter bounced around the cave and she felt his hands around her throat. With her last shred of strength, she cast a light over the room, revealing his face. As he bared his fangs and went to sink them into her jugular, she sent an image to the one person she was able.

CHAPTER 1

Awakening.

It felt like he'd been asleep for longer than he should have. His limbs felt heavy, as if they'd lost all feeling and when he tried to move, nothing happened. All he felt was the rage that'd been his last waking memory before the blackness.

Unconsciousness. It was such a strange word to describe this kind of slumber. He knew it wasn't natural and it made him burn with anger. He could scarcely remember why, though it'd felt like he'd just closed his eyes moments ago.

The biting metallic taste of magic burned in the back of his throat and somehow, he knew Isolde had something to do with this. Isolde, his stepmother Aoife's witch, had turned his sisters into monsters and saved him for last.

With a cry of twisted anguish, he sat bolt upright, his eyes opening for the first time. Everything seemed more defined. The strange blue of the rock that surrounded him sparkled with sunlight from a shaft in the ceiling that climbed upwards to the surface. Nature had reclaimed this place and he knew his father would never have allowed it. That could only mean one thing...

Gasping for breath, he covered his watering eyes. His heart thumped a thousand beats a minute. On beat, off beat, double beat...

"My lord?"

His head rose at the sound of a female voice. A pretty young thing stood beside what could only be described as his tomb. She was all ivory skin and flaming red hair, and he knew she was one of them— one of the humans who'd lived in this land before his people came—though she was dressed in strange clothing he'd never seen before.

"My lord?" she asked again.

It was then he realised it was not only his heartbeat he was hearing, it was also hers. Once he'd fixated on the sound, he couldn't hear anything else. He saw the vein in her exposed neck pulse and he suddenly felt hollow inside. Remembering the first taste of blood, he understood what'd happened to him.

He shot across the room faster than he thought possible, feeling as stiff and sore as he was. The woman let out a gasp as he pushed her against the wall, pressing her tiny body into the rock. His pale fingers bit into the skin of her neck, searching for the vein, and she cried out in pain.

"How long?" he asked, barely recognising his voice.

"Three thousand years."

He dropped her, drawing a sharp breath as her words sunk in. Had it truly been three thousand years? That bitch Aoife had trapped him in a tomb for *three thousand years?*

"What of this world?"

"The world has changed in a million different ways."

"Show me." He grabbed her again, this time sinking his fangs into her skin. The blood would show him what he needed... and if she was telling the truth.

She let out a surprised gasp as her flesh tore, but she didn't struggle. Warm blood filled his mouth and he swallowed, strength returning to his frozen body.

He was inundated with strange words and sounds... and he understood them all, just as the woman did. The world had changed, magic had declined, and creatures that once walked proudly now slunk in the shadows of the underworld.

He was a prince of the Tuatha de Danann—vampire, a Fae, a creature of power, and he could read her blood like a book. The human world dominated, and it was the ultimate insult. They'd changed the world with their buildings, technology... and carved it open with *war*. They were a blight on a land that was once rife with all kinds of life. Humanity... how it reeked with hatred.

He drank the woman's blood until there was no more, her heartbeat slowing until it stopped, and he let her lifeless body drop to the floor.

What was he to do now? Aoife was long dead and with her, any chance of revenge. It was the Celestine who'd betrayed his family, and if there was even a single Celestine left alive, he would find them.

If what the blood had shown him was true, then his kind were gone. Dead. Extinct. He wasn't one of them anymore; he was something else. He smiled thinking about the word he'd gleaned from the woman's blood.

Vampire. What a strange name.

Then he heard a sound echo from the tunnel adjoining his tomb and he cast out his hearing. After Isolde had changed him, he hadn't had time to adjust to the thing that she'd made him into. He remembered his vision had been clearer, every sound sharper, and every emotion that'd coursed through him was ten times more potent. Food did nothing for him anymore, only blood. *Blood.* The sweetest thing he'd ever tasted.

Focusing on his surrounds, he realised he wasn't alone. Someone else was coming. A witch who carried the scent of Isolde, and a human man.

He stood, listening, and felt their gazes on him, the intensity suggesting they thought he was a beast from the underworld. Perhaps he was. All he wanted was to feed. If he was to venture to the surface of the new world, he would need his strength and all the information he could.

The thrumming of their heartbeats assaulted his ears and it only told him one thing. They were afraid. *So, they should be.*

Then they were running. He laughed at the pointlessness of it all and walked across the cavern.

Darting forwards, he was on the man before he could blink twice, dragging him down to the ground and sinking his fangs into flesh. The man screamed as pain took him, but he wasn't listening. As blood ran down his throat, he was inundated with the most curious images.

"*Run*," the man gurgled and the witch, turned and fled down the tunnel.

No heartbeat came from beneath him so he followed the woman witch, wondering what her blood had to say. Grasping her arm, he turned her to face him, saw the terror in her eyes, and felt nothing. His fangs ached to taste more, so he ripped into the vein in her neck, a hand over her mouth to stifle her annoying screams. Screaming seemed to be a common denominator and he was already annoyed.

As the witch's body slackened, he let the visions come and what he saw surprised him—witches, vampires, a powerful coven descended from Isolde... She'd lived? The bitch who made him had lived while he was trapped down here?

He dropped the witch's body and held his aching

head in his hands. What had he done to deserve this? He'd done nothing but be his father's son. He'd been used along with his sisters. His sisters... If they were trapped like he'd been, he would find them and bring them back, and together, they'd build a new kingdom. The Tuatha would rise again, this time more powerful than before. This time they were immortal.

His eyes focused again, the pain from the visions subsiding, and he focused on his surroundings.

The witch was mutilated beyond recognition. Had he done that? He supposed he had.

There was a curious object lying in a pool of blood and he knelt to peer at it. Picking up the rectangular slab of metal and plastic he now knew was called a smartphone, he turned it over and looked at the glowing screen. *Curious.* It made a shrill ringing sound and he squashed it in his hand, shattering it into pieces.

There was one vision that'd stuck with him from both the man and the witch. A strange woman with blue eyes and raven hair that the blood told him was a hybrid, like himself. A Celestine hybrid. How strange that she would look like she did.

Aoife had been silver-haired and blue-eyed. Her skin had shimmered like a pearl from the ocean, a rare beauty, but this Celestine had been quite the opposite. Her hair was black as the night sky the stars hung from, not the silver glow a star would radiate. She had the same ice-blue eyes as Aoife, the same eyes that hid the secrets of the universe.

He was full of blood and a hunger for revenge he couldn't fathom. If this Celestine hybrid was still alive, he would find her.

He would find her and make her pay.

The sun was low in the sky when he finally decided he should go outside. The wards around the Tuatha's tunnels were annoying but didn't stop him from entering the human tomb above and following the scent of sun-warmed grass to the surface.

Emerging into the light for the first time in three thousand years, his eyes stung and he held an arm across his face. The grounds were silent, save for the wind rustling through the grass.

The air was crisp, despite the patchy sun, and he assumed it was winter, or close to it. He knew from the blood he'd ingested from the vampire woman and the witch that sunlight was lethal to vampires, but it didn't seem to bother him in the slightest.

Scanning the countryside, he saw the road and the car where the witch and the human priest had left it. In an instant it seemed he'd crossed the field and was standing by the machine, and he marvelled at his strength and speed. He'd been changed less than a day before Aoife had sealed him away and it was like he'd just been born.

There was nothing of use in the car and he didn't enjoy the thought of trying to master its operation, so he walked down the strange black tar road in search of civilisation. It wasn't long before he heard the rumble of a live vehicle approach from behind and it passed him by in a gust of cool air. It was a different shape and colour, and red lights appeared on the rear.

The vehicle slowed before stopping a short distance ahead and a young human male emerged. He looked down at himself and realised his clothing was nothing more than rags, eroded away by time, and he was covered in blood that'd begun to dry and flake. Not exactly attire fit for a Fae prince, especially not for the only son of Lir.

"Hey," the man exclaimed, jogging down the road towards him. "Are you okay? Do you need some help?"

He looked the man up and down and decided he was a suitable match. Same height, similar build. Grasping the front of the human's shirt, he pulled him close and snarled, "Give me your clothes."

The man's expression slackened into a vacant stare and he began to strip. Curious. He didn't know he could make the humans do things. That was an unexpected boon. It reminded him of Isolde and her ability to control people's minds. They'd had the same reaction to her power, though he suspected she had to cast some kind of spell. He'd just willed it, and so it was.

Gathering up the man's clothes, he walked away down the road, but as an afterthought turned back. "Now, forget you ever saw me."

The human nodded and while the going was good, he disappeared into the field, leaving the man to wonder why he was naked on the side of the road. Perhaps he should've killed him, but it seemed more amusing this way.

The sounds of a fast-flowing river reached him long before he found the source. Stripping his ancient shirt and trousers off, he waded into the water and ducked his head under, washing the dirt and blood away with a handful of gravel from the bottom. He scrubbed until his pale, dead skin was pink.

As the carnage he'd wrought underground washed away, swirling in the whirlpool of the swift current, he wondered how he was going to get to Briton. Boat or one of those airplane machines. Taking one of those ferries from the city called Dublin seemed the less likely to cause him annoyance. The humans were so suspicious of one another that they needed pieces of paper with their photographs to go anywhere.

Letting his fingers trail in the icy water, he thought about his family. What had happened to his sisters? Fionnuala and the twins, Fiachra and Conn... He had no idea where they might be hidden or if they were still alive. They hadn't deserved their fate, none of them did.

And what of his father Lir? His wrath would've been extraordinary when he realised what Aoife had done. He hoped his father had killed her and made a spectacle out of it.

Wading out of the river, he tossed his filthy rags away, watching them float downstream while he dressed in the modern clothing he'd stolen. The material felt strange against his skin, coarse and heavy, and he wondered how he would get something a little more refined. Perhaps he'd find out when he reached Dublin.

He was going to have a lot of fun in this new world and he wished Siobhan was here to share it with him. But his love was long dead and yet another he wanted to avenge. He never got to say goodbye to her, but in hindsight, he never got to say it to anyone at all.

Making his way back across the field to the road, he followed the directions he'd gleaned from the witch's blood and began his journey. Revenge was best served with a healthy dose of planning.

CHAPTER 2

I t all started with an image of death.

Blood, screaming... and eyes. Red eyes.

Gabby sat up sharply, gasping for breath, trying to shake off the disorientation from her dream. Her skin was clammy and sweat trickled down her face as she clutched the covers around herself. The dream had seemed so real, almost like a vision.

It took a while before she realised where she was and even then, her heart still raced.

The door slipped open a crack, letting in light from the hallway and with it, the biggest pain in the ass she'd ever had the pleasure of meeting.

"Gabrielle?"

Clutching her head, she'd hoped he'd leave her alone, but he'd heard her heartbeat and she'd probably called out in her sleep. He could hear everything.

"I'm fine, Regulus."

He inched the door open, his bulky frame blocking most of the light. "Your heart says otherwise."

She'd rather be a million miles away from this place right now. After Regulus had manipulated her into faking his death, she thought that might be the end of it. Aya had destroyed the Coven and any chance of them awakening whoever it was they were trying to find.

The Coven were insane, corrupted witches descended from the original witch, who was created with Celestine blood. Coraline had been one of them, but she'd been willing enough to help in their cause. She'd given Zac her power so he could kill Regulus, but it was all a ruse.

Zac, Aya, and their friends Nye and Tristan, all thought the Roman was gone for good. When they found out the truth, shit would hit the fan. Regulus was mortal enemy number one.

After she'd resurrected the founder, he'd brought her to a house on the outskirts of London. A safe place, he'd called it, but safe from what?

"I'm fine," she said again. "It was just a vivid dream."

"Vivid dreams are usually precursors to something else," the vampire told her. "Have you heard from the witch?"

She shook her head in the darkness, knowing full well he could see the gesture.

"Perhaps you should try to recall the dream.

They've had more than enough time to figure out if the Coven's spell had succeeded."

"You seem to know who it is," she said. "Why won't you tell me?"

"Because it's pointless unless the spell worked."

Regulus would tell her nothing. That ass with his schemes and threats had manipulated her into being a part of the biggest ruse of all—and she'd received nothing but silence in return. He'd made sure Gabby had no cards to play and delighted in reminding her.

"What was the dream about?"

He sat on the edge of the bed and she was overly conscious she was wearing nothing but a tank top and shorts. He was wearing little else and she looked him over. She was so used to seeing him dressed in crisp business shirts and slacks, not form fitting T-shirts and boxers.

"Gabrielle?"

"Eyes," she whispered, looking away.

"Eyes?"

"Red eyes and blood."

He frowned, his gaze wandering over her. "I know you don't want to remember it," he said, his fingertips grazing over her hands, "but it might have been a message from the witch."

She pulled her hands back, his gentle gesture making her uncomfortable. Nodding, she rested her forehead against her knees and closed her eyes, trying her best to focus with Regulus so close.

He really was handsome in an asshole-ish way. Ever since she'd resurrected him, he'd been—*no*. She hated him for what he'd done to her and her friends.

Letting go, she felt her mind slip back into the dream, recalling each scene. It came back in startling clarity and she realised that Regulus had been right. It was a vision.

Coraline and Max were together in a strange blue tunnel. She felt the witch's panic and desperation as if she was living inside her skin. They were being pursued by something... No, it was *someone*. They were running, her heart pounding and skin prickling. Max's horrified screams ripped through her and she stopped, spinning on her heel.

"*Max*," she screamed. A man was bent over him, ripping into the flesh of her love like a rabid animal.

"Run," he gurgled through a mouthful of blood and she realised he was beyond saving. She had to warn them.

Spinning on her heel, she kept running down the tunnel, back towards the wards, but icy hands—cold, like death—grasped her arms. Red eyes stared down at her; a face covered in blood. A monster had her in his grasp. A monster from the Hell of Max's religion. This overwhelming feeling of defeat washed over her as she called on her power one last time. Then nothing but white-hot pain.

"Gabrielle?" Regulus' strange eyes came into focus

and she realised his hands were cupping her face. He was frowning like he was worried about her.

Pushing his hands away, she rubbed her temples.

"Are you okay?" he asked. "You were crying out—"

"It was Coraline." She sighed, shaken up by the vividness of what she'd just relived. "Max tried to save her, but... they didn't stand a chance."

"Coraline? Ah, the Coven defector the Six kidnapped at that Halloween party. Can't say I'm sad, never got the chance to meet her."

"How can you be so flippant about it?" Gabby cried, wanting to slap him.

"Death is part and parcel with being a vampire. I've seen so much of it that it seems little to worry about. As for the priest... well, there aren't any gods. Just men and monsters."

How could he just sit there and not care? Surely, he'd lost someone he'd cared about? Or maybe he really was dead inside.

"Did you see what ended them?" the Roman asked.

"A man with red eyes."

He let out a lengthy sigh and shook his head like he'd decided something and as usual, he didn't let her in on it. Reaching up, he tucked a strand of hair behind her ear. "Can I do anything?"

She gave him a filthy look.

"You seem rather shaken."

"Why do you care?" She was just his toy after all; a

source of power to be used and abused for his own gain. He didn't have a right to care.

"I've seen many horrible things in my long life," he said. "You're young. Vulnerable. I remember the first time I had to kill, and it wasn't—" He stopped himself short, his jaw hard.

She froze, her gaze rising to meet his.

"Get some rest," he murmured, standing sharply. "We'll talk more tomorrow."

Gabby frowned as the door closed behind him. She'd thought Regulus was nothing but a cold-hearted predator and a master manipulator. But every so often, she caught fleeting glimpses of something soft underneath his hard surface that confused her.

It was absurd. If Regulus could actually be nice and give a crap about someone, then the world was more screwed up than she ever thought possible.

Sinking back into bed, Gabby didn't have the strength to think about it anymore. The vision still lingered, and she knew sleep wouldn't be on the menu. She thought about the man with the red eyes and understood that the Coven's spell had worked. *Who was he and why did they want to wake him up?*

There was nothing she could do about it now, so she let herself slip back into some semblance of sleep, but her dreams were plagued with red eyes and blood until the sun rose.

CHAPTER 3

Zac stood amongst the sea of tourists lining up to gawk inside one of London's most famous Medieval prisons, the Tower of London.

It wasn't an active prison anymore; the guards that lingered outside were more a draw card for all the visitors and latent ceremonial status than anything else. Nothing more than a photo opportunity in their regalia. Still, he wondered how many of these humans cared about the history of such a place.

Nye stood beside him, glaring at the occasional human who turned to stare at the ugly scar that marred his face. The scar ran from his left temple, across the bridge of his nose, over his right eye, and ended just past his cheekbone. Four hundred and twenty-seven years ago, he'd been a spy in Queen Elizabeth the First's court. The Tower of London was still at its terrible peak—executions and incarcerations were at an all-time high, despite it being the Golden

Age of Britain. When the Spanish Armada attempted invasion off the coast in 1588, he'd been lucky enough to have his face hacked open by a broadsword. It was only later that he'd been turned, so he was stuck with the scar for eternity.

"Why do we need the Three?" Nye asked with a groan, shoving his hands into the pockets of his heavy coat. "I don't like it."

"Because if the Coven completed that spell, then we need manpower. Preferably in the vampire category. Who knows what we might face."

"I could do without it."

Zac glanced from his friend to the Tower. "Not keen for a trip down memory lane?"

"Nope."

The Three had started out as the Six—Regulus' trusted thugs for hire. They did the difficult jobs that he'd trust no other with. Aya had killed Rob and Holly not long after Zac'd joined them, making them the Four, but then Nye had defected to Zac's cause. Now they were the Three. When Regulus had died his last death, they'd splintered and disappeared. Rebels without a cause. Zac needed to convince them their new cause—fighting the remains of the Coven's grand plan—was one worth fighting for.

The Three were the kind of men—both in life and in death—who needed a master to serve. Maddox had been an assassin, taking orders from a higher up. Rix had been a bodyguard to the kings and queens of

England. And finally, Pyke had been party to the many executions that took place here in the late 1500s. There was a reason for his nickname, and it was exactly what he'd imagined it to be.

Zac had been under the command of others at one stage or another, but he'd quickly risen to the rank of captain in the Confederate Army. He'd been a leader in his human life and a mess in his vampire one.

His human life was the one he was trying to connect with; finding the Three and convincing them to come with him was hopefully his ticket to finding a way for his two halves to exist together. That was the reason he felt he should leave Aya.

Thinking of her, he wondered if leaving her like he had was the right thing to do. The morning before, he'd stood with her in that hotel room with the whole world at their feet, and he'd denied her.

She was shaken, but free from her two-thousand-year-old war for revenge. The Romans had killed her family and turned her into a hybrid and now they were dead, too. She had nothing to avenge except her mission to guide the witches. The Witch Hunter was who she needed to be now, and Zac needed to find the man he was meant to be before he was worthy of her love. Always unstable, always in agony, always a hairsbreadth away from utter horror. That's who he'd been since the day he was turned, but it wasn't how it was meant to be.

"You can stay up here if you want," Zac said,

looking Nye over. "Just give me a few directions and I can deal with it." A trip down memory lane wasn't his idea of a good time, either.

"It's fine. That place is like a maze down there. Besides, Pyke isn't your greatest fan."

"True." He did crash a car with him and Maddox inside on purpose, which he had little to no regret on that one.

They walked the length of the bulwark, alongside the Tower to the Tower Bridge and back, weaving amongst the tourists, scanning the walls.

"They built this bulwark a few hundred years ago," Nye said as they walked. "The wall of the Tower used to go straight into the Thames."

"How do you propose we get into the dungeons?"

"There's an aqueduct at the foot of the wall, down in the river," the spy said, leaning over the edge of the wall and looking at the murky water. "The tide lines have changed in the last four hundred years, so I reckon the tunnel will be flooded."

"Tunnel?"

"Yeah, they used it to bring prisoners to the dungeons. If they were brought by boat, they had less chance to escape. Once they were inside the tunnel, it was game over. The guards used to call it the River Styx."

"Sounds cheerful."

"The river of Hell, mate. There was no such thing

as human rights back then, not for prisoners. They were fair game."

Leaning his back on the wall and scanning the crowd, Zac asked, "Do you really think he's hiding in there?"

"Pyke was apprenticed to the executioner at a young age. I suspect it was as good a home as any than he might've had otherwise. Like most of us thugs, he was a bottom-feeder in the slums until chance brought him out. He might've had death shoved in his face, but he was being fed and had someplace warm to sleep. For a kid like him, it would've been like living like a king. If I were him, I would've gone home."

"Then," Zac said, "we try for this aqueduct once night falls and look until we find him."

"Best option."

They went to a pub across the street and drank until the sky darkened and the crowds dispersed. Nye became more restless as the hours wore on, but he said nothing.

When the crowd thinned, they left the pub and wandered across to the Tower, which was almost deserted. The tide had dropped to the point where a few yards of sandy riverbed was exposed along the edge of the bulwark. Satisfied that no one was watching, Zac dropped over the side and landed with a thud. A soft splash next to him revealed Nye with one foot in the water.

"Shit," the spy hissed.

"We have to work on your landing," Zac said with a grin.

"Shut up."

"You're more antsy than usual."

"Bad juju in this place, mate." The spy pointed towards the opening a little farther up. "We should be able to get in there. It'll be locked with a grate."

Zac was at the entrance a second later, scanning the bars. "No door. Here, take one side."

Together, he and Nye used their strength against the steel bars, prying them open enough so they could fit through.

The tunnel within was damp and smelled like rotting earth and trash, but they pressed on, their boots sloshing in the sludge. The farther they went, the more signs of the Tower emerged. The concrete turned into the brickwork of the original foundation, and things became a lot more Medieval-looking.

The tunnel slanted upwards and they were suddenly inside the dungeon. Pitch-black, sense of foreboding, and all of that.

"It's changed more than I had thought," Nye whispered, his voice echoing. "This is where they received prisoners in my day. That tunnel we came through is new."

The ding of Zac's cell broke the eerie silence as he received a text message. Raising his eyebrows, he pulled it out and looked at the screen. It was from the witch, Coraline. She'd only written one word and it made his already cold blood run colder.

Awake.

He held up his cell so the spy could see.

"Blimey," Nye exclaimed. "Well, we're in the shit, hey?"

"Not much we can do about it right now."

"What I'm more worried about is how you got it." Nye waved his hands around. "There's no bloody reception down here."

Zac shrugged. "Witches."

"Bloody witches. What did I tell you? It's always witches."

"I guess we better hurry the hell up." He didn't know who was awake, if it was the original witch or something else, but any option was a bad one.

Turning on his cell's torch, Zac scanned the walls looking for a way forwards, but Nye was already making a move towards a passage farther ahead.

"Follow me," the spy said, disappearing into the darkness.

Putting his cell away and casting his senses out, Zac followed behind as closely as he could. Nye had his cell out, shining the way forwards, the harsh white light illuminating centuries-old prison cells. It stunk like human filth and damp earth from the thousands and thousands of souls that'd seen incarceration here. A place that'd seen such pain and torture would never stink like anything else—no matter what anyone did to scrub it clean.

Nye halted in front of him, lingering at a cell opening. Zac listened, but couldn't hear anything but their own breathing.

"What is it?" he asked but didn't get a reply.

Nye leaned his head against the corroded bars, his hands clenched into fists.

"Nye?" he asked again.

A low keening sound came from his friend and it sounded like pure anguish. Zac knew all about that.

"It was here, wasn't it?" he asked. It couldn't be anything else. He'd never seen anything get to his friend, not like this.

"Yes."

Zac waited, not wanting to ask, and let his gaze take in the cell that'd deteriorated with time and the putrid waters of the Thames. Remembering the night he sat with Nye on the rooftops over Regent Street, he knew the spy had been turned underneath the Tower. Judging from his reaction now, it'd been horrific. Who wouldn't want to avoid reliving that again?

"She was just a girl." Nye's voice was so quiet, Zac almost missed it. "A tiny waif of a thing."

"What happened to her?"

"They found her in a lane in Cheapside," he said, his hands curling around the bars of the cell. "She was accused of murder. They found her covered in blood from head to toe, sitting amongst the remains of a dismembered body."

Zac could see where this was going but didn't have the heart to say anything comforting. He just let Nye get it out, because holding it in was nothing but trouble.

"They threw her down here because no one knew what to do with her. She wasn't talking, she wouldn't go outside... she would fight anyone who neared." He stopped, drawing in a deep breath. "It was my first assignment after getting my face hacked open. After the Armada, after the Hunter pulled me from that fire ship, Reileigh got all the credit. Of course, they didn't believe the rambling fool with a torn-up face. They found me on the beach, half-dead, half-mad, and ranting about the woman on the ship. Lady Annabeth."

Zac remembered Nye had told him Aya had pulled him from the fireship. She'd saved his life but failed to take his memory of her.

"I was determined to show them," Nye continued. "They didn't believe a word I said about her, and I was smart enough to shut my mouth and play it as delirium from my wounds, but they forgot my part in saving England from the Spanish. I'd served the Crown for years, and they repaid me with silence and poverty. I would win the trust of the girl and find the truth. It was what I was good at. I'd solve what no one else could."

"The girl?"

"She was pale and sickly and wouldn't eat. She was afraid of everyone who came near, save for me. How could a girl do that? Tear a full-grown man to shreds? A tiny urchin, half-starved and freezing to death?"

"She was a vampire." Zac didn't have to ask; he could already guess what happened next.

"I brought her fresh clothing to replace her rags. I sat with her and told her stories, told her about my family, the loss of my mother. Anything to gain her trust. Eventually, she started giving in. A word here and there, and before long, she told me anything I wanted to know. Except, I didn't know the right questions to ask... She was starving," he scoffed, "but she'd already latched onto me, I'd seen to that."

"She thought you'd save her," Zac said, realising what the girl had done.

"She must have compelled me, because the next thing I knew, I was inside the cell. She fed from me, then gave me her blood. I don't remember how I died... just how I came back. When a guard finally came looking for me, blood was the only thing I wanted. You can guess how the rest went."

"What happened to the girl?"

"After I'd changed, I woke in her arms," he choked out. "She was singing, stroking my hair, cradling me like a child. She spoke of the things we'd do together, unspeakable horrors. I knew she was lost. There was no way back for her."

"What did you do next?"

"I knew she'd made me a monster like her. Everything was clearer somehow, and I didn't feel tired at all. I just felt... *hungry*. I knew I had a choice to make. I could either be like her or be something else. I couldn't chance her changing someone else, so when her back was turned, I-I ripped her heart out. *A little girl...*"

Zac knew the dangers of turning a child—they were too young, too emotionally undeveloped, and too prone to violence because of it.

"It was the right thing to do, Nye," he murmured. "She was a true vampire. Her humanity was lost."

"I know," he said, stepping back from the bars. "Afterwards, I dumped her body at the bottom of the Thames and disappeared. Regulus recruited me not long after, and believe me mate, I needed direction and he gave it to me."

"I'm not judging you, Nye. We do what we need to survive."

"I've never had a direction that wasn't someone else's," he said with a frown. "If we get through this, I don't know what to do."

"One day at a time," Zac said, slapping the spy on the shoulder. "One day at a time."

Casting a look back at the cell, Nye walked away and continued down the passage. They hadn't gone far when Zac clamped a hand on his friend's shoulder, stopping him mid-stride. Pressing a finger to his lips, he nodded in the direction they'd been headed. Through the darkness that'd turned into murky moonlight from high-set windows, they heard movement.

"The executioner's rooms," Nye whispered. He eased open the door and before he could call out, he was jerked inside. Zac ran after him and saw it was Pyke in full vampire mode.

The vampire pushed the spy back against the wall, fangs bared, and when he realised who he was holding, his eyes settled back into their ordinary brown hue.

"Calm down, mate," Nye exclaimed, holding his hands up.

"Nye?" Pyke dropped him abruptly and stood back a few paces.

"What a warm welcome," he replied, cracking his neck.

Pyke glanced at Zac and his eyes darkened. "And you."

Zac sighed. "Yeah, and me."

Pyke sat back down on the makeshift bed along the far wall, running his hand over his face. He looked strung out and his usual scruffy demeanour was all over the place. "I assume you want something."

"I'm sorry I had to deceive you," Zac said. "But I had to so I could end Regulus."

Pyke snorted. "Aye, I get it, but you didn't have to

put me through a windshield in the middle of nowhere."

"Would you believe me if I said I was sorry for that, too?"

"No."

Zac let out a laugh. "If you were in the same position, you would've done the same thing."

Pyke narrowed his eyes before shrugging. "Aye."

"What are you doing here, Pyke?" Nye asked. "You could've gone anywhere."

"I had nowhere else to go," he replied. "I didn't expect to be turfed out on my own."

"When I had nowhere else to go, I went home," Zac said, thinking of the manor back in Louisiana. "You never forget your first home, even in death."

Pyke looked up at him with a raised eyebrow. "You're different."

"I suppose so."

"I gather you've taken what was Regulus'. It doesn't mean I'll swear fealty to you."

"I've taken nothing, Pyke. I don't want it."

Standing to face Zac, the vampire signed sharply. "Then why are you here? Why are you bothering me?"

"The Coven has awakened something terrible."

"And why should I give a stuff?"

"You know the Hunter is a hybrid with a creature of power," Zac began.

"Yeah, so what?"

"So, the Coven woke a some*one*... not a some*thing*," Nye drawled.

"There's one of two people it could be," Zac went on. "The original witch, who was driven insane by the blood of a star... or a hybrid vampire belonging to a dead race of creatures like the Hunter. The difference being, they are an *original* hybrid. Created, not turned."

Pyke's eyes widened. He got it. Aya was a force to be reckoned with and it had taken her hundreds of years to learn control, and even now it was tentative. This hybrid could never grasp even a semblance of that notion. The witch would be just as dangerous, but at least Aya might have a chance at stopping her. The hybrid, not so much.

Coraline had mentioned to him before she'd left to go to Ireland with Maximus that it could be a Tuatha— a Fae from the old stories of Ireland—but that was one for the too hard basket.

"We need your help. Together, we have a chance. Alone, we have none at all." Zac stared him down, refusing to back away.

"And what are you doing down here anyway?" Nye asked. "Wasting away to a shadow. Living in a life long gone. You want a purpose? He's giving you one."

"Will you come with us?" Zac asked.

Pyke looked like he was going to cave but shook his head. "No. Not right now." Nye gave him a look that said not likely. "I'll meet you at the apartment soon enough. That's all I can give you right now."

"We could really do with your help," Zac said. "If a day or two is what you need, then we'll wait."

"Zac—" Nye began, but he held up a hand to stop him.

"He's coming." He glanced at Pyke.

"Aye," the vampire said. "I'll come. One last battle for old times' sake."

Zac offered him a thin smile. "Then we'll see you at the apartment."

Before Nye could say any more, Zac grabbed the spy's arm and they left Pyke to his misery. For this to work, the Three had to come willingly. Forcing the matter wouldn't do any good, it'd just piss everyone off. Trying to fight a common enemy with bickering and infighting would get everyone killed. No, they had to do this together or not at all.

"That was easier than I thought it'd be," Nye said as they made their way back through the dungeon.

"Pyke is the kind of man who needs a cause. The moral compass doesn't really matter."

"Rix may go along with it," the spy said. "Maddox, not so much. You might need to beat it out of him."

"We'll cross that bridge when we come to it."

Zac knew all too well that Maddox was a troublemaker. He was the one who'd tried to lead the others against him after he'd freed Coraline in that car accident. If it wasn't for Nye's intervention, their plan would've been shot to pieces. He was counting on Nye's presence to be the thing that turned the tide with the assassin, but he wouldn't worry about that until the time came.

When they finally returned to the surface, with the stink of torture and rot behind them, Zac's cell pinged with a text message from Gabby.

It was one word, but the worst one she could've sent.

Hybrid.

CHAPTER 4

Aya peered out of the window at the grey London sky, misery settling into every part of her body. She'd been alone for most of her afterlife and was content with it—being who she was—but now that so many of her friends knew, being alone wasn't high on her priority list anymore. Truthfully, she pined for Zac and he'd only left the day before.

She never thought she could love again, and it had taken her almost two thousand years to figure it out. She loved Zac with everything she had, but it still wasn't enough to stop him from leaving.

There was a knock at the door, interrupting her spiralling thoughts. Looking over her shoulder, Tristan walked into the room—the suite he'd produced for them at the Ritz hotel—a frown creasing his brow. His curly hair looked wilder than ever and sometimes she forgot how much he'd been through because of her over the years. It'd been a long time since they'd met during the Crusades—a thousand years long. Her only genuine regret was that he'd to suffer his change into a vampire on his own. She wished she'd been there to stop it from happening in the first place.

"Arrow," he said, coming to stand beside her. "We need to do somethin'. We can't stay here forever."

"It's been a day." A day since she'd lost control and ripped the Coven apart; a day since she'd almost taken Zac with them.

"I know, but what if you didn't stop the spell like Coraline said? Shouldn't we prepare?"

Aya let his thick Irish accent wash over her. Her heart ached over many things and he seemed to be a calm place in the chaos over the past few months. She knew what she needed to do, but after so long, what if she didn't like what she would find? Now, more than ever, was a time she needed to be strong. The Romans were gone, Katrin had been banished, and she was free. She was no longer hunted, but there were still many things left undone.

Looking back out the window, she murmured, "I have to go home."

"Home?"

"My birthplace."

Tristan knew she hadn't been back there since she found the mutilated remains of her family. She'd left to exact revenge on the Roman founders that day and never looked back. No longer a true Celestine, she felt like that place was lost to her. Now that her enemies were all dead and gone, she had to go and make her peace.

"You don't have to come," she told him. "I can go alone."

"Of course, I'm comin' with you," Tristan scoffed.

"Zac won't..." she began.

"He will understand, *leannan*." He used an old Gaelic word for love. "He let you go this time, after all."

He let me go, she thought. *He let me go because he didn't feel worthy.*

"Fine, but you can't come all the way."

"Vampires aren't allowed?"

She shook her head, wrapping her arms around herself.

"Okay, well, Nye left his car here, so we can go whenever you want. Just say the word."

"I suppose now is a good a time as any."

"I'll get our things and check us out."

Nodding, she turned back to the window once more, gazing at the bleak weather outside.

What would be waiting for her when she finally set foot in the field of white flowers again? The white flowers were the only thing that could truly kill her. Luckily for Aya, they only grew in her forest and she was the only one left alive who knew where it was. A witch could enter with the right intent, but if no one knew it was there, the secret would remain hidden.

Aya now had the freedom to choose her own death

and for the first time in her life, she didn't want it anytime soon.

Finally, she turned away and gathered her few items of clothing, stuffing them into the small bag Tristan had given her. The room had been trashed when the Coven kidnapped her comatose body, which was another story entirely. Tristan had done most of the damage trying to stop them, but what was a few pieces of furniture when insane witches were on the loose? He'd obviously kept himself busy the last day cleaning up the mess.

She looked around the hotel room one last time and with a sigh, she opened the door and left it all behind. That chapter was over and another one was beginning.

She waited downstairs as Tristan checked them out and spoke to the valet. She had no patience for those human nuances. Humans had grown more and more suspicious of one another, and the hoops they had to jump through to do anything was baffling. Privacy was a thing of the past.

"Where are we going to?" Tristan asked as they waited.

"Grasmere."

"Oh, in the Lake District?"

"Yes, I suppose that's what it's called now."

"It's about a five-hour drive," the knight said as they got into the sleek car that appeared before them. "We'll be there just after dark."

"We have time," Aya replied, fastening her seatbelt as he pulled out into traffic. "I gather someone will let us know if we're needed."

As the city gave way to countryside, she was content to let it go by in silence until Tristan's cell phone beeped in his pocket.

"It's from Zac," he said, peering at the screen with one eye on the road. Not exactly responsible driving.

Her heart beat double time. "And?"

"Erm..."

Aya scowled. "*Tristan.*"

"You didn't stop the spell."

"And who did it awaken? The witch?"

"No, it's a hybrid."

"A hybrid?"

Tristan looked at his cell like he didn't believe Zac's message.

"What else is there?" she asked.

"He says it's a Tuatha. That can't be right, can it? The Fae from the old Irish stories?"

Aya's blood ran colder than it already was. She knew the stories, the true ones, and it didn't bode well at all. The Tuatha de Danann and the Celestines were at war long before Aya was born. It was a long, heartbreaking tale that ended in both sides losing almost everything.

"Yes," she told Tristan. "The one and the same."

"You don't sound so enthusiastic."

"They're bad news, Tristan," she said, glancing at

him. "Our people were at war at one time. They're not the pretty fairies from your stories."

"War?"

"It was only three generations before I was born. The Tuatha were a race that came, conquered, and destroyed. It was everything the Celestines were against. We fought them to the brink of extinction."

"That's why there were so few of you left by the time you were born?"

"Yes. The whole reason the original witch came into play was because of Aoife. She was sent to marry the Tuatha's king, Lir, as a way to secure peace between our dying races. Now we know she had other plans."

"She made the witch so she could create hybrids?"

"And those hybrids were Lir's children."

"The Children of Lir were turned into swans in the stories," Tristan said. "But they were really changed into... founding vampires?"

"The Children of Lir were a casualty of war," Aya told him. "Their fate seems regrettable. Trying to destroy the Tuatha royal family was folly on Aoife's part—it seemed she couldn't let go of her hatred for the people who drove her family to the brink of extinction. Creating hybrids locked in eternal servitude to the enemy seemed like a good idea, but her mistake was using her own blood to make the witch that needed to cast the spell."

"Why couldn't Aoife cast it?"

"Celestine magic can't be used like that. It's used for nurturing the Earth, not creating monsters."

"Unstable blood made them and now one is awake."

"Yes, and whichever of Lir's children it is, they will be mentally unstable." Insanity bred insanity, after all.

"What do we do?" Tristan asked quietly.

"We keep going on to Grasmere. I may need to make peace with that part of my life, but there may also be something there about the Tuatha."

They drove in silence for a while, villages and towns passing them by. Rain turned to sleet and the sky cleared before greying again the farther north they travelled.

"How long does a Celestine live for anyway?" Tristan asked like he'd been thinking about it for a while.

"I was very young when I was changed," Aya replied. "A life span would sometimes stretch to a thousand years for the strongest of us, though it depended."

"On what?"

"On our power, our link to the stars, where we chose to settle... Many things."

"How long would you have lived if you hadn't been turned?"

"It's hard to say. I was strong, as my parents were. I would've been one of the oldest. Still, I've gone on for twice as long as nature intended."

"Through no fault of your own."

"No." For a split-second she considered telling him about the white flowers but decided against it. The secret was best left to her and her alone—she had plenty of experience keeping them. Instead, she said, "If there is one thing this long life has taught me is that there is no use dwelling on what can't be changed. We can only keep going forwards."

"And our next order of business is to find a way to stop this Tuatha-hybrid."

"You know I can't ask you to help, Tristan. There's no telling what will happen next and I can't protect you."

The knight laughed out loud and she glared at him. "When will you learn, Arrow? I'm with you till the end."

"A thousand years *can* addle your brain."

"And two thousand?" he asked with a wink.

"Don't even start," Aya replied and smiled her first genuine smile in days.

Tristan pulled the car into a spot behind the only pub in the main street of Grasmere. There were about five houses and a few little tourist shops with glowing lights in the windows. Christmas displays twinkled warmly through the misty rain and the fading afternoon light.

He looked across at Aya, who was staring out into the night.

"You can wait until morning," he said. "It'll be dark soon."

"It's not far."

"Do you want me to come with you into the forest?"

"No, it's raining."

He didn't know how he should answer that, so he replied with, "I'll wait in the pub until you return."

"I might be a while. Time acts differently there."

Nodding, he said, "I'll still be at the pub. They seem to have rooms there. Or I'll just wait in the car. I won't be far."

Without another word, she opened the door and slipped out into the dull winter air and disappeared across the street into the woods. He knew better than to worry about Arrow. She'd taken care of him when he was at his worst, and every time he tried to repay the debt, he never came close to doing anything that mirrored her efforts. When she said she would be okay, she really would be okay.

Getting out the car, he opened the side door into the pub and waved his foot through the threshold. When he found he was able to enter, he walked into the warm light and ordered a beer from the elderly man behind the bar. Finding a spot in the corner, he settled in for the long haul.

There were about half a dozen people spread across the homey room, some drinking with friends while others enjoyed meals by the open fireplace. If it weren't for their current predicament, he would've enjoyed himself.

Something was weighing on his shoulders and for the life of him, he couldn't figure out what. It felt like someone was looking over his shoulder, waiting. Glancing around the pub, he saw nothing out of the ordinary. He was certain everyone here was human.

As his thoughts turned to Arrow, the door opened and a man walked in. Tristan's eyes instantly fixed on the stranger. He looked out of place, wearing an expensive suit, sans-tie. The weight that'd been pressing on him since he'd sat down constricted heavily against his lungs and he knew something was wrong.

The stranger turned towards the corner and strange red eyes fixed on his. It suddenly became very hard to breathe. This man could only be one person.

Tristan knew his name from the old stories his people told a thousand years before—stories that were still told today. His name was Aed, the only son of Lir, Prince of the Tuatha De Danann.

The hybrid slid into the chair opposite, a sly smile on his face. "What gave me away?" he drawled.

"Your eyes have red irises."

"Do they?" he asked in genuine surprise. "How interesting. They used to be blue."

Tristan decided the best course of action was to remain silent and let the hybrid ask the questions. One poke in the wrong place might provoke him. Really, how was he supposed to handle a three-thousand-year-old psychopath on his own?

"This world really is something else," Aed continued. "Machines, electric lights... and these clothes." He tugged at the collar of his suit jacket. "I like them. Fit for a prince, are they not?"

"You look... refined."

"Yes, I do, don't I?"

"Is there something I can help you with?"

The hybrid narrowed his strange red eyes and leaned across the table. "The Celestine with the black hair... where is she? I know she's here. I can smell her flowery stink all over you."

Tristan's skin prickled. Arrow had made a point of telling him how their people had been at war. Something told him that this guy hadn't got the memo.

"You will tell me where she is, or I will slaughter these people. Perhaps I will anyway." Aed looked around the room at the various humans who were drinking and eating meals by the hearth. "What do you care, hmm? You crave blood just as much as I."

"I don't kill innocent humans."

"You don't?" Aed asked. "Why not? Isn't that against your nature? Don't humans eat animals? Cattle, sheep... humans are *our* livestock. Our only food source. It is nature's way."

"Nature didn't create us," Tristan told him.

"No, I suppose not." He stood, straightening his suit

jacket, pulling at the cuffs of his shirt just so. "Do you know what it's like to be trapped in a tomb for three thousand years? It's disorienting and cramped, and you wake with this insatiable *hunger*."

Before Tristan could open his mouth, Aed was across the room, sinking his fangs into any flesh he could grasp. The old boozehound by the bar was dead in seconds, his lifeless head lolling against the ancient oak countertop. The elderly publican was snapped in two as screams erupted through the remaining humans. The air was heavy with the stench of blood as it splashed against the walls and floors, staining everything red.

What could Tristan do? He could try to stop Aed, but it was too late for that. The hybrid sunk his fangs into a woman by the hearth, the air full of animalistic slurping sounds as he drained her dry.

"There," Aed declared with a gasp, dropping her limp body to the floor, "that's a little better."

Tristan looked around the pub dumbfounded. Seven humans were dead in just as many seconds and he hadn't lifted a finger to save them. Why was he still alive?

"Now," the hybrid declared, wiping his mouth on a serviette, "we wait for the star to return for her companion. There is much I wish to ask her."

That's why.

CHAPTER 5

Gabby stood in front of the fireplace, watching the flames crackle in the hearth.

The image of Coraline's last moments haunted her. The bloodstained face of her killer was all she could see when she closed her eyes, which was why she tried not to close her eyes.

"Gabrielle."

She turned slightly at the sound of Regulus' voice and sighed. He stood just inside the doorway, arms crossed.

The house they were staying in was cozy and well-furnished—every bit a traditional English cottage—but it wasn't home.

"What do you want?" she asked.

"Time is short."

She sat in one of the armchairs closest to the fire and waited.

"Can you show me his face?" Regulus asked quietly, sitting across from her.

"Yes." She'd avoided it for as long as she could.

As he leaned forwards, she reached up and placed her hand on the side of his face, cupping his cheek. To her disgust, he let out a small sigh—he enjoyed this.

Pushing thoughts of him away, she focused on Coraline's vision. The image that haunted her the most flashed through her mind again. Deep red eyes, *blood*. Coraline's pain. She pushed it all into the Roman and didn't hold back.

Regulus' hand shot up and grasped her wrist, severing the transfer.

"Enough," he said. "Do not torture yourself, Gabrielle, and do not torture me."

"Why do you care?"

He let her go and regarded her with a guarded expression. He was the master of containing his emotions. His two-thousand years compared with her twenty-one? No guess on who'd win that competition.

"If you want my help, you have to start talking," she said.

"That's what we're doing." He smiled slyly at her. The asshole she knew was coming back to the surface.

"Really?" she asked. "Because I've been doing nothing but putting up with your sarcastic ass so far."

"*Gabrielle.*"

"You love your games, don't you, Regulus?"

He smirked. "To an end."

"Tell me everything or spend an eternity on your knees."

"Do you say that to all the men you meet?"

She stood sharply. "I'm not playing your games, Regulus," she snarled. "Tell me everything or you'll be begging for your life."

"I don't beg anyone, Gabrielle, but I'd beg to you."

She narrowed her eyes at him, willing an aneurysm to explode in his brain.

"*God*," he hissed, clutching his head. "You really know how to turn a man on."

"Sadist," she spat and sat back down.

He shook his head as it healed itself. "I know it's difficult for you, but..."

"But what?" she asked when he faltered.

"You're you and I'm me."

She knew what he meant. One of the most powerful witches in the world and the last remaining original vampire.

"What is he?" she asked.

"The old stories of Ireland talk about a race known as the Tuatha de Danann."

"He's a Fae?"

"The Children of Lir," Regulus began, watching her reaction. "The stories say Aoife turned them into swans. They also say she was one of the Tuatha, but she was also a true Celestine, so that doesn't matter. In the end it was Aoife's witch who turned the four Tuatha into hybrids. Katrin was a human witch when she made us. Aoife's witch was driven insane by Celestine blood. Do the math."

"There's an insane, psychopathic, vampire-Fae-hybrid on the loose?"

"That's a mouthful." He leered, letting his gaze drop to her lips.

"How did they end up trapped in tombs?"

"Aoife. She realised she'd made a mistake and tried to fix it."

"What about the original witch?"

"She lived on and founded the Coven. They lost the hybrids and have been searching for them ever since. Well, *had*."

Gabby knew Aya had destroyed the Coven as they were casting the spell that would awaken the original. Now they knew the witches had succeeded. Who knew what this hybrid was capable of? If what Regulus said was true, then the hybrid's mind would be compromised.

"Do you want to know the reason the Celestines were reduced to nothing?" Regulus asked. "It was the Tuatha. They may have hidden underground for hundreds of years, but their demise was their own fault. The Celestines won the war, but they both suffered the same fate—extinction."

"The Celestine's were at war?" she asked, surprised. "I didn't think it was their style?"

"The Tuatha were a harsh race. They were known

as the devourers of worlds. They conquered and consumed. Why wouldn't the Celestines fight that?"

Gabby nodded slowly, not liking where this was going.

"The Tuatha are still revered in stories and heralded as gods, but they perpetuated those stories themselves. They wanted the people of the lands they conquered to think well of them, even after they slaughtered hundreds of thousands and took their homes. They were the ultimate brainwashers. And to think that one might still live?" He snorted and shook his head. "We're all screwed."

"We'll stop him," Gabby said defiantly. "Even if I have to work with you."

"You think I'm the bad guy?" Regulus scoffed. "Just wait until you meet this hybrid. Then we'll talk about bad."

"What do you know about him? Who was he?"

"He is the last remaining son of Lir. They called him Aed. The rest, his sisters, are dead."

"What happened to them?"

Regulus seemed to ignore her question. "Do you know who Katrin really was? She was born into the Coven without any power. They raised her to become one of the Five. They knew what the last Celestines were planning."

Gabby's mouth fell open. "They planted her?"

"Yes, but they didn't count on her betraying them." He let out a sigh. "Her plan for creating the first vampires wasn't only to learn the secrets of power from the Celestines; it was to hunt down the original vampires Aoife's witch created and destroy them. The Coven used her, and she wanted to see them undone... Out of the six vampires she hd created, she trusted me with this task. *Me.* You know why I've been trying to get into the Coven all this time?"

The enormity of what had happened sank in. "They woke one of the Children of Lir, a founder who can't be killed."

"They were my only lead to finding Aed. Now the Coven is gone, but their creature still lives on."

"You killed the others?" she asked, suddenly understanding. *He knew how to end them.*

"Yes."

"How?"

"There are some things only a founder can do."

"You're the only way to kill the hybrid?"

"Don't look so disappointed, Gabrielle. You're hurting my pride."

"How?" she asked, ignoring him.

"With my cold, dead hands, that's how."

"*Regulus,*" she scolded.

"I have to tear his heart out. Then, for good measure, rip his head off then burn him into a pile of ash. Only then, will I be satisfied."

Gabby fell back into the armchair and sighed. This was way too much, even after all the crazy that'd happened in the last year. It was like a three-thousand-year-old conspiracy. It had nothing to do with her, though if she didn't stand with Regulus, then who knew what would happen? Disclosure, for one. The hybrid would run rampant and who knew how many people would die in the process. So yeah, it had everything to do with her.

"So, what now?" she asked, locking eyes with Regulus.

"We go to this Brú na Bóinne. From there, I'll be able to track him."

"He could be anywhere by now."

"Yes, but there's no other way of knowing where he went."

"Fine," she said, standing. "Tomorrow."

Regulus rose as she turned to leave. "Gabrielle."

"What?" she said with a sigh.

"I will protect you."

He said it with such sincerity, her heart faltered. Gabby turned to face him, a frown on her face. He was standing right in front of her, a mere step away. He'd moved so silently, she hadn't noticed.

She shook her head. "I thought I was just a means to an end?"

"No," he murmured, letting his gaze rake over her face.

She should've moved. She should've said something. But when he stepped into her, she froze. He slid his hands over her waist and breathed in her scent deeply. What was this? Another of his games? As he lowered his lips towards the crook of her neck, she froze. *He wouldn't dare...*

"Stop me at any time, Gabrielle," he murmured, pressing his lips against her neck.

Instead of the sharp pinch of his fangs, she felt the tip of his tongue tease her skin.

"What do you want?" she asked, trying to keep her voice even.

"You know what I want." He pressed his lips against hers, his tongue sliding into her mouth as he tried to claim her and for a moment, she felt a searing need. Her body pressed against his of its own accord, and it was all the acceptance he was looking for. He backed her against the wall, deepening his kiss, letting his hands wander.

What the hell was she doing? Gabby's eyes snapped open as she reached for her power.

Abruptly, Regulus tore away and fell to his knees, trying to draw in heaving breaths.

Satisfied he'd learned his lesson, she let him go and he gasped, clutching his head.

"I've never met a witch like you, Gabrielle," he said with a strange look in his eyes.

"I've never met a bigger asshole than you."

"That mouth," he murmured, licking his lips.

"You'll never be touching it again."

"Never say never."

He was a two-thousand-year-old vampire. He'd been a Roman soldier who had attempted to assassinate his emperor. He had made Aya's life a living hell. He'd snatched the Celestine from her forest and imprisoned her. He hadn't been the one who'd turned her, but he may as well have. He had been one of the founders who had murdered Aya's family. He'd manipulated Victoria, making her fall in love with him, then sent her into the world heartbroken where she destroyed Zac and Sam's lives. Not to mention the threats he'd used to get Gabby to work with him—threats that included murdering her family.

How could she let him have her after all that? Even after all those things, it still wasn't even taking into consideration how he'd manipulated her into orchestrating his own death.

And now Regulus deigned that he was capable of genuine love? He wanted to protect her? What a joke. That man was only capable of one thing.

Evil.

And evil did not have a heart.

***

A vampire with a passport. Gabby stifled a groan at the notion. It was an Italian one. She guessed Regulus looked a little... well, Roman. Where was he from anyway?

She stood in the crisp Dublin air as Regulus worked his asshole magic on the woman behind the rental desk. She kind of expected him to compel what he wanted out of her, but he pulled out a platinum credit card instead.

When he saw Gabby look at him through the window, he winked like the sly bastard he was.

Groaning, she turned her back to the rental office and scanned the surrounding countryside.

The airport was on the edge of the city and the sky was grey with the promise of rain. An hour and fifteen minutes saw them tarmac to tarmac, and another hour or so would see them to Brú na Bóinne. Then they would know where to start. The sooner they found the hybrid, the sooner they'd find a way to subdue him and the Roman would finish the job. Then she could go home and never see the asshole again.

She jumped as Regulus appeared next to her, picking up her bag from the concrete.

"This way, dear one," he said with a grin, walking off through the line of rental cars. Pressing the fob on the keys, he opened the trunk on a modest-looking car. She thought he'd get something flashier—he looked the type to show off.

The Roman put their bags in the trunk, thumped it closed, and went for the driver's side before she could push him out of the way. Getting in the opposite side, she watched as he put the keys into the ignition.

"Do you even have a license?" she asked, eyeing him suspiciously.

"I might have been born in thirteen AD, Gabrielle, but it doesn't mean I don't know how to drive a car."

"Whatever, just hurry up."

"There's one thing vampires don't have and that's a sense of urgency."

"Even hybrids?"

"*Especially* hybrids."

With a sigh, she punched Newgrange into the GPS and it brought up the directions.

Without another word, Regulus backed the car out of the lot and merged onto the highway, following the directions on the GPS.

"Do you know what we're looking for?" Gabby asked. "Would he have been buried with the human dead?"

"No," he replied, not once taking his eyes from the road. "I suspect the human population built their structure as some kind of tribute in the centuries after. The Tuatha would never mingle with them, especially not in death. Aoife wouldn't have hidden him in such an obvious place."

"Then it's a smoke screen for something else..."

"It's a burial chamber on the surface," Regulus explained. "They call them mounds. The Celts, the name you know them by, built them so grass and flowers could grow above. A tribute to the dead."

"So why hasn't anyone found the hybrid before now?"

"What we're looking for is beneath. In the earth."

"Caves?"

"Yes."

She didn't have to ask the next question. Nobody knew they were down there because they were warded.

As the car wove through the green fields, Gabby watched the countryside flash by. She'd always wanted to visit Ireland, and London for that matter, but never expected it to be like this. She wanted to see museums and art, drink Guinness in a traditional Irish pub, and meet a hot Irishman so she could swoon at his accent. Cursing her terrible luck, she glanced at Regulus. She didn't think she could hate him more than she did right now.

He returned her look, his lips curving into a sly smile. *Ugh.* The air inside the car suddenly felt extremely close.

When they finally reached Newgrange, they turned towards the burial mound. From a distance it looked like any other hill they'd passed on the drive here, but underneath, it would be a warren of ancient chambers, full of ancient human burials. Regulus pulled the car into the small lot and killed the engine.

Opening the door, Gabby stepped out into the fresh air and could instantly feel a buzzing sensation tickle against her skin. It was different than the power she was used to, so she could only assume it was the lingering signature of the Tuatha.

Closing her eyes, she felt it out. Within, she could sense a tinge of Celestine that reminded her of Aya—it must've been Aoife's doing. She'd likely warded this place once she'd sealed Aed in his tomb.

"Gabrielle," Regulus beckoned, holding out his hand.

"Do I really have to go down there with you?" she asked, lingering by the car.

"I gather you can feel the magic around this place," he said, pointing to the mound. "Your expertise is required."

With a sag of her shoulders, she pushed past him and walked towards the entrance. He was beside her a second later as they approached the deserted historical monument.

"It's closed," Gabby said, noticing a sign near the entrance to the mound. It said, *Guided tours by prior booking only. No access.*

"Good," the Roman said, walking up to the modern door that'd been set into the ancient structure. He ripped the lock off and tossed it aside, pushing his way inside. Gabby had no other option other than to follow him into the darkness.

As they made their way through the tomb, the air stank of mouldy earth and dampness. She felt out her way with her earth sense, the power around them thick and metallic.

"Here," she whispered, her voice echoing against the rock. "There's a concealment in the wall."

Regulus grasped her hand in the darkness and despite herself, she shivered. "Lead on."

"Through the back of this chamber is an opening," she said. "There are stairs."

Magic pulled at her skin as she passed through the ward. Regulus came without hesitation, his footfalls light behind her as they descended through heavy clay earth and then dense bedrock. A strange shimmering light broke up the darkness and she hesitated.

"Keep going," Regulus whispered behind her. "Nothing lives down there."

Taking a deep breath, she continued, the light growing with each step towards the bottom. The staircase finally opened out into a small chamber and she gasped as she took in the subterrain.

The chamber and adjoining tunnel were lined with smooth rock, like someone had melted it into shape. She ran her fingers over the surface, studying the strange, sparkling blue hue.

Regulus still had a hold of her other hand and tugged her down the tunnel. The entire network seemed to be lit with some kind of natural phenomenon that'd been enhanced with magic. She'd never seen anything like it. She was content to let the Roman lead her as her fingers trailed against the rock.

"I suggest you don't look, Gabrielle."

"What?" she asked, thoroughly annoyed, but she looked anyway.

Ahead, bloody remains were strewn across the tunnel and splattered up the walls. Turning away with a horrified gasp, she closed her eyes, trying to will herself awake.

"I said don't look." Regulus was at her side. "Would you like me to carry you across?"

"Eat shit," she spat and glared at him. Turning back, she tiptoed her way through the remains, trying not to heave her breakfast all over herself.

It was Coraline and Max, or what was left of them.

Truthfully, she didn't know them that well. She'd met Coraline only through a mental link and one phone conversation. She hadn't met Max at all. Still, she'd been a witch and devoted to their cause, no matter her Coven heritage. They didn't deserve to die like this.

A few yards ahead, the tunnel opened out into a vast cavern. Stalactites hung from the roof, the blue hue of the rock brighter here, but it wasn't the only thing that dangled from the ceiling.

The body of a woman had been strung up like a star, arms and legs splayed out, each limb impaled on the natural cave formations. Gabby saw the sickly grey skin and instantly knew what the woman had been.

"Vampire," Regulus muttered, cocking his head to the side.

"What's a vampire doing down here?"

"I've encountered them before with the others. They're worshipers, followers created by the Coven long ago to watch over the hybrids."

"Then why did they lose them?"

"Hundreds of years down here? Can you imagine

how mentally stable they'd be after a decade, let alone a few centuries?"

"Good point."

The vampire, or what was left of her, was lit with the eerie light trickling down from the surface. Reflecting off the blue rock, it made her hair a brighter, almost neon shade of red. The entire scene was macabre to say the least.

"Well," Regulus said, his voice echoing around the chamber, "it's a little theatrical for my tastes."

Gabby shivered despite the coat she wore and wrapped her arms around herself. She wanted out of here as soon as possible. "Can you track him?"

"Give me a moment, dear one."

He ran his pale fingers along the tomb before pacing across the cavern, following the trail of blood. As he disappeared into the tunnel, back towards the remains of her allies, she stepped up to the hybrid's resting place and studied the rock. It was like the whole thing had been melted in place, like magma from the core of the Earth itself. Regulus had said Aoife had imprisoned them. It'd been Celestine magic, then. Strange to think she was touching something that'd been wrought thousands of years ago.

"He's been gone a few days. Two at most." The Roman's voice echoed around the rock, making her jump.

"How do you know where he's gone, then?"

"I was made for this purpose, among others," he

said blandly. "You have an earth sense. I have a hybrid sense."

"Is that how Caius found Aya? Arturius?"

Regulus snorted, "No. We could never track her like that."

So, just Tuatha tracking, then.

"We must return to the surface."

"Where has he gone then, smart ass?"

Regulus sighed and wiped his palms on his trousers. "He's looking for the Celestines."

CHAPTER 6

Aya made her way through the damp forest, climbing over moss-covered logs and leaping over the little streams that fed down into the lakes.

This forest marked the land around her home—the field of white flowers and the house she'd grown up in. It was a place that was of this world, but apart from it. A haven for the last of the Celestines... and the place that had marked their horrible end.

Despite the surrounding coldness, the air thickened the farther she walked. The boundary loomed, and as if it sensed her presence, it parted as she stepped through into warm summer air. Sunlight streamed through the canopy, warm dots of light dancing across her skin. Glancing back over her shoulder, the only sight she was greeted with was an ever-stretching forest, green and gold. It looked the same as it always had in her childhood, but something was missing.

The farther she walked, the more she felt apart from this place, like she didn't belong anymore. Nothing stirred, not even a birdcall reached her sensitive ears. This place was as dead as she was, and her heart sank.

Really, what'd she been expecting? After everything that had passed, would it still be brimming with the life she craved to nurture and protect?

Stopping at the edge of the clearing where she knew the white flowers grew, Aya's gaze ran over them. They'd flourished, spreading out across the field like a thick carpet, their yellow centres dazzling in the sunlight. They were the only things that lived here now.

Memories flooded her mind of the day she'd been standing in the centre of this very clearing, gathering the blooms for her mother. Now, she lingered in the same spot where Regulus had stood watching her go about her work.

Closing her eyes and taking a deep breath, Aya squashed the memories deep within and stepped out into the sunlight. The flowers seemed to tilt in her direction as she walked through them, as if they sensed her presence. A macabre welcome wagon—the one thing that could kill her and the one thing that reminded her of her family. It would deliver her to them, but she no longer wanted it. Not yet.

Finally, she glimpsed the house through the trees on the far side of the clearing. She almost expected to see her mother standing on the porch, her impossibly long silver hair fluttering in the breeze, her bright eyes and warm smile welcoming her home... But it was dark and empty. The windows looked out onto the forest like soulless eyes, the front door a portal to the abyss. The home she knew was long gone.

Glancing up at the trees where she'd last seen Grant and Lance—the men who helped tend to the family and the house—she found the branches bare. They'd been hanging upside down, blood running down their lifeless arms, dripping from pale fingertips onto the earth below. She'd smelled it before she'd seen them, but it didn't soften the blow. Closing her eyes, she could almost see them as they'd been all that time ago.

Inside the house, her mother and father had been placed together on their bed, hands entwined, their bodies mutilated, and their lifeforce had pooled over the floors and splattered on the walls. Her brother, *her dear brother*, had been the same. She'd been pure and strong, but he was so young. Together they would've led the witches into the new age and died together in peace. She couldn't do it without him.

"Aydrenn," she murmured, uttering his name for the first time in two thousand years. It wasn't fair, but life never was.

She'd come too far to stop now. Pushing open the front door to the house, she stepped into the darkness.

Spider webs clung to the ceilings and dust clogged

every surface. No one had been here since the Coven had sullied it a thousand years before.

There was no sign of her family's remains. There was no sign that her family had ever lived here. Their belongings—her mother's books, her father's works—were all gone. Venturing into their rooms, it was all the same. Nothing.

A sob escaped Aya's throat. What had she been expecting to find? The bones of her family? The stains of their blood in the wooden floors? Some kind of link to her past? Something tangible she could hold to remember them by? She didn't deserve any of it, but she still hoped.

There was nothing here. Nothing that could help. The Coven had been through the place and taken anything that might have been valuable to them, which was everything. The only thing that was left for her to do here at this moment, was to make her peace.

Outside, Aya's breath caught in the back of her throat and her already dead heart sputtered and almost stilled entirely. Her family stood a few paces away, hand in hand, smiling with all the power of the stars behind them.

But Aya knew they weren't really there. They were an echo, an apparition, merely leftover energy waiting for the day she'd return.

"I'm sorry," she whispered as tears fell.

Her father nodded, his skin shimmering with its familiar glow, marred by his translucency. Her mother smiled kindly, a sadness in her eyes that betrayed she understood her daughter's fate. And her brother raised his hand in a wave, and she knew it was goodbye. As they disappeared across the field, she raised her hand, tendrils of blue flame licking at her fingertips.

She didn't belong here anymore. Her mere presence was a blight upon the pureness of this place. The echo of her lost family tugged at her heart, but it made her realise the inevitable.

Aya said her last goodbye and left the clearing and went back into the human world. She would never set foot here again, not until it was time to join her family in the afterlife. She still had things to do, battles had to be fought and won in the name of the Celestines. She had to help her friends and she had to see the Tuatha dead.

She had to go back.

Aya smelled the blood before she found the source.

The air was thick with it and she instantly thought of Tristan. Emerging from the forest, she stood by the road, glancing up and down the street at the shop fronts that were still lit, the gaudy Christmas decorations twinkling in the darkness.

A terrible sense of dread chilled her bones and her gaze fell onto the pub.

The Tuatha were extinct by the time she was born,

but that didn't mean that she didn't know who was sitting inside waiting for her. There was only one reason the hybrid would be here, and she was it.

She'd been afraid of many things, but now was not the time for fear. Now was the time for facing danger head-on. Tristan would be counting on her.

Opening the side door, her eyes changed instinctively as the overwhelming scent of blood slammed into her. That wasn't the only thing that gave her pause. Her friend was sitting with a man who oozed nothing but dread, death, and destruction. It was so potent it made her stomach squirm and her skin prickle.

Tristan's gaze flew to hers as she stepped inside. Immediately, she saw the panic in them.

The knight sat at a table amongst the remains of an unknown amount of humans, body parts and blood strewn around the room. The Tuatha-hybrid sat opposite. It couldn't be anyone else.

He wore a dark tailored suit and a white shirt that was stained with dark splotches of blood. Sickly-looking skin made his otherworldly eyes stand out like pits of fire. Red eyes meant red death. The hybrid looked her over just as blatantly, a smirk of satisfaction on his handsome face.

"You smell like death," she said as the hybrid stood.

"Welcome," he drawled. "Why don't you join us?"

Rather than show any weakness, she sat next to

Tristan, never taking her gaze off the Tuatha for an instant.

"And whom do I have the pleasure of speaking with?"

"You can call me Aya," she replied, her head held high. This was one man she would never utter her true name to. Whether he learned it or not was of no concern, but he would never hear it from her.

"I am Aed, prince of the Tuatha De Danann. And who are you to be worthy of being the last of your kind?"

"I am not the last of my kind... I am the only one of my kind. I am neither Celestine nor vampire."

A slow smile spread across Aed's face. "You're a clever little girl, are you not?"

"To a degree."

"And your kind suffered their end at the hands of your own creations. You never learned the first time. I was of the understanding that stars were more self-righteous than that."

Aya's jaw stiffened, but she didn't rise to the bait. "The Five were created human. They were never gifted with Celestine powers."

"Ahh," Aed said, tapping the tabletop with a pale finger, "but humans are as corruptible as any other race. So easily manipulated. All you have to do is offer them a little power and they'll eat out of the palm of your hand." He regarded her for a moment, letting his strange red eyes rake over her body. "You were turned by one of their human vampires."

"And you were turned by a Celestine," she drawled. "Doesn't it burn you from the inside out knowing you have the blood of your enemies running through your veins?" She felt Tristan's knee press against hers underneath the table and she let her hand curl around his thigh.

"*Aoife*," Aed spat, slamming his fist down on the table. "The woman who would call me son? That bitch cast off her Celestine name and took one of ours, but she meant none of it. She betrayed us. She betrayed my father. The only thing I regret was not ripping her apart myself."

"Shame. What's it like being stuck in a tomb for three thousand years? Cramped?"

"Arrow," Tristan hissed beside her.

"Where are my sisters, Celestine?" Aed asked, his eyes beginning to swirl.

"I would hope they're dead."

The hybrid shot to his feet with a snarl. Curling his hands into the lapels of Aya's jacket, he wrenched her out of the chair. The wind was knocked from her lungs as he shoved her hard against the wall, betraying just how strong he was.

Fingers bit into her skin as he held her in place, and she watched his eyes swirl with a strange lustre. Hers were the silvery white of the stars when her vampire side took over; Aed's were an odd shade of red, almost like they were filling with blood, brimming on the edge with death.

"Oh, it's so romantic. The poor little Children of Lir, turned into graceful swans." He dragged his fingertips along her face, his red eyes taking in every inch of her features. "Do I look like a swan to you?"

"Then why don't you just kill me now and be done with it? Isn't that what you want? Why else would you come here?"

His strange eyes searched hers for a moment and a smile crept onto his lips. "Because you're like me. You cannot be killed."

"We'll see about that."

"The last original is gone. The spell is lost. You have nothing," he spat.

Understanding hit Aya like a sledgehammer. That's why Regulus had been so intent on getting into the Coven. He was hunting the Children of Lir... but why did he care? It didn't matter now—he was dead. All the founders were and there went their only known chance of delivering Aed his true end.

The only thing Aya could think of doing was reach for her power. It boiled up inside of her as she contemplated her next move. She could kill the founding vampires her family had created, so it stood to reason she could kill a founding hybrid, Tuatha or not. Before she could think twice, she pushed him back with all her strength and he stumbled a few steps before coming to a stop.

"Well," Aed said, "it seems we are on equal footing, no?"

Tristan was on his feet and Aya held a hand out to stop him from intervening. There was nothing the knight could do, not now and especially not alone.

"What are you going to do, Aya?" Aed edged towards Tristan.

Before he could take another step, she lunged forwards, her fingers outstretched. The familiar sensation of flesh cutting through sinew and bone prickled across her skin as she plunged her hand into the hybrid's chest. He let out a strangled roar of pain, eyes wide with surprise. She let her power slam into his heart, blue fire lighting up the room.

The pop and fizz of every electrical circuit in the place shorting out was the only sound for one sickening minute and she thought she'd done it. His heart stopped in her hand and it was over. She pushed Aed's limp body away and he fell to the floor with a thud.

"Is he dead?" Tristan whispered, the darkness eerie considering the carnage they stood amongst.

"I—" She was interrupted by a loud wheeze as Aed drew in a heaving breath and sat straight up, his eyes fixed on her.

"That... *hurt*," he rasped, clawing at the hole in his chest.

"Shit," she hissed. Well, there went that idea. Her power was useless against the Tuatha. Null and void.

Aed rose to his full height, blood oozing down his front as the wound in his chest healed, flesh knitting back together. He reached for a chair, the wood snapping in his hands. Aya didn't have time to dodge to the side as he lunged for her, a long sliver of wood slicing through her stomach, the tip imbedding in the wall behind her. Gasping in surprise, she tried to grasp the end to pull it out, but her hands wouldn't work. Fingers slid numbly against her skin as blood coated everything.

"How does it feel, star?" Aed asked, a satisfied smile playing across his lips. "Hurts, doesn't it?"

"What do you want?" Tristan asked, his voice wavering.

"What do I want?" The hybrid turned on the knight. "I want what is *owed* to me, and I will take it any way I can. I will make the world run red with blood if that's what I need to do. Do not stand in my way, vampire, or you will join them with your head on a pike." Turning back to Aya, he grabbed the splinter of wood and twisted it, enjoying the gasp of pain as it tore through her flesh and organs. "Did you know... even your blood smells like the earth? Like flowers in full bloom. *It's an insult.*"

"You smell like a rotting corpse," she gritted, blood trickling from the corner of her mouth. "I think we're done here, don't you?"

He stared at her, the streetlamp outside lighting his face like a macabre devil. Wrenching the wood from her gut, he tossed it at her feet as she fell to her knees with a gasp. He walked towards the door, but stopped mid-stride. Aed looked at his hand and then down at a man who was slumped over the bar. Touching the corpse's shoulder, the hybrid's expression changed into one of surprise. As his hand glowed a deep crimson, the dead man twitched and his eyes snapped open.

"Well," he declared, "that's interesting."

"*Arrow*." Tristan took a step towards her.

Aed pulled his hand away and watched the red flame envelop his arm. He still had his power and it looked like he could reanimate corpses. That was just fantastic.

The door swung on its hinges and Aed was gone. Just like the insane, unpredictable mess that he was.

"Why did you have to goad him on like that?" Tristan exclaimed, helping Aya to her feet.

"I wanted to see if he still had any power." She pulled up her shirt and smoothed her hand across her stomach. The hole was already closing over.

"Shit, Arrow. He could've killed us. I know you can come back and all, but what if he tore you to shreds? How the hell am I supposed to put you back together?"

"Can you sew?" she asked.

"You're makin' a joke at a time like this?"

"Better to make a joke than cry about it. At least now we know what won't work. I can't use my power against him."

"At least not to kill."

"No." She hobbled from the pub, desperate for some air clear of the foul stench of death.

"What do we do now? What about that guy? The zombie?"

"Leave him be. He'll drop dead soon enough."

"Drop dead?"

"Even corpses have expiry dates."

No use moping about how she wasn't all-powerful anymore. Her Celestine power was useless, and this was one scrap she couldn't get herself out of. She supposed there was a first for everything. There was only one thing they could do at a time like this.

Grasping Tristan's shoulder for support, she said, "We need to find our friends."

CHAPTER 7

"Rix is hiding out where?" Zac asked in surprise as Nye pointed to the arrivals display.

They stood inside the concourse at London's Waterloo train station, waiting for the platform number to show up for a train to Hampton Court.

"Hampton Court Palace." The number flashed up on the screen and the spy began to weave through the crowd. "He used to be a bodyguard of sorts to Henry the Eighth and his harem. He spent a lot of time out there, I assume. Roaming the halls, cracking skulls, and all that stuff."

"So, he was a good guy once upon a time?"

"Depends on your definition of *good*. Henry was a mental case. He was dead before I was born, but England still reeked of his legacy, even under his daughter Elizabeth. Rix was party to that, even if it was only under orders. Everyone on the losing side was doing shit they believed in until they got caught. Then they blamed it on 'orders'." He air-quoted the last part as they stepped into a train carriage towards the end.

"And you're sure he would've gone back there?" Zac asked as he sat in a seat next to the window.

Nye sunk down across from him, putting his feet onto the seat. "Rix never talked much about his life before that. Few of us had nice beginnings, so I don't blame him for keeping his trap shut. When he did talk about it—on the rare occasion he was off his face drunk—he always spoke about Hampton Court. It actually sounded like he was happy there, you know? It's the obvious place to look and if he ain't there, then I have no idea where he's gone."

A feeling of absolute sorrow washed over Zac and he leaned forwards, his elbows on his knees. Sinking his head low, he took a few deep breaths. It came out of nowhere, but if anything the past year had taught him was that it always meant something supernatural was going on. His thoughts went straight to Aya, and he knew it had something to do with her.

Nye sat up straight and frowned at him. "What's wrong?"

"I just..." he said, rubbing his eyes. "I think it's Aya. Something's happening."

"Like what?"

Zac didn't know what to say, so he just said what he'd felt, "Sadness."

"Do you think it's her blood? She is a little unpredictable."

"Her blood gave me dreams for a while," he said, glancing out the window. Impossible dreams that'd been windows into her past at a time he'd thought she was gone forever.

"Then maybe you're picking up on whatever she's feeling."

Zac shrugged and wondered if she'd gone home. He didn't think he was that special to warrant such anguish. He hoped she had worked up the courage to face her past and move beyond it. It was what he was trying to do after all, and she'd spent a lot more time than him running from it.

An overwhelming desire to ditch everything and go find her pricked at his skin.

"You said it yourself..." Nye continued, "we've got work to do. No running back when you're the one who broke it off, mate."

"Are you a mind reader?" he asked with a scowl.

"Don't need to read minds when it's written all over your face." The spy kicked his feet back onto the seat. "Besides, helping the Three find their way back is the aim, right? Helping them helps you find your own way. We've already got one out of three. Don't stop before we've got the complete set."

"Right."

"Then it's psycho fairy ass kicking time." He punched his fist against his palm.

The train pulled into the station and Nye led the way, pressing the button to open the doors. Only a handful of people got off, and they began to walk towards the exit.

"Thar she blows," the spy declared, pointing across the river.

Hampton Court Palace was pretty unmissable. It sat right next to the river Thames, its red brick façade and gardens stretched from the modern bridge for as far as the eye could see. The building itself wasn't that large, not like Zac'd been expecting, but the grounds went on and on.

They crossed over the water, walked through the front gates, and down the long driveway, past tourists wandering in either direction. There was a small building to the left that seemed to be the ticket office, and Nye strode in like he owned the place. Zac could only follow his lead.

No one else was waiting to be served, so the spy went right up to the counter, startling a woman who'd been filing her nails.

She looked them up and down, trying to hide a look that said, 'What the hell do you want to come here for?' They did look like a pair of thugs in their heavy black coats and boots. Combine that with Zac's constant scowl and Nye's pretty face, they probably didn't fit in anywhere, least of all Hampton Court Palace and its horde of tourists.

"You gonna give us a ticket, love?" Nye asked with a

wink. "Or are you just gonna stare? I can give you my number if you'd like? What time you get off?"

The woman swallowed hard and said, "Two adults cost forty-nine pounds."

"Forty-nine quid?" Nye exclaimed. "That's highway robbery!" Leaning over the counter, he said, "How's about just giving them to us?"

She shook her head, looking bewildered, and printed out a pair of tickets and handed them to the spy. "Enjoy your visit."

"Cheers, love."

"Smooth," Zac drawled as they walked outside. "We could've just compelled the guy at the gate. You didn't have to scare the poor woman."

"There's too many people around and we're too conspicuous." He nodded at the gate that led into the castle grounds. People milled about the entrance where a guy stood on one side scanning tickets with a hand-held gun.

"The place closes in half an hour."

"Good thing we got in before last admission." The spy slapped him on the shoulder.

They stood in the middle of the forecourt and Zac scanned the façade. He wasn't sure what he was looking for, but it was a weird sensation standing inside something that was older than he was. Considering he'd been born in another century, it was strange to think he could get any older.

"I suppose we need a map," he said, watching

tourists go in and out of different doorways and under archways, which looked like another outside court. The light was fading fast—being the dead of winter and all—but people still milled about, not bothered in the slightest.

"Don't need one," Nye said. "It may have been almost five hundred years ago, but I remember a thing or two about this place."

"Sometimes I forget how old you are."

"I'm an old musty man," the spy proclaimed. "But not as musty as the Irish knight."

Zac shook his head with a laugh. "Then where do you think Rix would be? I'm sure a place like this has a lot of hidden corners."

"He spent a lot of time protecting the king. My guess is that he would be around one of the passages leading from his apartments. Underground, not up here with this rabble."

"Okay, then. Lead the way."

They made their way across the cobblestoned courtyard and into a door that was marked with a sign reading, 'Henry VIII's Apartments'.

"Once upon a time, in a land far, far away…" Nye began as they walked through the first floor, "there lived a king who couldn't keep it in his pants."

"I'm sure it went another way," Zac said as a few tourists turned to stare.

"Who needs an audio guide when you've got me?"

"People who want the clean version."

His friend grinned as they found the stairs and walked upwards. "Henry liked to do a lot of things in his bedroom. One of them being coming..." he paused for dramatic effect, "and going."

Rolling his eyes, Zac thumped up the ancient stairway, past the Medieval tapestries and swords that hung on the walls. It really was lavish and nice to look at, but they hadn't come to gawk.

"Elizabeth lived here for a while," Nye continued. "I came here a few times. Being a spymaster meant I was privy to all the hidden passageways and hidey holes. They did them pretty well, and I could probably say with certainty that most of them haven't been opened in hundreds of years."

"Hidden stashes of Medieval jewels?"

"All kinds of things. Medieval spank boxes."

"Too much information."

The attendant at the top of the stairs gave them a look as they stepped onto the landing. Without glancing twice, the vampires went into the first room, which was a formal throne room where the monarch at the time would receive guests. Beyond, was another throne room for the more important people, then a formal sitting room for private audiences. All of them had painted ceilings and gold-leaf-encrusted carvings and furniture to match. Knowing how the other half must've lived made it a very stark contrast.

"Here," Nye said, waving him forwards into the next room.

The royal bedchamber was dark and small with a four-poster bed in the middle, flanked by ornate dressers and chairs. Rugs lined the floor, elaborate tapestries covered the walls, and the windows opened out to the manicured gardens below. The bed was smaller than Zac thought it'd be, not exactly 'king-sized', not by modern standards. He gathered people were shorter back then and going by Nye's height, he thought it must be the case—he was almost a whole head taller than the spy.

Standing beside the rope that blocked off the room from the designated walkway, Nye glanced back the way they'd come, looking for the attendant. "The one good thing about winter," he said, "is that there ain't that many people tramping through the king's bedroom."

When he was satisfied the coast was clear, he stepped over the rope and strode across to the tapestry that covered a large portion of the opposite wall. Lifting the corner, his arm disappeared behind it, feeling the paneling behind.

"A secret passage?" Zac asked, glancing over his shoulder.

"Escape route..." Nye's muffled reply came. "I don't know if anyone realises it's here. There's a trick with this one and if you don't get it in the right angle, you could be here for days." There was a dull thud and a click, and the spy stuck his head out from behind the tapestry and shot his friend a grin. "You coming?"

Zac followed Nye through the gap in the wooden paneling and the spy slid it closed. It clicked into place and they were thrown into darkness.

"It's a crawlspace for a few yards, then it drops a floor, then into the underground." The spy inched forwards, his back against the wall. The air stunk like soot and grime, and their boots kicked up a thick layer of dust as they shuffled the length of the first section of the crawlspace.

"So, it was used as an escape route for the king if the castle was ever breached?" Zac asked, his voice low.

"Yeah, and secret messengers and prostitutes and all kinds of debauchery."

"Why this one?"

"This is the only way down to the section of tunnel I think Rix would be."

The spy led him down a set of crude stairs that were only slightly wider than the crawlspace. At the foot, they opened out on a passageway that was wide enough for them to stand face on, but their shoulders still brushed the stone walls on either side. The path seemed to slope downwards before they came to another set of stairs that led down to the underground.

When they reached the bottom, Nye stopped and gestured down the tunnel. A warm light radiated ahead, breaking up the darkness. Someone was down here and chances were, it was Rix. Who else could it be?

Zac edged around the spy and took point, tiptoeing

forwards. The moment he stepped into the light, hands grabbed the lapels of his coat and flung him across the room. He collided against the stone with a bang, dirt and grit raining down on him as he landed face first on the floor. Powerful hands circled his throat and began to squeeze.

"Rix," Nye exclaimed, pulling the vampire off Zac. "Calm down, mate. It's only us."

"I know who it is." He shoved the spy away. Pointing at Zac, he snarled, "That is for the car crash and your lack of loyalty."

"I won't apologise for that," Zac replied, scrambling to his feet. "If honour is your thing, then you'll understand I was bound to others before Regulus ever showed up."

Rix didn't seem to care. "What the hell do you want?"

"We've come to ask for your help," Zac replied, dusting himself off.

"You want my help? *Not likely.*"

Nye stepped between them and if Zac knew what was going to happen next, he might have pushed the spy out of the way. "You think by hiding yourself away down here you're going to bring back Jocelyn?"

"Shut up," Rix roared, pushing Nye back into the wall.

"She's been gone five hundred years, mate."

The vampire's hands curled tightly in front of the

spy's shirt, chest heaving, and eyes starting to change. "Don't you dare say her name."

Zac watched the exchange, not sure what to do. Who the hell was Jocelyn?

"Do you really want to waste away to a shadow?"

"Who was she?" Zac asked and Rix's eyes fixed on him.

The vampire snarled, "I loved her... I loved her, and they took her away from me."

If it was one thing Zac knew about, it was lost love. "Let Nye go, Rix. Hurting him won't solve anything. It might shut him up, but it won't fix anything."

The vampire let go of Nye, taking a step backwards.

"Why are you down here?" Zac asked. "What is this place to you?"

"What do you think?" he spat. "I met her here."

"Who was she?"

Rix scowled. "Why should I tell you?"

"We're trying to help you, mate," Nye said. He pointed to Zac. "This guy loves the Hunter. If anyone understands twisted love stories, it's him."

Zac simply shrugged.

"Lady Jocelyn was a noblewoman at court," Rix finally said. "I protected the king, and she was his plaything. He cared not for her and when he was done and cast her from his bed, I would escort her back to her rooms."

Rix had loved the king's mistress. The vampire was

built with hard muscle, broad shoulders, and a hard face, not exactly what some would consider handsome. She'd loved him for who he was under all of that. No wonder the memory of whatever happened next still stung deep.

"No one defies the king..." he went on. "We met right under his nose, night after night. We were fools to think that no one would notice."

"He found out?"

"He killed her," Rix said, dropping to his knees. "He had her executed the moment he found out about us."

"Who did?"

"The king. He let the guards have their way with her and then they cut off her head. There was nothing I could do... I couldn't save her."

"Hiding down in your secret meeting place isn't going to bring her back," Nye said a little too bluntly.

Rix went to stand, his eye darkening, but Zac put a hand on his shoulder.

"He's right," he said. "He could be a little more tactful about it, but he's right. We need your help, Rix."

"You need my help?" the vampire scoffed. "You should've thought about that before killing Regulus. You have no idea what that man did for me."

"No, I don't. But what's done is done, and the future is still here."

"He saved my life, don't you understand?"

"He turned you," Nye said in disbelief.

"Yes, he turned me. I was left to rot in the dungeons

in the Tower, all for loving a noblewoman. He found my pathetic arse and we struck a bargain."

"Servitude in exchange for—"

"The heads of Jocelyn's murderers."

Zac glanced at Nye and frowned.

"I could never get close to the king," Rix said. "Not without a bloodbath and not without revealing what I'd become. Regulus forbid it. I was compelled not to destroy the Tudors. When it was done, I returned to him and never left. I was the first of the Six, but not the last." He looked at Nye, who nodded. "You know what it's like, Nye."

"Yeah, I know. He had a way with words you couldn't fault."

Zac scoffed, "Manipulation."

"Maybe with you," Rix drawled.

"I believe Regulus was trying to find something," Zac continued, ignoring the bait. "The Coven were trying to wake someone... something."

"So what?"

"We now know it woke a hybrid," Zac told him.

"A bad ass, magical vampire-fae hybrid," Nye added for emphasis.

Zac glared at the spy. "I don't know what Regulus wanted with him, but it's become glaringly obvious that we need to stop the hybrid."

"Why?" Rix asked.

"Do you understand what the Hunter is?"

Rix shook his head. "We were tasked with hunting her, that's all."

"She was once a creature of power. Arturius turned her, but she kept a lot of what she was afterwards. That's why she can kill a founder, and why she's strong and unpredictable."

"And what does that have to do with this other guy?"

"He wasn't turned, Rix. He was *created*. Corrupt, unstable, and totally unpredictable. Add to that whatever power he had before, and well—"

"We're all in the shit," Nye finished.

Rix rolled his eyes. "Yeah, but why the hell should I care?"

"Because the hybrid threatens us all," Zac told him. "He's a threat to exposing our kind to the human world. He's a threat to everything on this entire planet."

"He's Henry the Eighth on acid, mate," Nye butted in.

Rix looked from Zac back to the spy and then down at his hands. "You need numbers?"

"Yes," Zac answered. "But numbers are nothing without vampires we can trust and who can fight... willingly. I won't make you come with us. I won't bargain with you. That's our plea and you can hear it or not."

"And if I choose to stay here?"

"Then you'll miss one hell of a fight," the spy declared wryly.

Rix's fingers curled into hard fists. After a minute, he asked, "Where are you meeting?"

"The apartment in Camden," Zac said.

"Who else?"

"Pyke."

"What about Maddox?"

"We haven't found him yet."

"Good luck with that."

"So, are you coming?"

"Maybe," he said with a scowl. "Exit's that way." He pointed to an opening opposite to where they first entered.

Nodding, Zac shoved Nye into the passageway. There was nothing more they could say, and he just had to trust that Rix would show up along with Pyke. It was all part of the process.

When they were far enough away, Nye said, "Do you think he'll actually show up?"

"Yes."

"Mate, you've got some belief system happening there because I have serious doubts."

"No time for doubts, Nye. You didn't think it would've been a good idea to let me in on Rix's girlfriend?"

"Was it ever my place to tell someone's messed up story like that?" He grinned as they stepped out into the moonlight.

"I guess not."

The air was crisp and clear, heavy with ice, and stars twinkled down on them in the hundreds through the light pollution of the city. It was eerily calm. He could have gone as far to say it was the calm before the storm—because a storm was coming and who knew what it was bringing with it.

CHAPTER 8

Gabby sat in the car next to Regulus as he drove away from Brú na Bóinne, images of Coraline and Max swimming around her mind.

She'd seen it before... carnage. When Aya had first shown up back in Ashburton, she'd saved Zac from the werewolf pack in a similar fashion. Death was part and parcel with fighting supernatural evil, but she'd never seen it happen to her friends before, even if they were friends she'd never actually met in person. As the car rounded a bend, she felt a little green.

"Are you okay, Gabrielle?"

"Fine," she replied, not knowing which part should make her feel sicker—what had happened down in the Tuatha's hole or Regulus' concern. Both were equally disturbing. "What now?"

"Tomorrow we'll go to Grasmere," he replied.

"Why there?"

"I suspect he wants answers."

"Yeah, no shit. Three thousand years locked in a pile of rock would do that to you."

Regulus smirked but didn't say anything.

"Well?" She was inches away from putting her hands on her hips and pouting like a five-year-old. Maybe a few burst brain cells would loosen his tongue?

"Well, what, Gabrielle?" You need to ask me a question if you require an answer."

"Why Grasmere?"

"The village stands near the place where the Celestines had built their last home."

Aya's home.

She suddenly got it. Regulus had been there before, hadn't he? He glanced at her out the corner of his eye.

"How are we getting there?" she asked. "And what do you think you'll do if we find him?"

"We'll get the ferry from Dublin and drive the rest of the way."

"Now?" she asked with a scowl.

"Tomorrow, dear one." The Roman grinned at her with a stupid sparkle in his eye. Of course, he'd enjoy riling her up. It's all he did.

Before they hit Dublin's city limits, Regulus pulled the car into a driveway. When the tree line cleared and she could see ahead, her eyebrows rose. It was a castle. Not a huge thing with a moat and drawbridge and the stuff out of fairy tales; it was a Medieval castle, with turrets and stained glass windows and a cottage garden with manicured hedges. It was a place out of the history books that'd been brought up to modern speed.

"What..." she began, but the words died in her throat. This was the side of Ireland she had wanted to see, not the underside she'd been subjected to so far. She wanted the history and romance part.

"This is quite a lovely place," Regulus said, ignoring her. "It's been standing here for a few hundred years in its current incarnation, but I understand it's history goes back a thousand years or more. It's a hotel now."

"I suppose you remember when it was built," she snapped, annoyed that he'd broken the spell.

"Yes," he said with such bluntness that she snorted at the irony. "I am an old bastard." He shrugged.

"You're the master," she said, waving a hand at him.

"Gabrielle, you know all the right things to say."

"Pervert." She got out of the car and slammed the door, wrapping her arms around herself.

He was beside her a moment later, their bags in his hands. Snatching hers from him, she turned, but he placed hand on the small of her back that stopped her from storming off.

Regulus guided her through the front door and inside, and Gabby couldn't help it when her guard dropped.

It'd obviously been remodelled with electric lights

and heating, but most of the original castle remained. Tapestries hung on the walls, much like they would've when the castle was first built, and they stood on a long, woven rug that stretched across the stone floor from the entrance to the foot of a wide staircase. A suit of armour towered in one corner, gleaming silver in the warm light and holding an impressive sword.

The castle was beautiful and regal and all the above.

Footsteps drew her attention to the staircase and an elderly lady appeared, her grey hair tied back into a severe bun and a thick woollen cardigan wrapped around her tiny frame. Her shoes clicked on each step as she descended towards them, a huge smile on her face.

"Ahh," the woman exclaimed in a thick Irish accent when she laid eyes on the founder. "Robert, how nice to see you again."

Gabby gave Regulus a look that said, 'Are you kidding me?'

"Mrs. Cavanagh," he declared warmly, "it's been a long time."

"Too long."

Gabby watched the exchange with slack-jawed surprise. All traces of the asshole she knew were gone and some impostor stood in front of her talking sweetly with this old lady.

"Would you like your usual room?" Mrs. Cavanagh asked, glancing at her.

"Yes, thank you."

"And who is this? A lady friend?"

"This is Gabrielle." He gestured for her to come forwards. "Mrs. Cavanagh has been the caretaker here for almost fifty years."

"Fifty-five, but who's countin'," she said with a smile. "Now, come. I'll get you the key and you make yourself right at home."

Mrs. Cavanagh led them into a small office set to one side of the main foyer and pulled out a set of keys —the old-fashioned kind, tarnished with age. Regulus took them with a warm smile, and Gabby noticed he was careful not to let his skin touch hers.

"As always," the woman said, "if you need anythin', just give me a holler."

"Thank you, Mrs. Cavanagh. I will endeavour to let you know."

He took Gabby's bag from her hands and led her up the staircase, leaving the woman behind.

"What the hell was that?" she asked, glancing over her shoulder the way they'd come.

"Why, I don't know what you mean," he replied with amusement.

"Liar."

"She doesn't know what I am, Gabrielle."

"So, you compelled her, *Robert*?"

"Never. And Robert seemed so much more appropriate than Regulus, don't you think?"

"But how long have you been coming here? Doesn't she notice that you never change?"

"No, she doesn't notice because she's half-blind," he said as he guided her down the hall. "I lived here for a time back in the fourteen hundreds, and I was feeling nostalgic in the 1940s."

"If she's half-blind, then how did she know it was you?"

"Gabrielle, I'm surprised. Do I distract you that much?" He laughed as she scowled at him.

"Ugh, gag me."

"She's a *witch*. Only she doesn't know it and her power is so insignificant, the only thing it's good for is to recognise the people she looks at through the fog clouding her eyesight."

How Gabby didn't pick up on that was beyond her. Maybe she was distracted... just not by him, but by everything else. "So, you saw a witch and...?"

"The day I came back here was the day she lost her sight, Gabrielle. A group of men had her face down in the field by the stream and I happened by them. You can imagine what they were doing to her, so I won't elaborate. They'd rubbed dirt and grit into her eyes and there was nothing I could do, not without making it worse. Vampire blood isn't a cure-all, sad to say."

Why the hell was he telling her any of this? She was just his tool, here for her power when he needed it. All of this was pointless. Did he want to show her he had a heart?

"This place was a lord's castle when it was first built," he continued, "and his daughters were witches."

"Oh, so you were here manipulating them, too?"

His jaw tensed, but he didn't reply. Unlocking a small door set into the thick stone wall, he pushed it open and led her into their room. To her disgust, there was only one bed.

When he saw the look on her face, he said, "I'm a founding vampire, Gabrielle, not a rapist."

"I'm not... I didn't," she sputtered.

"I'm sure you're more than capable of defending yourself," he said with amusement. "You've tried to make my head explode on several occasions, so I know you're capable."

He set their bags down by the bed as she hovered by the door, feeling more awkward and out of her depth than ever before. She was supposed to hate him, and then he sprung that story on her? Gabby realised she didn't have any clue who this man really was, and that unsettled her beyond belief. Even her power tingled in her gut, but what it was trying to tell her, she didn't know. These things always had a way of bubbling to the surface when they were least expected.

"I was human once," Regulus said, closing the door. "I was capable of terrible things then as I am now. When I was human, I tried to kill my emperor. Everyone was quick to brand me as the evil one, but not one asked me *why*. Why did I try to kill him?

Because he was corrupt. Because he killed innocent people. Because he was the evil one."

"Regulus—"

"I was prepared to die for what was right. Does that make me evil? Everything I did after was what I believed in, even if I didn't have a choice but to follow Katrin's orders. I hunted the Children of Lir and I hunted Aeriaya. I saved people and I killed them all in the same breath. Do you really think I'm truly evil?"

Gabby pressed herself back against the wall, her heart thumping erratically in her chest as he loomed closer. She'd finally managed to piss him off and it hadn't taken much, just the right button. Regulus stepped into her, his hands winding through her hair.

"I can hear your heart beating, Gabrielle," he murmured. "Is it fear... or something else?"

She was too startled to answer.

"You think me incapable of mercy. Incapable of compassion. *Of love.*" His lips brushed against hers, sending a shiver down her spine.

His gaze searched hers for a long moment, looking for something she didn't understand. With a sigh, he pressed his lips against the corner of her mouth and whispered, "Get some rest, Gabrielle. Our work continues in the morning."

And then he was gone.

Gabby woke to a silent room. Rolling over, she found she was very much alone, and her first thoughts went to Regulus. Where had he been all night?

Trying not to think about it, she went into the small bathroom and had a quick shower before he decided it would be a good time to come back. Pulling on some clean clothes and sticking her feet back into her boots, she shoved the door open with her shoulder and jumped when she laid eyes on the founder.

He sat on the bed, legs outstretched, waiting for her to get ready. Her eyes glided over his long body and she noticed he looked brighter, his eyes a little less dark. He'd obviously gone out to feed.

He looked at her with a raised eyebrow at her blatant staring. "See something you like?"

"I hope you didn't kill her," she retorted.

Regulus snorted, shifting on the bed. "Jealous?"

"In your dreams, asswipe." Why was it so important to him that she see him other than what he was? The more she thought about it, the more it became a mystery. Her thoughts grazed over the story he'd told about the elderly caretaker downstairs and she was still confused. His part in Gabby's tale was that of the evil overlord; there was no grey area.

"Are you ready? I can get you something to eat on the ferry."

She nodded and put her things into her bag. Her hands shook a little as she folded her clothes, and she didn't know why.

"As much as I would like to linger in this place," he hesitated before continuing, "we have more pressing matters to attend to."

He'd been happy here. The notion slammed into her and she realised her power was latching onto his emotions. He felt strongly about this place and it was potent enough for her to sense it.

There was nothing she could add to that, so they said their goodbyes to Mrs. Cavanagh and were back in the car for the next stage of their hunt for the hybrid.

They drove in silence all the way to the ferry terminal just north of central Dublin. They sat in silence all the way across the Irish sea as the ferry dipped and rose with the currents all the way to Liverpool. They stood in silence as their passports were checked and as they queued in the long line of cars and trucks waiting to be let off.

It was becoming a ritual, the way they went from place to place, not having time to wonder about where they were. City became countryside again and again as they travelled in pursuit of Aed. They needed to catch up, they needed to finish him, but she wished they never did. What if she wasn't strong enough? What if something happened to Regulus? What if...?

As the car wove through the countryside everything became greener and sharper, the air heavy with moisture. Gabby had thought Ireland was green, but it had nothing on this place. The Lake District was brimming with life. Even with her earth sense, reigned in as it was, she could still feel it tingling around the edges. She longed to get out and wander in the woods and let it fly, but that was an indulgence she couldn't afford. She had to be ready for whatever awaited them here.

Regulus pulled the car off to the side of the road and killed the engine. They'd stopped just outside the village, the edges of buildings peeking through the trees ahead. She glanced at him, worry beginning to prickle her skin. She could feel something alien amongst the life of the forest.

Regulus' gaze met hers and she knew he felt it, too.

"Something's not right," he whispered, his voice sounding odd after not hearing it since that morning.

"I can feel it," she replied, everything she'd been fighting against the past day melting away.

"Stay here," he said, and went to get out the car.

Grabbing his hand, she shivered despite herself. "I'm coming with you."

He stared at her hand over his for a moment and nodded. "Stay close."

Standing together on the side of the deserted road, it was oddly quiet. Gabby glanced the way they'd come and back towards the village. Aed had been here, she was sure of it.

Regulus took her hand, his eyes darkening, lips pulling at his teeth.

"Regulus?" she murmured.

"I can smell blood," he said.

She'd never seen him look anything but human, and her heart skipped a beat at the sight of his body reacting to whatever he was picking up on.

"I won't hurt you," he said as his eyes settled back to their usual brown. "I'd never touch you like that. Not without your permission."

Not without her permission. The thought alarmed her a little. "We have to keep moving," she said. "I can handle myself if you get too frisky."

A grin pulled at his lips and he tightened his grip on her hand. "I know you can, dear one."

He guided her up the street, through the quaint little village, past shops selling gingerbread and local handicrafts, past houses built right on the edge of the road. He led her to the ancient pub and stopped outside the door.

They hadn't seen one soul. The feeling of dread was heavier here and whatever had happened had been inside the pub.

"You don't have to come in," Regulus said. "The scent of blood is overpowering. I can only imagine what waits inside."

"I need to," she replied. "We're fighting this together. Where you walk, so do I."

A sad smile tugged at his lips. "You surprise me more than you should, dear one."

"Let's go," she said, nodding towards the door. "No time like the present."

The first thing Gabby saw when she stepped into the pub was blood and bodies. Whoever had been in here when Aed had shown his face was a goner. Half a dozen people lay haphazardly about the room, all in different degrees of mutilation. An arm missing there, a head gone, exposed bones... and blood, lots of blood. It stained the carpet and walls, the stench overpowering.

She thought that would be enough to give her the creeps, but her gaze fixed onto movement behind the bar. A man stood there, a cloth in his hand. He was wiping down the bar in swirling motions, one continuous circle in the same spot, over and over. His eyes were blank and unseeing, dead.

"What the hell?" She watched as he went over the same spot again and again and wondered how long he'd been like that. Cleaning the blood of his patrons, staring blankly. Was he compelled?

"Can you sense that?" Regulus asked, peering at the man through narrowed eyes.

"Sense what?"

"Exactly." The Roman dropped her hand and poked at the bartender but got no response. "I was afraid of this."

"Afraid of what?" What hadn't he told her now?

"This man is dead, Gabrielle. He has no heartbeat, but he still goes on. What do you think happened here?"

Her breath caught in her throat. Aya still had her

power... and so did Aed. "Necromancy," she whispered in horror.

"The Tuatha led vast armies. Friend against friend."

"They had armies of the dead?" Regulus' words echoed in her mind. *The devourers of worlds...*

The Roman grasped the man's face and twisted, the snap as the human's neck broke echoed through the silent pub. He let the body slump to the floor behind the bar where she couldn't see. "Don't look, dear one." He grabbed a bottle opener that'd been lying amongst the blood and knelt out of her line of sight. The sickening sound of shattering bone and squelching brains assaulted her ears and she squeezed her eyes shut.

Then there was the sound of running water and the familiar presence that signalled Regulus was at her side. "Come outside," he murmured in her ear. "There is nothing more we can do in this place."

Opening the door, she stepped out into the cool air, the stench of blood fading away. It still lingered around the edges, but the heavy feeling of death eased. Grasmere would have a haunted pub to add to its tourist attractions now. The energy in that place was off the charts, and it would be there for a very long time to come.

"Why was he here?" she asked with her back to the pub.

"He obviously took it upon himself to seek out the Celestines at the source."

"Aya?"

"I gather she was recently here. It was her home, after all."

"This was Aya's home?" she asked, looking down the empty street.

"Not this village. This place was built many years afterwards. In the forest."

"Of course, you'd know where she lived. You kidnapped her."

"Yes," he said bluntly, and she felt like slapping him.

"Can we go there?" she asked, wondering if Aya was still here.

"No, I cannot. It exists on a plane next to ours. The only way in is with witch's magic. You are welcome to go, but I don't see the point."

Knowing what'd happened there, Gabby shook her head. It didn't seem right going to a place where the last of Aya's family and kind were slaughtered. Especially since she stood next to one of the vampires who was responsible.

"I was ordered to do it," Regulus said. He'd been watching the changing expression on her face, so it wasn't hard to guess what she was thinking about.

"Why does my opinion even matter to you?"

"Because it does."

"Ugh." She threw her hands in the air and strode towards the car. "You're so infuriating."

"How so?" Another game of words.

"You're such a know-it-all and never elaborate. You thought Aed might still have his power and never told me about it. I can't help you if you're not forthcoming."

"There was a nice bed and breakfast back down by the lake," he said, looking at his watch. "We will travel back to London in the morning."

"That's all you're giving me?"

"You must be tired, Gabrielle. Sleeping in the car mustn't be very comfortable for you."

"Just when I think there might be more to you, you turn around and be the asshole I know you are. Why do you have to do that? You're so exhausting, I hate myself for trying anything other than thinking the worst of you." She spun on her heel and stormed back to the car, not even sure why it had angered her so much. The day she could go home and forget about Regulus and this stupid saga, the happier she'd be.

CHAPTER 9

"I'm amazed you know so much about the Three," Zac said as he walked with Nye down a dark and seedy looking alleyway.

"Step one of being a spy is to know everyone's business, right down to the last detail. No one could fart without me knowing about it."

"Seriously?"

"Maybe not those kinds of bodily functions, but near enough."

The farther they walked into the secret, seedy underbelly of Shoreditch in east London, the more Zac's senses prickled. "Where are we going, anyway?"

"Friday night is fight night," the spy replied, pointing to a building at the end of the lane.

"It's Tuesday."

"Then every night is fight night."

Zac looked over at the building that Nye had pointed to and found there was nothing special about it. An abandoned brick and mortar number in the middle of the city that everyone but the undesirables had forgotten. There was a heavy-set man by the door who looked like he was a bouncer there to separate the rabble from the echelon.

"He's a vampire," Nye said, nodding towards the door.

"How do you know that?" The entire place radiated a smell that suggested something had been left to rot.

"I've seen him before. I've come here a lot over the years looking for Maddox. If he was on a downer, he'd either be out mauling some poor woman or beating the crap outta some vampires."

Zac gave him a look. "Beating the crap out of vampires?"

"It's an underground boxing ring. Vampires only."

"Is this like a *Fight Club* thing?"

"The first rule is, there are no rules."

"I thought the first rule was not talking about it."

"If you didn't talk about it, then how would anyone know to come?" Nye asked with a grin. "C'mon."

They walked up to the bouncer, who straightened when he caught their scent.

"No pussies allowed, boys," he said as they approached.

Zac rolled his eyes. "We're looking for Maddox." The guy stunk like blood, but then again, the entire place did.

"Who's lookin' to know?" the man rumbled, sizing up the two vampires.

"The Six," Nye said, narrowing his eyes.

The bouncer eyed them once more before opening the door and nodding his head.

As they walked inside, Zac gave his friend a look.

"Golden ticket with this lot." Nye shrugged. "We're lucky word hasn't spread far."

The entire place fell silent the moment they walked in. A cage was in the middle, empty for the moment, and a bar was set up on one side. Other than that, the only thing that stood out was the thirty or so vampires that were staring at them. Zac narrowed his eyes in annoyance and just as suddenly, they all turned around and began talking again.

"They're afraid of you, mate," Nye said, elbowing him. "You can smell the fear."

Zac guessed they were. He hadn't really been well-adjusted when he first came to London a few weeks ago. Murdering vampires in their homes and in the middle of the city was a great start. Now that word was slowly creeping around that Regulus was dust courtesy of his right hand, who'd want to mess with him? Nye had his own reputation—being head honcho of the Six —and them as a pair could only mean trouble. Too bad they'd given up on thuggery for the foreseeable future.

Zac grabbed the arm of the nearest vampire, a man

who looked like he'd been turned in his early twenties. "We're looking for Maddox."

"Maddox?" he asked, swallowing hard.

"You deaf as well as dumb?" Nye prodded.

"O-out b-back," he stammered, pointing to a door on the opposite side of the room.

Dropping the vampire's arm, Zac strode across the room, the crowd parting. This was getting tiresome already and they'd just walked in.

"Once, I would've lapped that shit up. Their fear. Now, it's just annoying," he said to Nye.

"That's called personal growth."

Zac eyed him.

"That's the point, right? Your missus locked you up and tortured your humanity back to teach you to be a better person."

"When you say it like that, it sounds messed up."

"It *is* messed up, but vampires don't do shit any other way. It's the thrill of the spectacle."

"Maddox will give us a spectacle," Zac said, his hand on the doorknob. "You ready for it?"

Nye shrugged. "He's gonna make *you* jump through that big hoop, mate. Don't look at me."

Without answering, Zac pushed the door open and came face to face with Maddox.

"Well, look what the cat dragged in," he drawled.

The assassin stood in the middle of the room, surrounded by empty liquor bottles and mismatched furniture, wearing nothing but a pair of jeans. Blood splotches were across his chest and he cracked his knuckles. He'd obviously been one of the fighters and was gearing up for more.

"You stink like stale piss," Nye said, screwing up his nose.

"Well, screw you, too."

"How many you won?"

"You're not here to talk about the weather, Nye. What do you want?"

"We want you," Zac said, trying to ignore the stench of stale sweat and blood. Hadn't anyone ever heard of air freshener?

"Sorry, I don't swing that way," the assassin said with a smirk.

"We want you to fight," he said more firmly.

"With you? Not likely. I suppose you think you can take Regulus' place," Maddox said, cracking his knuckles again. "Bring the Six back together... Oh, forgive me. Aren't we the Three now? As far as I'm concerned, you two aren't invited."

"Not likely." Zac sighed. "I wouldn't touch that with a forty-foot pole."

"Man, you're stupid," the assassin said. "You killed a *founder*. If you're too stupid to take power, then someone else will."

"And I suppose that someone is *you*?"

Maddox spread his arms wide. "And why shouldn't it be?"

"We have bigger things to worry about than a few

dogs fighting over scraps," Zac replied. "The Coven woke a hybrid, Maddox."

"Happy joy. Good luck with that." He turned his back.

"He's not just any hybrid," Nye said. "He's a three-thousand-year-old Fae-hybrid who can't be killed, is bloody insane, and nobody knows what the hell he wants. That's the most dangerous combination of them all. Who do you think he'd go for first?"

Maddox looked back at them and frowned. "The seat of power."

"We need to get rid of him," Zac said. "No one will be safe as long as he's around. Human, vampire, or otherwise."

"And I suppose you need my help. I can't see any other reason why you're here."

"We need as much strength as we can get, and the Three have it."

"The Three?" the assassin scoffed. "Rix and Pyke are going along with this?"

"Yep," Nye said, leaning against the wall. "You're the only stubborn old man out of the bunch."

"That's because I've got nothing to lose and no memories to give two tosses about."

"Yeah, yeah," Nye waved his hand, "you're the ultimate vampire. Tell someone who cares."

Zac leaned against the wall, crossing his arms over his chest. "You're either in or out. There's no grey area."

They watched Maddox as he mulled it over, pacing

back and forth, his bare feet shuffling across the concrete floor.

"I'll cut you a deal," he said, looking Zac in the eye. "Fight me, and depending on how much you amuse me, I'll consider it."

"Fight you?" Zac scoffed. "Are you serious?"

"I haven't forgotten the car crash. You know, the one you deliberately caused to free that Coven witch?"

"So what?"

"I have four hundred years on your arse, but I know enough that age doesn't matter in the slightest with you. I want to fight so I can see what you've got when you're not being a sneaky bastard."

"Fine," Zac said with a sigh. Fighting was his thing, after all. If Maddox wanted a few rounds of bloody violence, then Zac would give it to him.

"No shirt, no shoes. No belts, watches, or anything else that can be used as a weapon," the assassin said.

Without a word, Zac shucked off his coat and kicked off his boots, dumping them in the corner. His shirt followed and Nye let out a wolf whistle.

"Do you ever get tired of being a cocky bastard?" Maddox asked.

"Nope. It's second nature," the spy retorted.

"I'm ready," Zac said, cracking his knuckles. "Let's do this if we're doing it."

Maddox frowned at him. "You don't want to wrap your hands?"

"Don't be such a pussy, Maddox. If there's no blood,

then it's not a fight. We're vampires," he said, pushing the assassin towards the door, "that shit will heal in thirty seconds. Are you afraid of a little pain or something?"

"I'm not afraid of anything," he hissed.

Maddox was different than the others. He had no sad story or family that he cared for. He just wanted to practice his craft. Killing people before they knew he was even there and vampirism had only made him better at it.

"Then get in that cage and show me what you've got."

As soon as they walked out, the room fell silent again, only this time, it was a different kind of silence. Then the murmuring started when they saw the two vampires heading for the cage. Then it became full throttle, with vampires yelling to place bets before the fight began, and the space around the chain-link cage filled within seconds

Zac filtered them out and focused on the task at hand. It wouldn't matter who won in the end; maybe only his pride would suffer a little if Maddox beat him to a pulp, but they'd both get what they wanted. He had no doubt the assassin would meet them at the apartment. Maddox wouldn't give up the opportunity to assassinate a hybrid Fae—after all, it was the ultimate trophy. This was just a formality.

Nye locked them inside the cage and the vampires stared at each other, neither of them moving, waiting to see who would attack first. The crowd rattled the cage, eager for some action, but Zac wasn't going to be rushed.

Predictably, it was Maddox who moved first. He was fast, but not fast enough. Zac dodged to the side as the assassin's fist flew towards him. Grabbing his forearm, Zac pulled the vampire's body into his and flipped him over his shoulder. The cage rattled violently as Maddox hit.

Turning, Zac grinned. "You can do better than that."

The assassin picked himself up and advanced again, this time taking it slow. He feigned left and Zac realised at the last second and went to dodge backwards, but by that time, a fist was already connecting with his right side, the pressure almost cracking his ribs. While he was stunned, Maddox grasped his arm and shoved a shoulder hard into his chest. He was flung through the air, rolling to a stop at the other side of the cage. The assassin was fast enough that he was already there waiting, and he kicked Zac in the gut as hard as he could.

Groaning, Zac clawed at the assassin's leg, pulled him down, and they wrestled, trying to land punches on each other. Eventually, Maddox got the upper hand, pulling Zac off the floor. He had him by the scruff of the neck, fingers digging so hard into his flesh that blood dripped along his collarbone.

Maddox's knee connected with Zac's ribs and there

was an audible crack, and the air was pushed out of his lungs. Before the assassin could crack another, Zac wrapped his arms around the vampire's stomach and pushed him back into the cage with all his strength.

Maddox grunted in pain and fell onto his back and Zac was over him, a hand around his neck, and punched him square in the face. Another crack signalled that he'd just broken the assassin's nose and blood streamed down his face, adding to the already overpowering stench of blood. Both their eyes changed and the crowd roared around them.

Zac curled his fingers into the front of Maddox's hair and the assassin clawed at his arm, tearing it to shreds, trying to make him let go. No matter how much it hurt, Zac didn't slacken his grip and pulled the vampire half off the floor before smashing his head into the concrete.

Maddox's eyes glazed over, but he still fought. With a roar, he bucked Zac off him and rolled on top, and this time, the assassin's fist connected with his jaw. Bone shattered and white-hot pain shot through his face, stars prickling through his vision.

"You like that?" Maddox exclaimed, his fist connecting again.

Zac raised his hands and grabbed the assassin's arm mid-punch and squeezed with everything he had. Bone snapped with a sickening crunch and Maddox fell back, shock plastered on his face. His right arm hung at an awkward angle and his already pale complexion turned white. He wasn't healing fast enough to keep going, that much was obvious.

"You can tap out, you know," Zac said, scrambling to his feet.

"Never," Maddox hissed and lunged upwards with his left hand, fingers outstretched.

Zac dodged as flesh grazed against his side. Last thing he wanted was a puncture wound in his gut—those took forever to heal and it was a pain in his ass he'd rather not deal with. Swinging around, he grabbed the assassin's head between his hands and pushed him down to the ground, a knee firmly in the small of his back. One simple move and Maddox would have big problems. One being a broken spine, the other a shattered skull or a broken neck, or if he was lucky, all the above.

The assassin roared in annoyance, his entire body tense with pent-up anger. He knew he was done, and he tapped the concrete floor with his good hand. Zac pressed his knee harder into his back, a warning not to try anything. A tap out was a tap out. This fight was over.

Letting him go, Zac stood, ignoring the crowd who'd become rowdier once there was a clear victor. Maddox rolled onto his back with a groan, holding his limp arm to his stomach. He looked majorly pissed off, but he'd lost fair and square.

Zac held out his hand as the assassin glared up at him and wiped his bloody nose with a scowl. "We don't have to be friends, Maddox. We just have to get along."

With a shake of his head, Maddox grasped Zac's forearm. "I'll help you with your hybrid problem and that's all."

Zac hauled the vampire to his feet, his bones cracking as they healed. "Deal."

CHAPTER 10

Pushing open the door, Gabby looked over the room and saw there was only one bed. *Again.*

The little bed and breakfast just outside of Grasmere was quaint and English and all of that, but it was ruined with everything that'd happened since she'd stepped off the plane back in London. It was romantic, but she supposed the only consolation was that Regulus was paying for everything. Him being here was the dampener... or so she kept telling herself.

The Roman chuckled behind her, reading her thoughts again.

"Oh, shut up," she hissed, dumping her bag beside the bed.

"Are you hungry?"

"Starving."

"Stay here," he said curtly and went to leave.

"Why?" she asked stubbornly. "I'm capable of looking after myself."

"I'm fully aware that you're a grown woman, Gabrielle... and a witch—"

He looked at her like she was something to eat, so she interrupted with, "Why do you keep me locked away, then? I'm not going to run away, you know."

"Aed is gone, but it doesn't mean he knows we're following him. He might come back and I can't let you face him alone."

His sincerity was unnerving. Her only answer was to sit on the edge of the bed.

"Any preference?"

"Well," she said, waving her hands around the room, "since we're in England and I've never been before, how about something a little more English and a little less hybrid?"

Regulus' lips pulled into an amused grin. "I do like that mouth of yours."

Before she could retort, he was gone in that annoying disappearing vampire way of his. Looking at her cell, she considered calling Zac to see how they were doing. She hadn't heard from him since she'd texted him yesterday.

Aed had been in Grasmere looking for the Celestines, and Gabby wondered if he'd found it because Aya had been here recently. At the thought of the hybrid, the good one, she smiled. Aya would have a plan and paired with Zac, they'd know what to do.

She had to take Regulus to meet them. That would go down a *treat*. She knew the Roman wouldn't go along with it and once Aya laid eyes on him, she'd try to kill him on the spot. Zac... well, she wasn't sure what Zac would do anymore.

The door opened and Regulus came in, holding a plate of steaming food. "English enough?" he declared, waving a hand.

With a sigh, she sat at the little table in front of the window that looked out over the cottage garden. He set the plate down in front of her like she was at a Michelin star restaurant, sat in the chair opposite, and proceeded to stare at her as she poked at the food he'd obviously gotten at the pub next door. Fish and chips with a side of mushy peas.

Deciding that ignoring him was the best option, she started to eat, her stomach finally beginning to settle after the afternoon's carnage. She'd confront him about Zac and Aya tomorrow. Today, that'd go into the 'too hard basket' because the Roman was riled up and nobody could deal with that.

His gaze never left her, and it was impossible to concentrate on anything else. Did he think she was that delicate? She'd seen dead bodies before, maybe not as mutilated as they had been in the past few days, but she'd seen them before.

Finally, when Regulus didn't stop staring, she asked, "Don't you need to eat or feed or whatever you call it?"

"I'm not hungry."

"Do you have to stare at me?"

"I don't have to, but I will."

Rolling her eyes, she turned back to her fish and chips, poking at the mushy peas. "You've got a strange way of doing things, even for a vampire."

"As opposed to what?"

"Zac."

"Zachary?" Regulus scoffed. "He so desperately wants to be human again. I'm content to be exactly what I am. That's the difference."

Clamping her mouth shut, she finished the last few bites of her dinner and pushed the plate aside. "Don't you have anything else you can amuse yourself with?"

"Like what?" He smirked and she instantly knew he was goading her.

"I'm sure there's some hussy down at the pub you can play with, and if she doesn't want you, you can go play with yourself."

"You're feisty tonight, dear one."

Gabby grunted, looking out the window at the garden. She needed space to breathe and just wished he would go someplace else and leave her alone. His closeness was doing stupid things to her.

"Do you think of your family often?" he asked and she looked up in surprise.

"Uh, yeah, considering you've threatened their lives..." She stood, not wanting to entertain whatever stupid thought was going through the founder's head. A hot shower and sleep were the only things she wanted, not some demented deep and meaningful conversation.

Before she could take a step towards her bag, Regulus was blocking her way. He slid his hands onto her waist and she realised he was having another go. Took him long enough.

"Let go of me," she hissed, put off because a small part of her liked the fact that he was attracted to her.

"Spend one night with me and I'll let them go. One night is all I'm asking." His hands caressed her waist, pulling her against him. "I've never bowed down to anyone, Gabrielle, but I'm bowing down to you. I'm yours."

He was bowing down to her?

"I'll let your family live in peace if you let me love you for one night."

She tore herself away, a twisted look of anger on her face. "That's blackmail."

His eyes darkened and he wound an arm around her, pulling her roughly towards him, his mouth on hers. He kissed her deeply, the breadth of his passion overwhelming. Tearing away, he said, "See it how you will, Gabrielle, but my intentions are true."

She gasped, her entire body aching. "What the hell do you want from me?"

"Deep down, everyone wants to be loved, even heartless bastards like me."

A shudder ran through her and she blinked hard, trying to clear her head. He couldn't compel her, so what was this? Another game, or did he really mean what he was saying?

"I won't force you," he whispered, placing his palm over the vein in her neck. "Only if you want me."

"I don't want to play your games anymore," she managed to rasp.

"This is not a game, dear one. Not to me."

Her head, scrambled as it was by the Roman's grasp, was screaming at her to push him away. He was not just a vampire... he was an original, a founder. The things he'd done were unforgivable.

Since arriving in London, Regulus had tried to shield her from the carnage every step of the way. Their relationship—if you could call it that—had begun with threats and manipulation, but something had shifted since she'd brought him back. For the life of her, she didn't have a clue what.

She thought about her heart and tried to make sense of what it was telling her. Since the day he invited her to that café in New Orleans to demand her help, every fibre of her being was telling her not to trust, but she'd still thought about him. Obviously, there was more to Regulus than met the eye.

His thumb brushed the curve of her jaw as she hesitated. How could something so wrong feel so right? Why try to fight it when it was inevitable?

Pressing her body against his, she caught his mouth with her own and kissed him. It was all the answer he was looking for. He deepened the kiss, sliding his tongue against hers, hands underneath her top. Letting her arms snake around his neck, he picked her up, coaxing her legs around his waist. As he dropped her onto the bed, she gasped as he kissed a trail along her neck, pressing his weight into her.

He was good at this... which made it so much worse.

It was bad enough that she'd helped Regulus fake his own death, but to fall for him as well? Zac... *Aya.* The hybrid would never forgive her and there was no way in hell she'd allow the Roman to go on living once the truth was revealed.

Gabby realised she needed Regulus. More than a means to kill Aed and from the way he touched her now, she knew he needed her just as much. Whatever stupid thing she was feeling, he felt it, too.

And only thinking about herself, she let him take what he wanted.

The last place Gabby thought she'd ever find herself was in the arms of the founding vampire, the asshole extraordinaire, Regulus. Her head rested against his very naked chest and surprisingly, it didn't feel awkward at all. She'd do it again and again. Tightening her grip around him, she snorted at the irony.

"What?" he asked, moving underneath her.

"Nothing." Closing her eyes, she tried to forget all

the complications and looming danger she was in just by being here. She could enjoy this for a few more hours at least. Her entire body still tingled in a good way. She'd had boyfriends before, but sex with a vampire was something else entirely.

"Gabrielle, you are my sun."

Her eyes snapped open at his words. A vampire was a slave to the night. Not Regulus, he was immune to the whims of the sun, but to say that to her... She knew what it meant. Vampires who couldn't walk in the day, longed for the touch of the sun's rays on their skin. This was more to him. More than a one-night bargain.

His eyes met hers and she knew he meant what he said. When she didn't move, he pulled her closer, his body flush with hers.

"Regulus," she murmured against his neck as he breathed in deeply. Is this what Zac felt for Aya? If it was, then she understood all the crazy things he'd done for her—she was a hairsbreadth away from doing them herself.

"A vampire and a witch," she whispered.

"It doesn't matter to me." He brushed his lips against her shoulder. "Who you are matters. Nothing else."

Lying here with him felt good, but it didn't mean it was right. She'd already crossed the line, but she could still end this. It wasn't too late.

"How can I prove it to you?" he asked, sensing her

doubt.

How could he prove himself to her? He had to do the one thing they needed to, but the one thing he didn't want to admit. That and so much more. "We need to find Zac and Aya."

Regulus' eyes darkened.

"You know we need their help."

"No."

"We're stronger together," she said, not backing down.

Regulus let out a long, sharp breath, his fingers tightening on her waist. "You're going to break me, Gabrielle."

"You tricked me into your bed and now you want to prove this is more. Truth isn't easy."

"I didn't trick you and I also didn't hear you complain," he murmured, his lips against hers. "You sounded like you were thoroughly enjoying yourself."

"*Regulus*."

He was trying to distract her, but it wasn't going to work. Even when he cupped her face and tried to kiss her again, she turned away. What a fool she was for trying to fight it. Her stupid human heart was falling for Regulus and she was powerless to stop it.

"You know I could make your head explode," she told him.

"How could I forget? You're particularly good at that little trick."

"Then stop being an ass."

"We will talk about it another time," he said, placing a finger over her lips. "Not now. Don't ruin this, Gabrielle. A night in the grand scheme of things doesn't matter. *Please*."

He was pleading with her? Gabby never realised the power she'd had over him all along. "Fine."

They lay together for a few minutes and she realised how cold his body really was. When she shivered, her skin prickling with goose bumps, he sighed and rolled away.

"Where are you going?" she asked, reaching for his hand.

"Not far," he said.

"I thought you wanted to stay?"

"Yes, but you'll catch cold. My blood is ice, dear one. We can't have you falling ill."

With a smile, she tugged on his hand. "Let me show you something."

Regulus took her in his arms again and she placed the flat of her palm against his hard chest. Calling on her power, she let it slowly trickle into the Roman, feeling his blood heat—just enough so he would be warm and not have to go anywhere.

"Well," he said with a sigh, tightening his grasp. "Thank you."

"Oh, so you do have some manners."

"Only a few."

Gabby took in his features, wondering about the Roman's life. Two thousand years was a long time, and she knew next to nothing about where he came from, his family... Everything about him was a mystery. The only thing she was certain of was his intentions toward her.

"What's your full name?" she asked, taking in his dark eyes.

"Marcellus Caelius," he whispered almost resentfully. "Regulus is my family name."

"Why doesn't anyone call you Marcellus?"

"I was named for my father," he said sharply, rolling onto his back.

"You weren't on good terms?"

He sighed, his gaze firmly on the ceiling.

"I'll take that as a no."

"What's with the questioning? There are things you'll never know about me. Things I've forgotten over the years... things that I don't want to utter."

"I don't know who you are," she replied, running her hand across his stomach. "You know me. Why can't I know a little more about you?"

He regarded her for a moment. "Ask what you will, but I can't promise I'll answer."

Gabby thought for a minute and could only come up with the most dangerous questions of all. "You and Aya..." she began, but he looked at her with such ferocity that her mouth snapped shut.

"She's told you the story."

"Regulus—"

"We've a lot of history, Gabrielle. We've all done

horrible things to one another. Things that are unforgivable. We've all the reasons to hate one another."

"Perhaps you need to learn how to forgive."

His jaw tensed. "You're going to be the end of me."

"Probably." She smiled. She knew she was pressing her luck big-time trying to get him to talk about things. If he cared for her as he claimed, then trust was one of the ways he'd show her.

"Tell me about them... the other founders. What were they like?"

His eyes narrowed. "You don't need to hear about that."

"Tell me."

"Gabrielle. You ask things you don't want to hear the answers to."

"Regulus," she breathed. "I can argue with you forever if I have to."

"Why do you want to know?" he asked, his brow furrowing.

"Because if you say you feel these things for me, you should be able to tell me. That's what a relationship is."

He closed his eyes, groaning.

"You know I'm right." What good was caring for someone if they didn't return the feeling? "I would answer any question you asked me truthfully."

"Do you care for me, Gabrielle?" he asked, calling her bluff. Good thing it wasn't one.

"Yes."

His breath hitched and he rolled back to face her, a hand caressing her cheek. "Why?"

"I don't know. That's what I'm trying to figure out."

He seemed to accept her answer and pressed his lips to her forehead. "It's not a pretty story. It doesn't have a happy ending."

"I know, but I'd still like to hear it."

Regulus hesitated for a moment before he began, "The founders... they were all evil in their own way. All save for Arturius."

"I have a hard time believing that." Gabby sighed, remembering how the Roman had abducted her.

"You've met him," Regulus said. "That's not who he always was."

"Who was he before? Did you know him?"

"I only knew him in passing before that night— that night Katrin brought us together. Arturius was good. I was the one who convinced him to turn. I showed him the truth of what the Empire was, and he agreed to Katrin's offer. If it wasn't for me, he wouldn't have become the monster he was."

"So, you didn't hate him?"

"No."

"He hated you."

"And rightfully so."

"Do you regret it?" she asked carefully, her eyes searching his. "Turning?"

He traced her lips with his fingers and whispered,

"Arturius' fate is the only thing I regret."

Gabby couldn't help but cast her eyes downward, taking in the lines of his bare chest. Out of two thousand years of what could only be described as carnage, that was the only thing he regretted?

"I can't change who I am," he said, picking up on her thoughts. "Everything I ever did, everyone I manipulated, tortured, killed... it was to stop the Coven awakening the Children of Lir."

"Not all of it," she said sharply.

He knew she had him. "No, but can you fight your true nature, Gabrielle?"

She shook her head, not trusting herself to speak.

"What does your heart tell you?" he murmured, running his hand over her breast.

"You have a gift, Regulus," she said wryly.

"For what?" His lips curved into a smile.

"Words."

"Is that all?"

She shook her head. "Cocky bastard."

"Don't dwell on the past, Gabrielle. It will do neither of us any good. We can only focus on the path before us."

"Killing Aed."

"Killing Aed," he echoed. "And only then can we think about what's next."

If there was any future after all of this, Gabby wondered if Regulus would be in hers. It was a thought too farfetched to even contemplate.

CHAPTER 11

Aya stood in the shower of the small hotel room Tristan had gotten for them, washing the dried blood from her skin. The wound in her stomach had healed a while ago now, but she could still feel the pain —a phantom splinter of wood slicing through her skin.

Aed. A Tuatha prince.

She thought back over the history her parents had taught her as a child. The Tuatha had appeared four thousand years ago and had wasted no time in claiming what was not theirs. The human population had no chance against the Fae and at first, they had fought back despite the odds. Soon, they realised they would lose, and submission was the best course of action to save their children and themselves from certain death and slavery. Unfortunately, they still got the slavery part.

The Celestines had stepped in when they could

take the suffering of the Earth and its people no more. The Tuatha had scarred what was sacred to them and it was enough to compel the peaceful race to war.

There had been a lot of atrocities committed on either side, but one of the worst was Aoife's betrayal. So much hope had been placed upon the alliance and she was the last chance for an end to the fighting. If the two races didn't stop, it would cause extinction for all, though it'd happened anyway. If things had gone differently, then the world today would be a very different place.

Stepping from the shower, Aya glanced at herself in the mirror. She looked as she always did. There was no mark from her encounter with Aed, but a lot of things had changed beneath the surface. Throwing her ruined clothes into a plastic bag, she changed into her only set of clean ones and went back out into the room, a waft of steam following her.

"Feel better?" Tristan asked, looking up from the newspaper he'd gotten at the front desk.

"Much. A hot shower does wonders for aching stomach muscles." *But not so much for rambling thoughts*, she declined to add.

"You're still hurt?" he asked in alarm, sitting up straight.

"No, nothing like that. Sometimes the memory lingers a while."

"I know you're tough and all, but maybe you should get some sleep."

"I'm not tired." She could go a few days without if she needed, longer than any ordinary vampire. "I doubt I could sleep anyway."

Aya sat on the bed next to Tristan, stretching her legs out across the mattress. Looking through the window into the darkness beyond, her thoughts went straight to her family. Their memory had lived on in her mind, but it had nothing on seeing them again, even as apparitions. It seemed like the universe was playing a cruel trick on her. She could look, but not touch.

"What did you see?" Tristan asked. "You've been quieter than usual."

She sighed, glancing at him before closing her eyes. "I saw them. I saw... my family."

"What?"

"They were an afterimage. Lingering energy, but they were there, and they knew I was, too."

"Did you speak to them?"

"I don't know how real it was, but it seemed as if they heard me."

Tristan shifted so he sat next to her. "You got a chance to see them again. A chance to say goodbye. Properly, this time."

"I always seem to get more than I deserve."

"Arrow, we all do things we're not proud of. Sometimes we don't get a choice. I know you're good."

"What about the horrible things I did because I wanted to?"

"We're all human."

"That's where you're wrong," she said. "I was never human."

"Perhaps not," he said, narrowing his eyes. "But Arturius was human once and it was his blood that made you. Who's to say that didn't change you in other ways? How do you know?"

Aya sighed, taking his hand. "You're ever the chivalrous and loyal knight, aren't you?"

"You shouldn't be so hard on yourself. You've done a lot of selfless things in the name of the Celestines."

"It's been nothing but selfish revenge."

"It may have started out that way, but what about all those witches you've helped? It was meant to be your callin', yes? I've seen it, Arrow. I've seen you do these things with my own eyes."

Aya looked back out the window. "We have more pressing matters to attend to than arguing about the things I may or may not deserve."

"Do you have any ideas?" Tristan asked thinly, and she didn't have to look at him to know he was annoyed she'd changed the subject so bluntly.

"We can't do anything on our own. My power can't stop him, so we need to find another way."

"You mean to find the witch Gabby?"

"Yes. She is one of the most powerful witches I've ever met. Together we could banish Katrin. Perhaps together we might have a chance at binding Aed."

"Or kill him for good."

"Or that."

"Do you have a way of contacting her?"

Aya shifted uncomfortably. Gabby had been in London and in contact with Zac. It had been less than a week since he'd left her to find the Three. Did she dare seek him out so soon?

"Arrow?" Tristan prodded.

"She was in London."

"So, we go back. Then what?"

Instead of asking the obvious, she asked, "Do you think the Three would have remained in London?"

"They all came from there in their human lives. I doubt they would've gone far. I heard Nye mention they would've gone home."

"Then we go back to London and look for them."

"But Zac left you behind..." Tristan began, realising she meant to seek out Zac, not the Three.

"I know. I gather he hoped he would come back when he found whatever it is he's looking for, but our predicament with Aed is a little more pressing, no?"

When she finally came face to face with Zac again, she hoped it wouldn't be awkward. She wanted to give him his space and not put any pressure on him, but... There was always a but. The only place she wanted to be was in his arms, but he wasn't ready for it yet.

"I don't think he'll like it," Tristan muttered. "His humanity was thin at best."

"We don't have a choice," Aya replied. "We're working towards the same goal and together, we have a better chance."

"If you say so..."

Aya narrowed her eyes and sighed. There was only one way to find out.

Zac couldn't think of anything worse than sitting around the apartment in Camden waiting for the Three to arrive, so he slipped out, bound for the pub or whatever watering hole he could find open at this time of night. It was well past midnight, and most were already shut or had put out their last calls. He didn't much like hanging around people anyway, so he walked instead.

They had to work out their next move as soon as possible. His thoughts went to Gabby and found he actually missed the witch. Since they'd first met, they'd never gotten along that well. In fact, he'd annoyed the hell out of her on purpose. When he thought that Aya had died her true death, she'd been there to help and something between them had changed. A mutual respect had sprung up out of nowhere. They'd both changed so much in the past year, it was incredible.

As Zac wandered the streets and lanes of the city, the more his thoughts kept circling around to Gabby.

Once they had the Three back together, he would seek out the witch. He didn't want to think about it, but it would be highly likely they'd need Aya and Tristan. He'd walked out on her a week ago, but what was a week in the grand scheme of things? A piss in the ocean. They might have to put their feelings aside to fight a common enemy.

Could he do it? Did he have to?

Rounding the corner into a small lane, he wondered what had happened to Coraline and Maximus. He assumed that's whom Gabby might be with. The last he'd heard from them was the single word text message that said *'awake'*. What was it with witches and single word text messages?

Listening to the surrounding city, he slowed, a weird tingle spreading across his skin. It was like the sensation he got when he knew someone was watching... only this time, it felt different.

Zac stopped, casting his hearing out into the night. Something was definitely there, but he couldn't tell what. Glancing over his shoulder, the lane was empty. Before he could turn back, he was shoved hard against the brick wall beside him, his head cracking against the masonry.

"Who are you?" a male voice snarled.

Shaking his head, Zac looked up at his assailant and his eyes widened.

Unnatural red eyes stared back at him. Even in the

darkness he could make them out, and weird stuff like this usually meant trouble. There was only one person this man could be.

The hybrid didn't look that bad for having been stuck in a magical tomb for three thousand years. He wore a stylish-looking suit, well-cut but without a tie. He had short, cropped blonde hair, and his sickly pale skin completed the picture—not to mention the bat-shit crazy red eyes. Zac was on his own and there was no prizes for guessing the winner if this came to blows.

"Who am I?" Zac asked, his back flat against the wall, eying the man. "Who are *you*?"

"I am a prince of the Tuatha De Danann, and the lack of respect you human vampire scum show me is insulting to my heritage."

"And your name is?"

"I'm offended you don't already know."

"You've been locked in a box for a couple of thousand years. Nobody gave a shit. That's probably why I don't know your name."

The hybrid's jaw stiffened as he tried to reign in his anger. "I am Aed and who are you? I will not ask so politely again. If I have to draw it from your blood, I will."

Zac wasn't quite sure what that meant, but the first time he'd tasted Aya's blood, it'd given him dreams of her past. Maybe this Aed could read his blood the same way. He couldn't chance that. Who knew what he'd give away?

"Zac Degaud. Puny vampire weakling. You have a nice way of introducing yourself to people." He pointed to his head. "Very nice."

Aed just stared at him. Zac thought he understood how insane people worked, but this was something else.

"Did she make you a vampire?"

"Who are you talking about?"

"The Celestine with the black hair. I assume she did because you stink like her."

Zac pushed off the wall, his anger boiling. "Be careful what you say to me."

"Oh, on the contrary... you should be careful what you say to *me*."

"She didn't make me," Zac snapped. "A defector from your precious Coven did."

Aed's eyes darkened. "They are not precious to me. Isolde did this to me against my will. Do you think I want to be like this? The Celestines will pay for their crimes. The Celestines and their witches. They're using us all, don't you see?"

The only Celestine left was Aya. That meant... "Whatever war you think you're fighting, it's long over."

"The war for revenge is never over."

"Give up, Aed. You and her are the only ones left of your people. You're not pure anymore and neither is she. Your war is over."

"*It is not over*," the hybrid roared, pushing Zac back into the wall again. "They attacked my people.

They were so worried about their precious Earth that they started their war on us. Instead of letting us conquer the humans, they destroyed us all. If it weren't for the Celestines, I wouldn't be this... this *thing*."

This shit was getting crazier by the minute. "And if you get your revenge, what then?"

Aed cocked his head to the side, confusion flashing across his face.

"How do you kill the un-killable?"

With a snarl that sounded almost like some kind of animal, Aed's eyes changed. Not into the black of an ordinary vampire, but they looked like they were filling with crimson blood. Red, glowing eyes like some kind of demon from hell. Zac was in the shit now.

Aed was tearing at the collar of his shirt and there was nothing he could do. Zac grunted in pain as the hybrid's fangs tore into the flesh of his neck. He tried to shove him off, but it was like he was swatting at thin air. He'd never felt so weak in his entire life.

Aed stumbled back with a gasp, blood running from his mouth. Zac reached up to his neck, feeling the wound. He edged along the wall, putting distance between them. The sting subsided as he healed, but his heart still thudded a billion miles an hour.

"What's this?" Aed asked, his eyes looking glassy.

Zac didn't answer. The guy was mental *and* angry. He wasn't dealing with that.

With a strangled cry, the hybrid fell to the ground,

clawing at his throat and Zac just stood there in shock, watching Aed writhe like his blood was boiling.

What the hell?

"You have her blood." He coughed, blood splattering on the cobblestones. "You would poison me?"

Zac shook his head as he watched the hybrid vomit everything that he'd just drunk. It must be his Celestine blood. Well, at least the hybrid wouldn't be chowing down on him again. At least he had that going for him.

"You love her..." Aed said in disbelief. "*You love her?*"

Zac didn't know what the hell Aed had learned from his blood since he'd just thrown most of it up, but he hoped that was it. He hoped the hybrid learned nothing at all, but that part was out of his control.

"Yes, I love her," he replied, standing over him. "What's it to you?"

The hybrid roared in anguish, stumbling to his feet. "How dare she get to love when they took *everything* from me." He lunged forwards again but stumbled to the side, his shoulder slamming into the wall.

If Zac was getting out of here in one piece, it had to be now and it had to be fast. He took a few steps backwards, but Aed grabbed him by the scruff of the neck and threw him halfway down the lane.

Rolling to a stop, Zac sprung to his feet, but the

hybrid was already on him. A shoulder slammed into his gut and he was on his back. Fisting his hand into the hybrid's hair, he slammed Aed's head into the wall with all his strength, the sickening crunch of bone echoing through the close air of the lane.

He grunted in surprise as the life bled from his red eyes until he fell limply onto the cobblestones. Zac scrambled backwards, putting as much distance between them as he could.

Shit, was he the luckiest son of a bitch ever, or what?

Aed was dead for now, but who knew for how long? The more Zac thought about it, the more he thought it was because Aed still couldn't understand what he'd been turned into. That'd been the only thing that'd saved him. If the hybrid was in control, he would've been deader than dead.

While the going was still good, Zac disappeared into the night, leaving Aed to wake up on his own.

After leaving a winding path behind him to throw the hybrid off his scent, Zac wasn't expecting the welcome wagon to be out in force back at the apartment.

Maddox was hovering outside, and when he laid eyes on Zac, he jumped like he hadn't expected to be found. "What the hell happened to you?"

"I didn't think you'd show," Zac said, leaning against the wall.

"Thought I'd miss out on something juicy," he

replied, narrowing his eyes at the bloodstain on Zac's shirt. "Looks like I was right."

"I ran into the hybrid on my evening walk."

"He took a piece outta you?"

"Don't worry, I got him back." He glanced at the entrance to the apartment and back to Maddox. "Haven't gone up yet?"

"Nope."

"Why not?"

He shrugged and glanced over his shoulder.

"Still undecided? Or still worried that you're pledging some kind of allegiance to the guy who kicked your ass?"

"You beat me fair and square... that time."

Zac laughed and shook his head.

Maddox shifted uncomfortably. "You're not the most tactful of guys, but you're trying, which is more than most do. Giving up is easy. Going on is harder."

Zac didn't have to ask to understand what Maddox had meant. A respect had emerged between them since the fight and now he was the one people looked to as an example. Crazier shit had happened.

"We better go upstairs and wait for the others," Zac said, pushing off the wall. "I take it you're in?"

"I suppose I am. The others are already here."

Zac raised an eyebrow. What was that about crazy shit?

"I saw them go in a while ago," Maddox explained with a shrug.

Zac looked the assassin over and wondered about his demeanour. Something had changed, but at a time like this, he wasn't going to look a gift horse in the mouth. Maddox was in and he was going to take it. "Then you better come in for a beer before they drink them all. I know I need one."

CHAPTER 12

Zac stared out at the dreary London sky and sighed. He had a lot to be depressed about, but no time for it.

"Cheer up, sad sack," Nye said behind him. "Does your neck still hurt from being a hybrid's chew toy?"

"No. It's fine."

That was last night's excitement. Tonight, they stood in the apartment that'd once housed the Six. It already had a different feel about it; it'd been claimed for another purpose—Hybrid Revolution HQ.

Zac had won the Three's trust and they were all finally together in the apartment below, brought up to speed and waiting for the next move... whatever that would be.

Truth was, he missed Aya. He wondered what she was doing, where she was. If she'd found it in herself to go home and face her past. He hoped so. Of course, he missed the life he'd tried to forge back in Louisiana and his brother, Sam, but that was a dream still somewhere in the future... if they had a future.

"You look like you need a beer," Nye said, opening the refrigerator. "And it's a Christmas miracle. There's still a six-pack in here."

They sat together at the kitchen table, drinking in silence. He gathered their next step would be to track down Gabby. If anyone knew what to do next, it would be her. She did have Alisandra's grimoire, or at least he hoped Aya had gotten it to her.

"Do you feel that?" Nye asked, breaking him out of his depression.

"What?" As soon as he asked it, he felt someone coming up the stairs.

"Someone's coming."

Casting out his senses, it was unmistakable. There were only two people he could recognise by sense alone, and one of them was coming up the stairs. When he left her, he thought it was going to be years before he'd get the chance to touch her again, but he supposed their hybrid situation didn't factor that in.

Nye went to stand, but he grabbed the spy's arm, pulling him down. "It's Aya and Tristan."

"How the hell do you know that?"

"It's one of the great mysteries of the universe."

Still, he wasn't prepared when she walked through the door, all blue eyes and black hair, and his heart did this thing in his chest he wasn't expecting. When her gaze met his, he knew... He'd never let her out of his sight again.

Standing abruptly, it didn't register when his beer bottle fell from the table and smashed on the floor. Nor did he notice when Nye gave him a look that said he was mad. He was across the room in two seconds flat.

"Aya," he whispered, a hand caressing her cheek.

"Hello, Zac," she said, smiling.

He pulled her roughly towards him, his lips finding hers, drawing her desperately into his kiss. It didn't matter one iota they were being watched. She kissed him back just as forcefully, and he was alive again. She made him alive.

"Get a room," Nye yelled.

Zac felt Aya's lips curve into a smile at the cocky vampire's jibe. He pulled away and grinned.

"I wouldn't mind that," she whispered.

"You have no idea how glad I am to see you."

She placed a cool hand on his cheek, her eyes running over his features. "I can feel it."

"What?"

Her face split into a grin and she grabbed his hands. Zac knew Aya had a sense for emotions, but his state of mind? That was new. She'd forever be surprising him.

She pulled him towards the table where Nye now sat with Tristan, and his hands tingled with her touch.

"I gather you lot are here because of the mental fairy," Nye said, handing Tristan a beer.

"How much do you know?" the knight asked.

"Enough to know he's a few sandwiches short of a picnic *and* a homicidal maniac."

Aya glanced at Zac and he grimaced. Clutching his hand, she asked, "What aren't you saying?"

"I had a run-in with the guy," Zac said.

"Aed?" Tristan asked. "He's here?"

Zac shrugged. "Was, is... perhaps. He jumped me in the street yesterday. Said I stunk like the Celestine with the dark hair." He glanced at Aya.

She cocked her head to the side. "You stink like me?"

"So he said."

"I hope it's a pleasant stink."

"Like rose petals."

"Ugh," Nye said. "Give us a break, mate."

"He bit my neck—"

Aya spun and pulled at his shirt.

"It healed," Zac said, pulling her hands away. "He seemed to be able to read me like a book from a drop, though he didn't much like the taste."

"What did he learn?" Tristan asked, glancing toward Aya.

Zac was suddenly glad that he'd stopped her from telling him how she could be killed. If Aed had learned that... "He knows I love Aya. That's all he seemed to be interested in. If he saw anything else, I don't know."

"He wants me anyway," Aya said, the way she held herself betraying her doubt. She didn't need to doubt his love. "If he knows about your feelings, then I don't see any different consequences."

"We saw him a few days ago," Tristan said.

"Where?" Nye asked.

"We went to Grasmere," Aya began. "I went home and when I came back, he was waiting for me."

"Tore the locals to shreds in seconds," Tristan said with a shiver.

"My power was useless," Aya added. "I tried to stop his heart, like I did with the other founders, but he just came back."

"What's his game plan?" Nye asked. "He can't be wandering around having a grand old time for the hell of it. If I was locked in a magical fairy dust slumber for three thousand years, I'd want to crack someone's skull open."

"Yeah," Tristan said, "but who's? Arrow's the only Celestine left. The war between their people ended a long time ago."

"He's after revenge, that much I could glean from Grasmere," Aya butted in. "He had a good time showing us his power, but he wandered off after that."

"I get that he's mentally unstable, but seein' it was another thing entirely," Tristan added. "Seemed with it one minute, and off with the fairies the next."

Nye almost choked on his beer and slapped the table, bellowing with laughter. "He *is* a fairy, mate."

Aya shook her head at the spy. "Point is, he could

do anything. We know he has a motive for revenge, but that's all we know about him."

"And he could do absolutely anything," Zac finished her thought.

"He has the power of resurgence. That's worrying enough."

"Resurgence?" Zac asked.

"Necromancy," Aya explained.

Nye let out a dramatic sigh. "Zombies?"

Aya snorted. "I wouldn't go that far."

"He's looking for his sisters," Tristan added. "He only mentioned it once before focusing on something else."

"Sisters?" Zac asked. "There's more of them?"

"They were called the Children of Lir. There was Aed, his older sister, and twin girls. It's a story still told in Ireland today," Tristan explained.

"Do you think the spell woke them all up?" Nye asked, his expression falling. "One's bad enough."

"I don't think so," Aya replied. "I wouldn't know how to find them even if they were still bound. That's a power that died the day I was turned. Besides, I think Regulus was hunting them. Aed said the only way he was going to be killed was by an original's hand."

"Damn," Zac said. "That must've been why he was so intent on getting into the Coven."

"Why would he have bothered?" Nye asked.

Zac snorted. "The all-powerful Regulus would've

been threatened by the reemergence of a family of founding hybrids.”

They sat in silence for a while, letting everything sink in.

“Have you heard from Gabby?” Aya asked.

“Not recently,” Zac replied, his brow furrowing. “I got a message from her a few days ago. All it said was ’hybrid’. Then nothing but radio silence.”

“What’s she doing then?” Nye asked.

“Hopefully trying to find a way to kill Aed before he kills us all.”

“Then that should be our next move,” the spy said. “Find Gabby and then figure out how to kill the psycho fairy, or if there isn’t a way, at least trap him again.”

“I agree,” Aya said, deep in thought. “We can’t go after him without knowing more. He and I are evenly matched strength wise, at least I think we are.”

“Even with your mystical blue power?” Nye asked. “I mean, he can raise the dead, but your power is different, right?”

“Yes, it’s different. But Aed was created. I was turned. That fight is over before it’s even begun. Together is the only way we have a chance. We have no original vampire. There has to be another way.”

“Your power is cancelled out when used against each other,” Zac mused.

“Yes, it seemed like it.”

“Well,” Zac said with a snort, “no use worrying

about it tonight. I'll try to contact Gabby tomorrow. One step at a time."

"Yes," Tristan said with a sigh. "In the mornin'."

As the vampires dispersed for the evening, Zac took Aya's hand. There were too many questions left to be answered between them and he was dying to touch her again. Without a word, he led her back towards the room he'd taken when he first got here, back when he was under Regulus' thumb. There would be no sleep tonight, not for them.

———

Zac closed the bedroom door behind them as Aya wandered around the room, looking out the window, over the tiny balcony and across the low-lying urban sprawl that was Camden. His hands slid over her waist from behind, pulling her body against his.

Aya knew their relationship had started out all wrong. She'd tried to possess him and he in return. They were both the kind of people who could never belong to anyone else, but when they were together, it just fit. Whatever happened next, it would be as equals.

"I didn't expect to see you again so soon," he murmured, pressing his lips against her neck.

"I wanted to," she replied. "I wanted to find you the moment you left, but I understood. I hope you're not mad with me for showing up unannounced."

"It's understandable, considering."

Closing her eyes, she breathed in his scent, letting it wash over her until there was nothing else. He was different since the last time she'd seen him. Just a week ago, he'd still been a tangled mess of emotions. Now he seemed... together.

He turned her around to face him, his eyes searching hers like he was trying to find the answer to some unasked question. She knew the one she wanted to say aloud but was still too wary of letting it be heard.

"Helping them... helped me," Zac whispered, seeming to understand what was in her heart. "I know what I need to do now. I know who I'm meant to be."

"Who you always were underneath that asshole exterior."

"Ouch."

"Still could have done without the Three."

"We need them if we're going up against Aed. We're not enough, even with them."

"I still don't trust them."

"The Three have agreed to help us." He shrugged. "They needed something to work towards. They're not Regulus' lackeys anymore."

"What about Regulus' network?"

"What do you mean?"

"You killed him. Couldn't you take it over?"

"I suppose I could," he said. "But I'm not a puppet master. I'm a lone shark."

"Hey." She nudged him.

"Okay, okay, we're Bonnie and Clyde."

"Bonnie and who?"

He frowned, shaking his head. "Never mind."

She pressed her lips to his and he circled his arms around her, closing the gap between them. They stood and kissed for what felt like an age before parting. Undressing each other, they fell back onto the bed, thoroughly reuniting again and again. Afterwards, they lay together, limbs tangled, listening to each other's heartbeats.

"Do you want to talk about it?" Zac asked, his fingers combing through her hair.

"Do you want to know about it?" she asked, knowing exactly what he was getting at.

"It doesn't matter if I do or not. I'd rather you share it if you want to, not because you feel obligated."

Sighing, she shifted against him, running her hand across his stomach. "You know what my home looks like. You saw it from my blood. It was the same, but different."

"How so?"

"It was dead. Empty. The Coven had been there, and any trace of my family was removed. Their belongings, memories... even their bodies. Nothing remained in the physical world but an empty shell."

"Physical world?" Zac asked.

Feeling tears prickle her eyes, she rolled onto her back and stared at the ceiling. "I saw them. I saw them and they saw me."

A firm hand cupped her face, drawing her gaze back to his. "You got a chance to say goodbye."

"I didn't deserve it."

"Whose place is it for anyone to decide who deserves what? Even for ourselves."

His gaze flickered down to her lips and she rolled over, her hand trailing downwards. "I love you, Zac Degaud."

"I love you, Aeriaya," he whispered, the sound of her true name coming from him reverberated straight through her soul.

Zac pushed open the door to the rooftop, icy air blowing inwards. The morning was overcast and the sky looked heavy with the promise of snow. He was going to call Gabby without the audience downstairs, but his eyes focused on a black form sitting on the edge of the roof, feet dangling over the edge.

"Tristan," he said gruffly, the door closing heavily behind him. Once, Zac would've loved to put a fist right in the knight's face, but not anymore. The thousand-year-old vampire had proven himself and had come to realise that Aya's heart would never be his. A tentative truce had formed between them, but things could still go either way.

"You and Arrow are on good terms again?" he asked without looking up.

"Yes."

Nodding, the knight looked at his cell and back out across the grey sprawl of the city.

"I know we never got along," Zac said, sitting beside him, "but I think we ought to."

"For Arrow's sake?"

"For no one's sake."

Tristan grunted, looking the younger vampire over. "We're more alike that you realise, Zac. Perhaps if we'd been better acquainted in the beginnin', I could've imparted some wisdom on you and saved all the angst."

"You know I seriously doubt that. You're so well put together, like the chivalrous knight you're supposed to be."

The knight laughed. "I can see this recurrin' thing with us. I take a jab and you take one in return."

"Rinse, repeat."

"Did Arrow ever tell you how I was turned?"

That was the last thing Zac was expecting to hear. "No," he replied. "The day you turned up in Louisiana looking for her, she told me it wasn't her place. She mentioned it wasn't pretty, and that it was during the Crusades, but not much more."

"I think you ought to hear it. I understand you've gained some wisdom over the past week, but no one changes overnight. Especially not the immortal."

The old Zac would've pushed the knight off the edge of the roof, but this one simply shrugged. He had a point. Everyone was a work in progress that was never completed. "If you think it's necessary."

"I was born in Ireland in the 1100s to a poor lord outside of Dublin," the knight began. "When I was twelve, I was sent to London to squire for a man who would turn out to be one of the first Knights Templar—the soldiers of God. It was a great honour and I soon became one of the few men to be knighted that wasn't a lord in his own right. My blood was good enough for them and so it was. I was happy for a time and then word came that the Crusades were to be resurrected."

Zac just let him go. This was a time he couldn't possibly understand, not like Tristan. Humans fought other kinds of wars then, no less brutal, but for beliefs and ideology that were beyond him.

"I left a wife and baby daughter behind in London and marched with not one but two Crusades to the Holy Land. It was my duty as a Christian and a Knights Templar to follow the orders of the Church and Crown, and so it was. On what history knows as the Fourth Crusade, it was I who turned the tide and allowed the city of Constantinople to be taken. But when I saw the horror my brothers inflicted upon its people, I was horrified, disappointed... *betrayed*. This was not God's will. Rape and murder in his name was not what I was fightin' for. That night, after the city fell, I went with a detail of soldiers through the sewers lookin' for any of the enemy that hadn't been accounted for. Anythin' to get away from the accolades that were bein' showered over me." Tristan shook his head, his jaw hardening.

"They lived in the sewers?"

"Yes. I didn't find any sign of the enemy, at least not the enemy I was expectin'. The vampires who lived underneath the city were rabid, foul things. Monsters with no sense of humanity left in them. They mauled me within an inch of my life, but not before I fought back. Their blood and mine coated everythin'. That was the only way I could've ingested it. I scared them away and by the time I was brought to the surface, my wounds were too great. The healers could only make me comfortable. So it was that I died in the night and was reborn into somethin' I didn't understand."

"But Aya said she found you?"

"Yes, but not until many years later. They called me the Devil Who Walked." Tristan shifted uncomfortably. "I plagued the forests of Austria so much that the villagers left me offerings. *Live* offerings. I wasn't much different from the beasts that changed me. If it wasn't for Arrow, I would either still be there or someone would've gained the courage to stake me. She gave me some tough love and brought my humanity back."

"That's why you're so loyal to her," Zac mused.

"Yes, of course. We were companions after that for a long time and yes, I loved her as you do, but I would never do anythin' to break what you have with her apart. She is my family now. It took me hundreds of years to find her after we parted, and I am loathe to take my eyes from her again."

Instinctively, Zac felt jealousy rise in his gut but pushed it back down. He had nothing to be worried about where Tristan was concerned. Theirs was a different kind of love. The knight obviously grew up with a code of honour and loyalty and felt the same way towards Aya as he would anyone who'd saved him like she had.

"Do you know what happened to your wife and daughter?"

"It'd been almost twenty years since I'd seen them. Who was I to go back? If she'd seen me... It was too great a risk to go back. I was unchanged from my thirty years. She would've been almost fifty. Back then, there was a chance she would've already have passed on. It was better they think me a dead hero than a live monster."

"Well, you have one up on me."

"It's not a competition. Just a way of understandin' my intent towards Arrow."

"I get it." She saved him from endless torment and if there was anything he understood completely, it was torment.

"We're not that dissimilar," Tristan said. "We were both created by monsters and not taught anythin' about control."

"Yes, I guess we were."

"And whatever happens next, know that I have your back."

"As long as I have yours, right?" Zac asked with a grin.

Tristan laughed at his jibe and thumped him on the back. "It goes both ways, my friend, or not at all."

Zac took out his cell, glad for the change in conversation. "I'm going to call Gabby. I'm starting to worry about her."

"I'll leave you to it," the knight said. "We'll wait for you downstairs."

Zac watched as the knight disappeared inside. Dialling the witch's number with the uneasy thoughts of Tristan's story echoing through his head, he pressed the cell to his ear and hoped to God that she'd pick up. If she didn't, then they were out of breadcrumbs to follow.

CHAPTER 13

Gabby stood in the middle of their room in the bed and breakfast outside of Grasmere glaring at Regulus.

They'd become a lot closer since the night before—in more ways than one—but he was still fighting her when it came to Aed. He knew as well as she did what they needed to do, but as per usual, he was having none of it. That meant they were arguing about it. *Again*.

"I thought you were meant to be this diabolical asshole," she said sullenly. "Not a child who throws a tantrum the moment you don't get your way."

"You're beautiful when you're angry," he said with a grin, knowing it'd annoy her.

"You know we have to meet with Zac and Aya. Why are you being so difficult about it?"

He drew her into his arms, using his strength when

she tried to push him away. "Stubborn pride, dear one."

"Your stubborn pride is what'll get you killed."

"Is that what you're worried about?"

"I worry about a lot of things."

"And it warms my heart to knowing you worry about me." He pressed his lips against the top of her head and she crumbled against him. Why did it have to feel so good?

"I have to call Zac. He'll know what to do."

"The last time I saw him, he was committing suicide by tearing out my heart. Do you really want to trust what he has to say?"

"*Regulus*," she snapped.

"I'm acting on experience."

"So am I."

He looked down at her with a frown and pushed her away, hands on her shoulders. "You want me to trust you, so call him if you believe it's in our best interests."

"Really? You're giving in?"

"For you," he murmured. "Just don't complain when Aeriaya tries to murder me."

Gabby hardly believed what he was saying. For the first time, she felt like she had an even footing with him. Before he could change his mind, she picked up her cell phone from the side table and turned it on. As it sprung to life, Regulus backed away.

"I can't be here for this," he said thinly.

He was still annoyed with her and it wasn't ideal, but contacting Zac and the others was the next logical step. They had to do this together. Regulus wanted to be all-powerful on his own, but this time it wouldn't be enough. He didn't have Katrin to back him up, or a network of witches and vampires—they all thought he was dead, and their plan counted on it staying that way.

"Don't be stupid," Gabby said, glaring at him. "And don't even think about doing your little vampire disappearing thing."

He raised an eyebrow. "Vampire disappearing thing?"

"You know what I mean." She waved a hand at him.

His lips curled into a smile and he sat on the bed, stretching his legs out.

Just as she went to scroll through her contacts, the cell rang, making her jump. Looking down at the screen, she saw it was Zac and relief washed over her. She wondered if she'd been mulling it over so much that the universe had sent out a subliminal distress call to the vampire.

Raising the cell to her ear, she said, "Zac."

"God, Gabby," came his familiar voice, "you know how worried we are about you?"

"Sorry," she replied. "I've been tracking Aed."

"What? How?"

"I've got someone with me." She eyed Regulus, who looked at her smugly. She might be softening towards him, but she still wanted to slap that stupid smirk right off his face.

"Who?"

"We'll come meet you. Where are you staying?"

"We're in London at the Six's apartment in Camden. I'll text you the address."

"Are you okay?"

"Yeah. A lot better... if you know what I mean."

"Good. I'm glad. Who's with you?"

"Everyone. Tristan, Nye, the Three. Aya. We're all here trying to figure out our next move. We need you, Gabby."

"I need you," she answered. A snort came from behind her and she turned to find the Roman glaring. Making a kissy face at him, his expression instantly softened. Jealousy suited the founder, especially when it was over her.

"Zac?" she asked, turning away.

"Yeah?"

"I'm glad you're okay. You and everyone else."

There was silence on the other end for a minute before he said, "Yeah. Me, too."

"I'm coming. I won't be long."

"Okay, but just to let you know... Aed is here in London."

"He is? When did you see him?"

"A day and a half ago. He jumped me in the street. Said I stunk like a Celestine."

"Are you okay? Aya? Where is she?"

"I'm fine. He took a chunk out of me, but I fought him off. Aya is here and she's in one piece. She had a run-in with him in Grasmere a couple of days ago."

"I know. I saw the aftermath."

There was a moment of silence, then Zac drawled, "You're getting around."

"Did he take your blood?" she asked. "He can read it like a book. Zac, if he—"

"He did," the vampire interrupted. "But all he seemed to get was that I was in love with Aya. Then he threw it all up in spectacular fashion."

"Celestine blood," she began. "It's..."

"Poison or something. Chucked it up and tried to claw his throat open."

"Well, whatever happened, it saved your life."

"It seemed to weaken him enough so I could crack his head open and get away. Haven't seen him since, so who knows where he's gone."

"Okay... We can do something with that." She sighed, resisting the urge to pinch the bridge of her nose. "I'm leaving now, we should be there tonight."

"Gabby?" Zac asked before she could hang up. "Who's with you?"

Hesitating, she glanced at Regulus, who stared back at her like he was goading her on. Narrowing her eyes, she said, "I'll see you soon." Hanging up, she shoved her cell into her pocket.

"The apartment?" Regulus asked. "That's original."

"You listened in?"

"You wanted me to stay."

"The shit will hit the fan the moment they know you're alive," she warned. "You could at least be a little nice."

"I don't know how to be nice." She gave him a look and he snorted. "Oh, okay, Gabrielle. I know how to be a *little* nice, but I'm much better at being *wicked*."

She felt her cheeks burn and he chuckled.

Regulus gathered their things and they checked out of the bed and breakfast. Then they were back in the car for the trip back to London. As they wound their way through the Lake District towards Liverpool, several police cars roared past, their lights and sirens blazing.

"I guess someone finally found the carnage," Regulus said dryly.

"Sometimes I don't know where that man is," she said with a scowl. "The one that was with me last night. Sometimes I think I'm hallucinating. You don't seem to care about life or death."

"I care a lot, Gabrielle."

"Could've fooled me."

"I know how to pick my battles and when to walk away from them. I know how to fight."

"I'm not talking about fighting," she said. "I'm talking about *caring*. There's a big difference."

His fists tightened around the steering wheel, but he didn't answer, his steely gaze fixed on the road ahead. This was probably something they'd argue about forever and a day without resolution.

"When did you…" She didn't quite know how to end that question.

"The day you walked into *Devil's Kitchen*."

That day back in New Orleans? An unknown witch had summoned her, and it'd been Regulus who waited in that café. He'd threatened and manipulated her into linking him to Zac, and now he was telling her that it was the first moment he felt an attraction to her?

"You do know that your family is under my protection, now and forever…" He hesitated and she was taken aback. This was unfamiliar ground for him as much as it was for her.

"Once this is over and you take back your kingdom of thugs."

"Yes."

"It's no use thinking of the future," she told him. "Not until this is over."

If there was a future, she couldn't see things working out without a hell of a lot of heartache. It was like she was the prom queen dating a mob boss. In what universe was that morally right?

"Will you teach me how to track Aed?"

He glanced at her out the corner of his eye. "Why?"

"We need to be ready for every possible outcome," she said. What if something happened to him? She would have to go on alone and without knowing how to find the hybrid, it would make her work much more difficult than it already was.

After a moment he said, "Tomorrow. There are more pressing battles to be fought today, dear one."

<hr>

The apartment building loomed above Gabby as she gazed up at the façade. The top two floors radiated warm light and even without it, she knew everyone was at home waiting. Six vampires and a Celestine-hybrid.

Regulus was beside her, a hand on the small of her back. "No time like the present, Gabrielle."

"Wait," she said, taking his hand. Pulling him towards her, she pressed her lips to his. He kissed her back, sliding his tongue against hers with a moan. Pulling away, she rested her forehead against his, her skin tingling.

"What was that for?" he asked, running a thumb across her bottom lip.

"Courage."

"They will forgive you in time. It was my fault, after all."

"You may have started this, Regulus, but it's different now."

"It's no one else's business," he growled. "You and I, whatever this is... it's between us and no one else."

She took in his black eyes, the curve of his

cheekbones, his annoying mouth and sighed. "You're right."

"I love it when you say that."

"Don't get used to it."

The Roman took her hand and led her inside, holding the door open for her. It was only a few flights of stairs to the top, so they walked together, their footsteps echoing off the walls.

Zac had told her they were staying in number six, right at the top, and when she stood outside the door, she knocked before opening it and walking into the fray.

At first no one did anything. Four sets of eyes shot straight to her, then focused on where she knew Regulus was standing just outside the door. Aya, Zac, Tristan, and Nye sat around the kitchenette, and every single one of their expressions fell into shock.

Aya shot to her feet like a lioness, her eyes beginning to change and before Gabby could stop her, she lunged forwards with a roar. The hybrid's hands circled around Regulus' throat and they fell backwards onto the floor with a crash.

Aya's hands emitted a dull blue glow that shone through her skin, and the Roman let out a roar of anger, trying to pry her fingers away. Gabby knew once Aya had a founder in her power, that was it. It would be too late to stop her, so there was only one option.

Focusing her will, Gabby poured it all into the

Celestine, and she froze, her expression falling into surprise.

"*No*," Aya wailed as her power subsided. She fell back with a cry of rage, holding her head as Gabby willed a few thousand synapses in her brain to misfire. Regulus sat up the moment she let go and went to lunge for the hybrid, but Gabby focused her will on him and his jaw stiffened.

"I'm not above hurting you both," she snapped.

"*I'll kill you*," Aya hissed at the Roman.

Gabby stepped forwards, putting herself in between Aya and Regulus and let them go at the same time. They were both on their feet, eyeing each other with a disdain she couldn't fathom.

"No," she said, glancing at the hybrid. "We need him, Aya."

"He's supposed to be dead," she cried, as Zac grasped her hand, pulling her away.

"I'm sorry I had to keep it from you, Aya, but surely you understand why?"

"No, I don't. What will stop him from trying to end me?"

"Probably the fact you cannot be killed by conventional means," the Roman drawled.

"He's the only one who can take Aed down for good," Gabby countered.

"That much we gathered," Tristan said.

When everyone stopped and stared at Aya, she

sighed dramatically. "I tried to burn his heart to ash, but it didn't work."

"You fought Aed?" Regulus snorted. "*You?*"

"We voided each other out," she continued, ignoring the Roman. "His power won't work on me and mine won't work on him."

The Roman laughed. "So, the all-powerful Aeriaya can't save the day anymore."

"*Regulus*," Gabby hissed.

"Don't you dare say my name, filth," Aya said through gritted teeth. "I can still end you."

"And what would that solve?" the Roman asked, walking around Gabby and picking up a bottle of alcohol off the table.

Gabby watched the vampires as they eyed each other, and she caught Zac's gaze. He frowned and shook his head slightly before turning back to Aya. She respected the Celestine as a witch, but Zac... He was different. His respect had been hard won and she was about to lose it if she couldn't explain herself to him. He'd gone to kill Regulus believing he was going to die, and it was all her fault.

"How is it that only you can kill the mental case?" Nye asked, breaking the silence. "Why not the Hunter?"

"I don't understand how it works," Regulus said, putting the bottle back. "I always assumed it had something to do with the spell that created us. I'm not sure Katrin did, either."

"But that doesn't make sense," Gabby said. "You said she created you for that reason."

"Yes, but who knows how these things work." His gaze flickered to Aya.

She rolled her eyes. "Don't look at me."

"For a Celestine, you have quite the attitude."

"Regulus," Gabby scolded. "Fighting will get us nowhere."

"Perhaps not," he said, his gaze never leaving Aya. "But I do love getting a reaction from the fearsome Witch Hunter."

"Why do you care about the hybrid?" Aya asked, her gaze burning. "Why not leave us to him?"

"Because, dear star, I was made for this purpose. Aed is a threat to all out kind, not just a lone remnant of a long dead war."

"You were made for this?" she scoffed. "Then why try to steal the Celestine's secrets?"

"I didn't say it was my *only* purpose," he said with a smirk.

"Enough," Zac said, stepping between them. "I doubt any of this matters right now. Not with a mental case on the loose. Leave your fighting for after he's dead."

Gabby knew she was right in trusting Zac. He'd changed and even though she was obviously on the outs with him now, he still did what was needed to be done.

"I can track the hybrid and we can end him for good," Regulus said. "Then all is fair in love and war."

"I'm counting on it," Aya muttered.

"Where are the Three?" Regulus asked. "I assume they're still around here someplace?"

"Downstairs," Zac replied, narrowing his eyes.

"Oh, calm down, Zachary," the founder snorted. "I'm not going to take away your playthings."

"I don't order them around. They're free to do whatever they want."

"Regulus," Gabby murmured. "Leave them be."

"You're not welcome here, Regulus," Aya said. "The moment you step out of line, you'll have to deal with me. Got it?"

"As clear as a starry night, precious."

"There's a spare room at the back," Nye said, nodding to a hallway that led off the dining room.

The Roman narrowed his eyes at the spy.

"If you've got something to say, mate, then just say it."

"Don't think I haven't forgotten your betrayal, Nye." He looked the vampire up and down before walking down the hall and pushing open the door to the bedroom. A slam echoed through the apartment a moment later, and Gabby glanced at Nye, who just shrugged.

"He's got a good memory," he said like it didn't matter and went back to the table, picking up the drink he'd discarded earlier.

The front door slammed as Zac left and Gabby looked to Aya, who just rolled her eyes and stalked off in the opposite direction. A third and final slam signalled her last word on the matter.

Gabby's gaze returned to the door Zac had stalked through.

"He's gone to the roof, I'd say," Tristan said, joining Nye.

There was no putting it off, so Gabby went out the door to the apartment and found the only set of stairs leading upwards. Zac was still unpredictable and there was no telling which way this was going to go. It was alarming how much he'd changed in such a short amount of time. Still, all she had was the truth and hopefully, he'd hear her out.

At the top of the stairs, Gabby eased the heavy door open and cold air rushed inside, taking her breath away. She instantly saw Zac sitting on the edge of the roof with his feet dangling over the edge. He knew she was there, but he didn't acknowledge her existence.

Letting the door close behind her, she gingerly propped herself on the edge beside him, the wind whipping icicles around her and she shrunk down into her coat.

"I'm sorry," she whispered.

"You let me believe I was going to my death," he said thinly.

"I'm sorry, Zac. It had to be believable to everyone. Aed can read blood like an open book. If he'd got hold of any one of you, it would've been over. The element of surprise is the only thing we've got going for us right now."

"You could've told me I wasn't linked with him. You could've told me that at least."

"I'm sorry," she said. "I did what I had to."

"Did Regulus threaten your family? Liz? Alex? Is that why you're with him? Is that why you did it?"

She sighed and looked at her hands. "In the beginning, yes. He threatened my family and yours."

"But?"

"But the Coven's spell worked and as a witch, I have a duty to see this to the end." The lie came so smoothly, she surprised herself. But it wasn't a lie, not really. She'd just left out one important little detail. "I'll do whatever it takes to keep you all from harm."

"You can't. Not from Aed."

"I might not be able to, but I'll die trying if I have to."

"You don't need to die for me. You're not going to be a martyr... not while I'm around."

His disappointment in her sliced deep. After everything, Zac mattered the most. He was her only link to home, her only link to what she'd left behind. She couldn't lose that, and she couldn't lose his hard-won respect. She couldn't lose *him*.

"We never started out as friends," she said. "But now we are. Please don't let this ruin it."

He snorted, wringing his hands together.

"This entire thing is bigger than us. It scares the shit out of me, and I don't think I can do it without you." She wound her hand around his thigh, pulling him against her. "I'll do whatever I can to get you home to Sam and Liz. *I promise.*"

Finally, Zac looked at her, his expression shifting into something she didn't understand. Snaking an arm around her back, he pulled her against his side. She took it as a white flag and rested her head against his shoulder. The irony of their embrace didn't escape her, considering how much they'd fought when they'd first met back in Louisiana. She'd been trying to protect Liz from his bad boy ways long before her friend knew they were vampires. This was a one-eighty from that, and it was hard to pinpoint exactly when things had changed. That kind of nostalgia brought up all kinds of memories.

"Remember that summoning spell?" she asked.

"Do I remember?" Zac asked wryly. "How could I forget?"

CHAPTER 14

Gabby's eyes opened slowly, taking in the living room that was flooded with silvery grey morning light. Her entire body felt sluggish from her night on the sofa and she rolled onto her back, stretching.

A pair of icy-blue eyes were staring down at her and she jumped, sitting upright.

"I have Alisandra's grimoire," Aya said blandly, holding out the leather-bound book to the witch.

Gabby took the grimoire gingerly, like it might zap her with Celestine payback medicine. The hybrid still wasn't thrilled and would probably be difficult until this whole mess was over—just one more thing she had to deal with on top of everything else.

Things seemed slightly better with Zac and she hoped they would stay that way. Aya, on the other hand...

Last night was the first time she'd seen Aya since

the day the hybrid had left Ashburton, and shouldn't she be just as angry with her? After she left Zac in such a callous way and after leaving them all? She should be angry, right?

"You know I can sense your emotions?" Aya asked, tilting her head to the side.

Gabby nodded, clutching the grimoire tighter to her chest.

"All I can sense is confusion," Aya said suspiciously. "I hope it's not the kind of confusion I'm thinking it is."

"Aya."

They both looked up at the sound of Zac's voice and the hybrid frowned. Gabby smiled a little at him in relief and he nodded. Things were bad enough without any of them finding out that she was falling for Regulus. That was exactly why she slept on the couch and not in his bed where she'd much rather be.

Zac held out his hand for Aya and she walked away stiffly, probably annoyed that she was interrupted from her interrogation.

"Let us know if there's anything we can do to help," he said. "We'll be waiting."

Gabby nodded. "I'll go over the grimoire this morning. Regulus is going to teach me how to track Aed later on."

Aya sighed sharply, wanting to put her two cents in, but Regulus chose that moment to walk into the room, looking all refined and collected, like nothing was wrong at all. The hybrid narrowed her eyes at him and dragged Zac towards the front door. A moment later, the door slammed closed, the boom echoing through the empty apartment.

Regulus sat next to Gabby, not in the least bit annoyed at the two vampires' abrupt exit.

Gabby glanced at the front door. "Should we go someplace else?"

"No, they won't be able to hear from down there. Too many walls and slabs of concrete in the way."

Nodding, she opened up Alisandra's grimoire. It was the first time she'd had a chance to look it over. When Coraline had taken it from the matriarch, she'd given it to Aya the day after the hybrid had ripped the witches to pieces. Now it sat in her lap and she wasn't sure she was going to like what she found inside.

The Coven itself had been corrupt from day one—not only by blood, but by cause as well. The spells and incantations in here would be all kinds of wrong. Still, this book was their last remaining relic and the personal grimoire of the matriarch. If there was any clue left, it had to be in here.

As Gabby opened the cover, she felt the book resonating in her hands, almost like it was trying to suck all the light from the room. On the first page, there was an epigraph written in an elegant hand. It was a manifesto of sorts for the Coven written in witch-speak, talking about revenge and birthright. She could taste a metallic bile rise in the back of her throat and she quickly turned the page.

As she flipped through the grimoire, the things she read became worse and worse. Spells for harm, curses on the soul, poisons to leach power from another witch, and more besides. Horrible, painful rituals that went against everything she stood for.

"This is all kinds of messed up," Gabby said, feeling sick. "There are spells and curses for all kinds of nasty shit."

"Nasty shit?" Regulus asked, amusement in his voice.

"Get with the times, old man."

He chuckled, running a hand over her thigh. "The Coven were not known for their kindness to all creatures."

"You've been dealing with them for a long time... what else aren't you telling me?" she asked a little too forcefully.

"You keep saying that like I deliberately withhold everything from you, dear one."

"Do you?"

"The Coven," he said, ignoring her, "were working towards one goal for the last three thousand years. Awakening the Tuatha-hybrids so they could resurrect a dead race."

"But that was never going to work. They'll never be as they were."

"Try explaining that to a coven of mentally unstable witches."

Gabby frowned, turning back to the grimoire. "But

Katrin was a part of the Coven," she said, running her fingers along the heavy parchment.

"Who was betrayed by her own kind. Used for something against her will. She would've been cast out for having no power; instead, they used her as a tool against the Celestines."

"And to bring back the Tuatha."

"She was intelligent enough to understand that it would be devastating if it ever happened. I've explained it to you before, dear one. She created us for her own revenge."

"Against the Celestines and the Tuatha."

"And those who would claim her as family as long as she did what she was bid to do."

Gabby stared at the grimoire, not trusting herself to look up. Everything had been so black and white for so long, and she was confused with all the blurring lines. Katrin was on the bad side. Gabby was supposed to banish her to the other side. Turned out that even the bad guys believed they were doing things for the greater good.

But Katrin was gone, along with the Coven and the other five founders, and they were the only ones left. The lines had to blur a little more to end a greater threat.

She flipped the page again, hoping the next one would have some kind of answer. Instantly, the ritual jumped out at her, the witch-speak word for awakening dominating everything else. The long, spidery handwriting looked like it'd been scrawled eons ago, the ink bleeding deep into the brown parchment.

"There is the awakening ritual," Gabby said, pointing to the page.

"Does it mention anything about the binding?"

Scanning the page, she shook her head. "It's talking about awakening lost brethren. Finding hope which was lost."

"Not our hope," the Roman said, looking over her shoulder.

"There is nothing about binding in the whole thing. There's glyphs for weakening, those might help, but nothing about putting a hybrid back inside a stone box. Aoife bound them with Celestine magic, maybe Aya—"

"If she knew, don't you think she would've already told you?" Regulus interrupted.

"Yeah, she probably would've."

She must have sounded more morose than she intended, because Regulus pulled her into his lap, a hand cupping her face. She instantly tensed and glanced at the door. If they found them like this...

"I know you didn't mention our relationship to them," he murmured. "I understand."

"I told them you're only here because of me."

"And I am."

"And you're not their master. We're equals."

Regulus snorted. That obviously didn't sit well with him.

"I've hurt them enough," she said, setting the grimoire onto the coffee table.

Regulus breathed in her scent and pressed his lips to her throat. "I thought this was between us, dear one. No one else, especially not those imbeciles."

"Please be nice. No fighting."

The Roman's only response was to capture her in a kiss. As he deepened it, he set her down on the sofa and pressed into her, letting his hands wander. A master of manipulation indeed.

"Are you going to teach me how to track the hybrid?" she asked breathlessly.

"Your wish is my command." When a smile spread across her face, he pressed a finger over her lips. "Don't take that too literally." Standing, he took her hand and pulled her up from the sofa. "You better put on your coat, dear one. We're going outside."

When she was ready, they trudged down the stairs and stood outside the apartment block, beside the canal that ran through the centre of Camden. The entire world passed them by as if nothing was in the least bit wrong.

"Do you think I'll be able to do it?" Gabby asked, putting the human world out of her mind.

"I don't see why it wouldn't work with you," he said. "I was made by one of the Five for this and you are descended from one of them, so it stands to reason."

"Then guide me through it and we can try."

"When I sense him, I can feel his power," Regulus said taking her hand. "If I'm quiet enough, I can feel it against my mind like a strange fizz."

"Fizz?" Gabby asked with a small laugh, squeezing his hand.

"Yes. A strange fizzing sensation, much like the white noise of a modern radio."

"How can you tell it's the Tuatha?"

"It's akin to tuning into the signal, like one of your radio stations. You'll know when you've got him, and you'll know which way to go like a magnet. I was told it's a similar feeling to a witch scrying with a crystal."

"Except you become the crystal."

"Yes, that sounds about right. It tells me where I need to go." He closed his eyes and breathed in deeply. "Give it a try, Gabrielle."

She stood next to him, fitting her small body against his side, and closed her eyes. Tuning out all the noises from the surrounding city, she cast her mind out, feeling for the white nose Regulus had mentioned. Zac had said Aed was hanging around London, so there was a high chance they'd get a hit. It wasn't long before she felt it at the edges of her thoughts. A strange fizzing sound, just as the founder had said, and the more she focused on it, the more she felt a tug at her soul. It was leading her towards the Tuatha.

"Can you feel that?" she asked, looking up at him.

Regulus stared off into nothingness, and she knew he did. He took a few steps, pulling her with him.

"Regulus, *no*," she said. He meant to go after Aed right now. "We can't go alone."

"We can and we will. This could be our only chance and I'm going to take it."

"He knows who you are. He knows from Coraline and Max. When he sees you—"

"It will be too late."

"He's just... sitting there," Gabby said as they peered through the wrought iron fence that surrounded the private garden. London was littered with them—they stood in the centre of a ring of old townhouses in the West End. Private, key-only exclusivity for the rich residents... and one hybrid who seemed to do whatever took his fancy.

"There is no reason for the insane, Gabrielle," Regulus muttered.

Aed was sitting in the middle of the garden on the edge of a fountain, trailing his fingers through the spray of water. He didn't look like an insane supernatural creature. He actually looked handsome in a posh suit and his hair styled just so. If she was just a regular human, he wouldn't have looked out of place, but her witch sense told her a different story, one that didn't feel nice at all.

Now that Gabby had laid eyes on the Tuatha himself, everything suddenly became real—a hundred percent more deadly—and her entire body shook.

"I will protect you," Regulus said. "I won't let anything happen to you. *Ever*."

"I know, but—"

"The glyphs you mentioned in the Coven grimoire... do you remember them?"

"The glyphs for weakening? Yes, they're simple enough, but I'd need a lot of them. At least one at each corner of the garden and one on his body."

"He'll notice the moment you cast. I will distract him while you ward the corners."

"Regulus, this isn't right. We need the others here." Gabby didn't like this at all. Something was about to happen, and all of her senses told her it wasn't going to be good.

"I have to take this chance. It may be the only one we get." Regulus pressed his lips to hers and was gone.

Not wasting any time, she circled her fingers around the fence at the corner, calling on her power. She began to weave the glyph as she'd seen it that morning in Alisandra's grimoire, imbedding it in the iron. As she worked, she sensed the hybrid's attention had shifted to her and she hoped Regulus was there.

"You..." She heard Aed say. He was hesitating, which meant... "You're supposed to be dead. I saw it in the blood."

"Sorry to disappoint you," came Regulus' voice, calm and clear as ever.

"I won't let you stop me before I've even begun. I won't let you deny me my revenge."

As the glyph finally seeped into place, Gabby jogged to the next corner and started weaving the next. She had to be quick about it. There was only so much time before Aed would focus on her instead of the Roman.

"You won't get a chance, Aed. There's no one left to exact your revenge on. No one who cares."

"You lie, you filthy human half-breed. You are nothing compared to me."

The second glyph was in place and she ran to the next corner.

"You are the last. There's nothing for you in this world. Not anymore."

"Stop with your lies," the hybrid roared. "I will find my sisters and together, we will destroy you all. I will tear everything you care about into pieces in front of your eyes. Then you can see how it feels."

"I'm delighted to be the one who tells you... You won't be finding anything."

The third glyph was in place and Gabby sprinted to the last corner, but she wasn't quick enough. She slammed into something hard and fell backwards onto the sidewalk. She looked up and her heart almost stopped beating. Aed stared down at her with blazing red eyes—the same eyes that'd stared at her through Coraline's vision.

"Celestine *witch*," he hissed taking a step forwards, but Regulus was there. Regulus grasped the hybrid around the neck and flung him back over the fence into the privacy of the garden.

"Quickly, Gabrielle," he said and was gone again.

She scrambled to her feet and with shaking hands, cast the fourth glyph into the fence. All there was to do now was cast the final onto the hybrid himself. She scaled the fence and landed in a flower bed with a dull thud, approaching the fountain where the two vampires were facing off.

"Your flimsy wards will do nothing, witch," Aed spat as his eyes fixed on her. "You think you can weaken me with your pathetic magic?"

"Don't listen to him," Regulus said.

"You will listen to me, vampire, and you will listen and do well to heed every single word. This world is *mine*. These humans are *mine*. And your witch," he glanced at Gabby, "is *mine*."

Aed launched himself at her and she stumbled back with a surprised cry, falling onto the ground. Regulus wasn't fast enough, and the hybrid straddled her, his hands circling her neck. "What does your blood taste like, pretty one? What stories does it have to tell?"

Regulus let out an agonised roar of fury and pulled the hybrid off her.

"The glyph," she gasped, catching her breath.

The Roman ignored her as he went in for the kill, but it was as if Aed could sense every move before the founder made it. Every blow was parried and every time he dodged to the side, the hybrid was there, sinking his fists into flesh.

Aed had the Roman from behind, and before Gabby could cry out, he sunk his fangs into Regulus' neck and blood poured down his skin, staining his shirt.

"*No*," she cried, taking a step forwards, but the Roman held out a hand to stop her.

Aed's eyes widened and he shoved Regulus away so hard the vampire's knees left cracks in the ground.

"No," Aed cried, clawing at his face, blood dripping down his chin. "You killed them. *My sisters...*"

"Gabrielle," Regulus wheezed, on his feet in an instant. "*Run.*"

He had her in his arms before she could turn, Aed's tortured cries following them down the street and into the darkening city. She ran for what seemed like miles and miles until he finally slowed to a fast walk in a back street somewhere she didn't recognise.

"He's not following," she said, casting her senses behind them.

Regulus dropped her to her feet roughly, a hand on the wall. He hung his head, seemingly out of breath, and she noticed he'd broken out into a cold sweat. Vampires like him didn't need to rest.

"Regulus?" she asked quietly.

Standing to his full height, he grunted, wiping his face. "We need to go back to the house. I need to keep you safe."

His shirt was still wet with his blood and it could've been because it hadn't dried yet, or maybe he was still bleeding. He noticed her gaze on his shoulder and with a frown, he took her arm and led her.

"Regulus, your shoulder," she protested.

"*It's fine.*"

His response was clipped and she knew he wasn't saying something. When his hand came up to his forehead, he halted, letting go of her arm. Before she could reach out to him, his eyes unfocused and he fell to his knees, breathing hard. With a cry, she was beside him, her hands on his clammy face.

"Regulus," she murmured. "What's wrong?"

He seemed to look at her, some kind of recognition flashing through his dark eyes. "Katrin?"

"No." She shook her head, beginning to panic. "It's Gabby. Gabrielle."

He frowned. "That's what I meant."

Trying not to let her concern show, Gabby wrapped an arm around his waist and helped him to his feet. "We've got to get off the street. Let's go home."

"Home?" he asked in a childlike voice.

"Yes, home."

There was only one explanation for Regulus' odd behaviour. Aed's bite had somehow poisoned him. She hoped the Roman's body would heal itself, because she had no idea how to do it. No matter her feelings, they needed him. Regulus was the only way they could kill Aed for good.

He was their last hope.

CHAPTER 15

Gabby tried to mask her worry as she helped Regulus back to the apartment. He seemed to have lost his strength all at once and hauling him up the stairs to the top floor was no picnic. He hadn't said a word since he'd called her Katrin, and she knew his pride had been hurt more than anything. The Roman didn't seem concerned that his wound wasn't healing, but he probably should be.

Zac shot to his feet when they came in the door and Regulus stormed off into the bedroom without making eye contact.

"Gabby?"

"Not now," she said, shaking her head.

"Yes now," he said. "Where have you been? I thought—"

"He was teaching me how to track Aed."

"You obviously found him. I can smell the blood."

"He made me go confront him, but it didn't work...

It…" She hesitated, glancing at the bedroom door. She wanted Regulus. She couldn't leave him. Not like that.

"It obviously didn't go well," Zac said thinly. "And here I was thinking all we had was the element of surprise."

"Please, Zac. Can we talk about this later?"

He narrowed his eyes and nodded. "Later."

Without looking back, she followed Regulus into the bedroom, closing the door softly behind her. He had his back to her, looking out the window at the dark city. She didn't have to ask if something was wrong, she could feel it crackling in the air.

Without acknowledging her presence, he took off his shirt and inspected the bite mark in the reflection. Even in the dark room, she could see it was red and angry. Blood still seeped from it, but that wasn't what made her look twice. It had been maybe an hour since Aed had bitten him, but it looked infected. The Roman's skin was marred with black veins that seemed to spread the longer she looked.

"I was never going to be a match for him on my own," he said, his voice stretched thin.

"You didn't know that," she said, her voice barely a whisper.

"There was a reason there was six of us."

Gabby shook her head. "Fail safes."

"And in the event one of them woke… strength."

"You knew and you still went after him?"

"I believed I could stop him on my own. Obviously,

I was wrong." He poked at the wound in his neck and hissed.

"Regulus," she said, tugging his hands away.

He shrugged her off, pulling his shirt back on.

"It's not healing."

"No," he said gruffly, not looking at her, "it's not."

"How—"

He turned on her, eyes blazing. "The only way I'm going to be cured is with Aed's blood. Can you see that happening? Because I can't."

"There has to be another way."

"I'm dying and that's that."

No, she couldn't believe it. But he was right, wasn't he? The hybrids hadn't seen the light of day since they were turned. Anyone who might have known about them were long dead and their secrets lost to the ages. Even if there was a cure, she wouldn't be able to find it in time.

"Did you know?" she asked. When he turned away again and didn't answer, she grabbed his arm and forced him to look at her. "Did you know this would happen if he bit you?"

His jaw tightened and he shook his head. "There was no way to know."

"But you suspected."

"Yes."

"I can't believe..." she said but cast her gaze away. She was going to say, she couldn't believe he didn't tell her, but she knew why he didn't. He was just trying to protect her from the aftermath.

"It'll be fast or it'll be slow."

"No. I won't let it happen."

"I can already feel my mind slipping."

"No, you can't."

"I called you *Katrin*." He cupped her face in trembling hands. "I called you Katrin and you're my Gabrielle."

She froze. *His Gabrielle.*

"It will only get worse."

"Do you want—"

"No," he said, pre-empting what she was going to say. "I don't want her to touch me. I don't want her to see me like this."

She nodded. Damn him and his stubborn pride.

"Only if I try to hurt anyone. If I try to *hurt* you. Only then."

The poison was running in his veins—she could feel it through the skin of his hands—spreading throughout his system.

But Aed had bitten Zac and his wound had healed, so why wasn't Regulus'? The answer was obvious, really. He'd been created to counter the Tuatha-hybrids and nature had still found a way as it had with his other purpose, the Celestines. Even the immortal had a way to end it all. What use was the word when he could be taken away from her with one little bite?

For once, she didn't want to believe Regulus wasn't as indestructible as she thought he was.

<hr>

After leaving Regulus to his stubborn melancholy, Gabby went back out in the living room. Zac was slouched in the oversized couch with Aya at his side. There was no sign of Nye, Tristan, or the Three, and she guessed they might have escaped to the pub when she returned with Regulus.

"Gabby?" Zac asked, sitting up straight.

She sunk into a chair across from them and rubbed her tired eyes.

"What's wrong?" he asked when she didn't acknowledge him.

"Aed bit him." She sighed. "He went for me and… he bit him."

"It's not healing," Aya said blandly, earning herself a glare from Zac.

"No," Gabby snapped, narrowing her eyes at the hybrid.

"What do we need to do?" Zac asked. "Is there a way to heal him?" He got it even if Aya didn't, and that was a role reversal if she ever saw one.

"He says the only way to heal it would be with Aed's blood."

"Well, we're screwed. Try getting within five feet of the guy," Aya said, splitting the wound further.

Biting her tongue, Gabby glanced away. Fighting between themselves wouldn't solve anything. Regulus was dying and there was nothing she could do. Going after Aed was a suicide mission. Anyone who tried would be dead the moment the Tuatha laid eyes on them. She knew she needed to ask, regardless of Aya's reaction.

Glancing at the Celestine, she asked, "If it comes to it, would you?" She didn't need to elaborate any further than that.

"No," Aya snarled. Her entire body seemed to glow with the force of her voice.

"Aya," Gabby sighed, trying to keep her emotions in check, "I'm asking you as a witch. As a sister. As a friend. If it comes to it, will you end his suffering?"

"No."

"Please—"

"You're forgetting it was Regulus who snatched me from my forest. His actions sealed my fate and that of my family. I will not help you."

"He was ordered to do it," she cried, her control beginning to crack. "Katrin ordered him, and he was compelled to do it."

"He may have been ordered, but he wanted it to do it regardless."

"It was two thousand years ago," she exclaimed, rising to her feet. "Two thousand years, Aya. Learn a little forgiveness. Aren't you supposed to be the embodiment of nurturing and care? How about you care a little for once in your screwed-up life?"

"Gabby—" Zac began, but she didn't want to hear it.

"I'll never forget this, Aya. *Never.* Don't even think to ask me for anything ever again because you will already know my answer."

Aya rose to her feet, her pale hands clenched into tight fists. "You have no idea what you're dealing with, Gabby."

Gabby felt her power tingle in her stomach, aching for release and before she could lose it and turn on the hybrid, she stalked from the room, tears threatening.

"Let her go," she heard Zac say, but she didn't stop to listen to more.

Easing open the door to Regulus' room, she frowned at how sick he looked. He'd collapsed back onto the bed fully clothed, too tired to even pull the covers back. Sitting beside him, she tugged his boots off and set them on the floor. Placing a hand on his forehead, he stirred, his eyes fixing on hers.

"I heard you arguing," he wheezed. "Your devotion warms my cold, dead heart, Gabrielle."

"Oh, shut up."

"It appears it's going to be slow. Which is probably what I deserve. Just let me die in peace."

"Never," she said. "You annoyed the crap out of me since the day I met you. I'm not about to let you stop now." Kicking her boots off, she curled up next to him, winding an arm around his waist.

"You don't have to stay, dear one. I don't want to hurt you."

"You won't." She stroked his cheek, trying to hold back tears. "Where do you want to be?"

He frowned like he didn't understand her question, but then he said, "Home."

"Think of it and I'll take you there."

She let her power meld with his thoughts and the surrounding air shimmered. If this was the last thing she could do for him, then it wouldn't be enough. *Nothing would ever be enough.*

Closing her eyes, she felt a few stray tears slip between her lashes and roll down her cheek. When she opened them again, it was to blue sky as far as the eye could see and golden fields broken up with a square patch of green—an olive grove—and just beyond, a white-washed house with a terracotta roof.

She sat on the rise of a hill, Regulus at her side, a slight breeze fluttering her hair. There was the slight tang of salt, which meant the ocean mustn't be far from the villa and its fields. He wound his arm across her back and squinted in the sunshine.

"It's so real," he said with a sigh.

"Where are we?"

"This was where I was born. Italy, as it was when it was part of the Roman Empire."

"It's beautiful."

"See that field just below the rise?" He pointed to the left. "That's where my father taught me to ride."

"What was he like?"

"He was a hard man. He loved my mother and I, but he was a centurion. Most of his life was spent fighting. He was absent for most of my childhood, such were the Legion's campaigns back then. It would be years at a time before he came home and for most of it, my mother did nothing but worry that he wouldn't return at all. Every time he came back, he was a little less... himself. Ultimately, it was his wish that I follow him into the Legion and so it was."

"Did you want to? Join the Legion, I mean."

He shrugged. "If there was another option, it never occurred to me. I wanted to be like my father. He seemed like a hero to a young boy. I never understood it at that age, not until I was living it. I soon grew up and the truth of life was revealed to me in the most horrific way. Conquering, war... death. Killing comes natural for a vampire. Perhaps it comes easily for a human but," he tapped his temple, "it doesn't come easy in here."

"Did you have any joy in your life?" she asked, leaning her head against his shoulder.

"Joy?" he asked in surprise. "I suppose I've been happy at times."

"That's not what I meant."

He let out a lengthy sigh. "No."

Gabby didn't know what to say, so she just linked her fingers with his.

"I hoped that after this was done, then things might've been different," he said. "That I had a reason to go on for myself and not for others. No more orders to follow but my own."

"What would you have done?"

"It's no use dwelling on things that will never happen." He looked down at her, his eyes full of sadness.

"Regulus..."

"I'm over two thousand years old, dear one. No one should live that long."

She clutched his arm, not wanting to let go. It was strange how she found herself here, falling for the one man who made life a living hell for so many of her friends. A witch and a vampire. "But... I've only just found you."

"It's a shame I can't spend more time with you, Gabrielle. It's a shame I have to leave you with this burden. If I could change it, I would."

They sat together for what felt like an age, looking over the valley. Whatever memories the Roman was reliving, he didn't share. He didn't have to; this was his time to say goodbye to whatever he wanted.

"I promised I'd protect you and your family," he said, breaking the silence. "When I'm gone, look inside my bag. You'll find what you need."

"What do you mean?"

"Everything that is mine is yours, dear one. My houses, my money. If I can't be there, then at least this will help you and your family in the future."

"I can't."

"You can, Gabrielle."

"I'm not ready to let you go yet," she said, curling her fingers around his arms.

"Neither am I, but the world stops for no one... not even the supernatural."

"Are you afraid?"

"How could I be afraid with you by my side?" He cupped her face in a warm hand, brushing away her tears with a thumb. "I never thought anyone would miss me when I inevitably died."

"I will."

"I know." He pressed his lips to hers, his kiss slow and full of all the things he couldn't say. Drawing back, he leaned his forehead against hers and let out a long, shaky breath.

"Thank you," he whispered, "for taking it away."

"You're welcome," Gabby replied, running her hand along his jaw.

With a sigh, he tore away and laid back in the grass, eyes on the sky. "I'm so tired..."

She curled up against him, her head on his chest as his eyes drooped. "It's okay. I'm here. I won't go anywhere."

"I could have fallen in love with a woman like you, Gabrielle. I think I already was."

"And I, you."

He let out a contented sigh and stilled beside her. As the vision dissolved, she knew he was gone.

Her tears flowed freely as she lay on his bed again, curled into his side. It was too soon. It couldn't end this way. It just couldn't. Regulus was gone and with him any hope for the future. Aed would wreak havoc on the world and that would be that.

They'd lost before it'd even begun, and she'd just lost the man she'd fallen in love with. If there had been any hope at all... it was just gone.

There was nothing.

CHAPTER 16

Gabby didn't know how long she'd been lying there, curled up next to Regulus' lifeless body. Not until Zac pulled her away and into his arms.

"Don't," she cried, pushing against his chest.

"Gabby, you can't stay here forever. Please, come away."

"No, I don't want to leave him."

"He's gone. *Please*."

He was, wasn't he? She crumbled into Zac as he held her tightly and didn't try to protest as he carried her from the room. A moment later, he set her down on the sofa.

Looking up, she saw Aya stare at her with a confused expression. Like she couldn't understand how she felt. The hybrid had lost her entire family; surely, she could understand? Even just a little? Her heart had just been ripped out of her chest, not in the literal sense, but it was gone.

Zac sat beside Gabby and went to put an arm around her, but Aya was still staring like she was some kind of puzzle and it made her want to snap her in two.

"He was a good man," she cried, standing up. "He was a good man who was driven to do evil things."

"You loved him," Aya said like it was the craziest thing she'd ever heard. Maybe it was.

"Yes. I loved him. So what?"

"Gabby." Zac stood and went to take her arm, but she stepped away.

"You've lied, killed, and tortured just as much as he did," she said through gritted teeth. "You do not get to judge me for this, Aya. You don't have the right."

Zac stepped into her, circling his arms around her small frame and she didn't have it in her to fight anymore. She couldn't justify Regulus' actions, she couldn't understand. She didn't have the time to even try. Her tears came hard and fast, staining the front of Zac's shirt.

"We have to bury him," she said desperately. "We have to…"

"Of course," he murmured into her hair.

"I don't know what to do."

"He has a house in Hampstead," Zac said after a moment. "We can take him there. There's a large garden out the back and if you ward it, no one will find him there. No one you don't want to."

She nodded, her entire body feeling numb.

"I'll get Nye to take you, and we'll meet you in an hour. I know it's soon, but we can't wait."

"I know."

"Don't worry about anything. I'll take care of it."

***

Nye drove Gabby to Regulus' house in Hampstead in silence. It didn't bother her, talking seemed to be too much effort right now.

When the spy pulled the car into a driveway, she looked up at the house and it didn't surprise her in the least. It was a mansion.

Roman columns held up a small verandah over the front door, landscaped gardens stretched around the grounds and probably out back as well. It was two stories of red-bricked, ivy-covered extravagance.

Nye was around to her side of the car in a flash, opening the door for her. He held out a hand and she took it, grateful for the help. Their footsteps crunched up the gravel drive and they stood outside. Looking at the door, she still couldn't fathom the selfless thing Regulus had done.

"I don't suppose you have a key?" she asked.

"It's my home away from home." Nye stuck his hand in his pocket and produced a key with a flourish. Unlocking the door, he went to step inside, but he smacked into thin air. "Hey. What gives? What happened to Happy the butler?"

"Butler?" she asked, then understood. "Oh, vampire safeguard."

"Only in the houses Regulus lived in," the spy said. "He had a lot of enemies, but it wasn't often someone thought they were the bee's knees and acted on it."

"I guess he split after Zac..." She couldn't say the rest, what with everything still hours fresh in her mind.

"Then what's the deal?" He kicked empty air and his boot connected with the invisible barrier around the house.

"I guess it's mine now."

To her surprise, Nye flung an arm over her shoulders and gave her a squeeze. "As long as you invite me in, we're sweet."

"If Zac trusts you, then so do I."

He raised his eyebrows. "Just like that?"

"I'm a witch. I know things."

"What kind of things?" he asked, looking worried. "Because—"

"No, nothing like that."

The spy watched her for a moment and said, "Everyone believes they're doing the right thing. Even if the majority is against them. Regulus was doing what he believed was right. He brought order to the seedy vampire underworld. He may have been king of the bad guys, but without him, this place would've been chaos."

"And what now? Who's going to take over?"

Nye shrugged. "Who knows?"

Gabby glanced his way. She knew Zac wouldn't be interested. That wasn't his game anymore, but Nye... He seemed to be the kind of vampire who'd be up for the job. He was two parts honourable, one part diabolical.

"Don't look at me, lovely," he said. "I don't think I have the stamina for it."

She smiled thinly. "It's in there."

"Bloody witches," the spy said with a laugh, "always causin' trouble."

"Always trying to restore the balance," she retorted. The spy hovered at the door, waiting for an invitation, but she wasn't done yet. "Consider it, Nye. You'd have my blessing."

"The blessing of a witch?" he asked, letting out a slow whistle. "You know I couldn't do it without being at least a little bad, right?"

"I understand. That's why there's a balance between light and dark. There can't be one without the other."

"I still don't like it."

"You're a good guy, but you have the right amount of fear. I've heard stories through the grapevine about Zac's short stint, but they also talk about you."

"There's talk about me?"

"Don't be modest, Nye. You know there is."

"You going to invite me in, lovely?" he asked with a wink.

"Come inside," she said with a slight smile and the spy guided her into the foyer.

Nye stopped by the door and let her wander the house as they waited for Zac. She flipped on light switches as she walked through room after room, running her fingers over the kitchen counter and dining table. Walking up the stairs, she found his bedroom, still full of his things, and her heart leapt into her throat again.

Finally, she found the study and closed herself inside. It smelled of leather and scotch and ash from the cold fireplace. Old, leather-bound books lined most of the walls and knowing how old Regulus had been, she wondered the age of some of them.

She couldn't believe he'd left it all to her. The wealth he'd amassed over his lifetime, he'd given it to her. All of this, his memories, his life, whatever his houses contained... it was all hers to do with what she wished.

Nye found her sitting behind Regulus' desk, leafing through a book that'd been left facedown on the antique mahogany. He rapped lightly on the door to get her attention. "They're here."

Glancing up, she sighed. "Okay."

Following him down the stairs and into the garden out back, she found everyone had assembled on the grass—the Three to one side and everyone else on the other. Aya stood behind Tristan, her gaze cast away, and

Gabby could only shake her head and keep moving forwards. Zac was the only one who stood between the groups of vampires like some kind of symbol of friendship. When he saw her, he came forwards.

"There's a grove towards the back of the garden," he said, taking her hand. "Full of all kinds of roses and daises. It isn't much to look at right now but come spring, it will be something else. I've put him there, but..."

"No, it's fine," she said, picking up on his hesitation. "It's perfect."

He led her down a path lined with grey pavers to the spot he'd described and to her relief, he'd already buried Regulus' body. If she saw his withered, desiccated features, she just might have snapped.

Standing there, oblivious to the group behind her, Gabby thought about the past few days. They were all she had, and it would never be enough. Gazing at the disturbed earth, she thought she should probably say something, but there weren't any words that could do Regulus justice. She'd only known the smallest piece of him, but the part he had given was the most sacred. Nobody made a move as she stood there amongst the miss-matched group of vampires, so she stepped forward, crouching by the upturned earth where Zac had buried the founder.

Calling on her earth sense, Gabby held out a shaking hand over the fresh earth. She'd seen her grandmother, Sofia, do it, so there was no reason she could as well. Remembering where Regulus wanted to spend his last hour on earth, she thought about the olive grove by his childhood home.

It was like planting a seed with her mind and she felt a tiny spark as it struck. The earth shifted beneath her hand and the tiniest hint of green sprouted from the soil, curling upwards, finding its way towards the light of the moon.

As the sapling grew taller, she rose with it, standing to her full height as the trunk grew thicker, branches multiplied, and a canopy arched overhead. When she was finally done, the tree was fully grown, laden with olives ripe for the picking. It was out of season, but somehow the notion fit with what Regulus' and her relationship had been. *Out of place, but right.*

Without a word to the assembled vampires, she walked back inside, just utterly tired of missing him already.

***

Zac sat on the roof of Gabby's house in Hampstead, Aya beside him. It felt strange calling it that. *Gabby's house.* He still couldn't understand how the Roman could've been so selfless after all the terrible things he'd done. He must have really cared for her.

The clear night sky stretched out above them, dotted with thousands and thousands of tiny stars, some with slight imperfections in colour, and he wondered if they were planets or satellites he was staring at.

Glancing at Aya, he saw that she was staring at the newly grown olive tree in the backyard. He couldn't read her expression, but he didn't have to. None of them had seen this coming, least of all her, and he knew her pride would have one hell of a dent right about now.

As he slid an arm around her, she looked up at him and said, "Aren't you angry?"

"No." Because he wasn't. "I have every right to be angry with Gabby, but I'm not. I don't want to be. I know she did what she had to for the greater good, and if that meant making me believe I was going to die, then so be it."

"I can't believe you're not in the least bit annoyed."

"If someone as pig-headed and selfish as me can sacrifice myself for the ones I love..." He shrugged.

"Regulus used you too, Zac. Don't you hate him for that?"

"Maybe I should, but maybe I just need to get past it and go on living."

"You don't want to do anything about it?"

"Maybe you need to learn how to forgive." He felt her tense beside him, her hand clamping down on his. "Two thousand years of revenge and hate. Aren't you exhausted?"

"Zac, I'm not above hurting you."

"And that's your answer for everything."

"I can see you've learned a thing or two about life."

"I know you can't see clearly where the Romans are concerned."

"Perhaps not, but I cannot overlook the fact that he sucked Gabby in. He made her—"

"Stop it, Aya." He gave her a look.

"He was a master at manipulation. Victoria was a prime example."

Zac let out a long sigh, allowing his eyes to search Aya's icy blue. Who knew what he was trying to find, but something inside him wanted to make her understand. Gabby's feelings weren't wrong, not by a long shot.

"There have been so many times that I thought I'd never get to kiss you again," he said. "The worst pain I'd ever felt was when I thought you had died. The thought of never touching or arguing with you again was too much to bear. So, I, more than anyone, understand what Gabby is going through. Completely."

"Zac, please," she argued.

"You have a horrible history with Regulus, I get it. But, Aya, you can't choose who you fall in love with. Gabby needs us right now. All of us. She doesn't need to be told how horrible the man she fell in love with was. She needs her friends."

"I don't think I can, Zac. This has been my entire life. How can I change that? How do I even begin to understand?"

He sighed, looking up at the stars and wondering if that's where Aya'd really come from. "Why does anyone love anyone? It's one of the great mysteries of the universe and hell if I know how it works."

"Who are you and what have you done with Zac Degaud?" she murmured.

"Ironically, the thing I was looking for was just under the surface all along. I was too fixated on being the monster and getting rid of it, rather than just making peace." Aya pressed her forehead against his, her thumb stroking the edge of his jaw. "I was always me. I just didn't know the way back."

He watched her thoughts play across her face and for the first time, she guarded nothing—confusion, anger, love, exhaustion. It was all there, and he didn't even try to understand how anyone could feel all of that at once.

"I know I need to make my peace," she said after a minute. "I've started but..."

"The Romans are gone. Katrin is banished to the other side. You had your chance to say goodbye to your family. The last peace you need before we face Aed is with Gabby."

Aya pulled back. "I know and I will. I think I should leave her be tonight."

What Zac didn't want to talk about was the fact they had nothing to use against Aed. No weapons, no secret plans, no spells. Regulus was their only chance at killing the hybrid forever and now that he was gone, they had a big fat zero. No one even knew how to bind him.

"What are we going to do now?" he asked with a grimace. "We're screwed, right?"

"I don't know," Aya replied. "We need Gabby."

"We do, but there's no one alive who knows about the Tuatha other than the fairy stories. What about the Celestines? Isn't there something in your history that could help?"

"Our answer may have something to do with the Celestines, or it may not. Anything I have to contribute might just make things worse. My power won't work against Aed. I just... I don't know."

"We'll think of something," he told her, hoping he was right.

Their answers weren't going to come all at once and this fight might take weeks, months, or even years to end. That was a thought too much to handle.

He longed for home. He wanted to see Sam and Liz, but until this was over, he'd stay as far away from them as he could.

Aya left Gabby alone for three days. In fact, nobody had seen her for that long. The witch had locked herself away in Regulus' study doing God knew what and they were beginning to worry.

The Three had gone back to the apartment in

Camden, but Aya had stayed behind with Zac, Tristan, and Nye to look after Gabby and think about their next move, which they still had none. Aed had all but disappeared for the time being and it was hardly a surprise. Perhaps he was mourning his dead sisters.

Aya hovered outside of the study and after a moment of hesitation, she opened the door and walked right in unannounced. Gabby sat in the leather armchair, curled up with a blanket, leafing through a leather-bound book. Her grimoire, along with Alisandra's, sat on the desk, unopened and untouched.

"Gabby?" Aya asked, closing the door behind her.

The witch looked up and scowled when she saw who'd interrupted.

"We're worried about you," she said. "I'm worried."

"I'm busy," the witch replied.

Aya walked over to where Gabby sat and glanced at the book in her hands. "It's a grimoire," she said surprised.

"There's a whole case of them," Gabby said, her voice betraying how tired she really was. "This is Victoria's."

Aya frowned, looking again at the grimoire in Gabby's hands. She had no love for the witch turned vampire who ruined Zac's life, but found herself curious over what was in it—especially since Victoria was a castoff of the Coven.

"There's nothing in here," Gabby said with a sigh. "I've been reading them all."

"So, there's nothing about the Tuatha, but what have you learned?"

"A great deal about other things. None of which we need right now."

"That's not the point," Aya said, sitting across from her in the other leather chair. "You've come a long way since I first met you. Growing trees from nothing. Glamours. Glyphs. It's impressive."

"So now you pretend to care? Now that you see how powerful I really am, you come crawling back? After you refused to help him? I can't believe you."

"I'd never use you, Gabby. You have to know I would never—"

"You've used and abused for the greater good, Aya. Don't deny it."

Aya grimaced. She had her there, but it was never without regret or shame. "The Celestines legacy is my priority. I am the last, even though I'm no longer complete. It's my eternity. You know it. Zac knows it. I've always been up front about that."

"You only showed me your true form because it was convenient for you," the witch snapped. "If Katrin hadn't revealed herself to you that night at Alex's, you would have revealed nothing to us, let alone me."

"If Katrin hadn't cursed Zac; if the Coven didn't... I wouldn't have revealed myself to anyone else but you. You know I can't compel you to forget. I wouldn't even if I could. I doubt I would've told Zac willingly and what does that say about me?"

Gabby eyed her suspiciously.

"I've never trusted easily," Aya said. Casting her gaze to the ground, she hesitated. She'd never had to explain her motives to anyone before. Forever cold and calculating. "I've kept myself secret for so long, sometimes I have trouble finding the right words."

"You think I'm a fool for loving him," she said. "You think I somehow changed sides. Betrayed you and the Five's legacy."

"No, I don't. I don't claim to understand it, but I don't think you're a fool."

The witch looked up at her like she was mad.

"My feelings towards Regulus will never change. I cannot apologise for that, and I hope you understand why. And my feelings towards you will never change, either."

Gabby sighed loudly, shifting uncomfortably. "And what are those?"

"You really have to ask?"

"I wouldn't ask unless I wanted to know the answer."

"Respect," Aya said firmly. "Love. Loyalty. We may disagree on many things in the future, but I see you as a sister. Not because you're descended from Ismena. Not because my mother gifted your line their power. Not because you are probably one of the most powerful witches alive right now. It's because of who you are. Never forget that." The witch's emotions were all over the place, and she had a hard time keeping it together as they washed over her. "I get it. Love is a wonderful and terrible thing all at once. If I lost Zac... Well, I would understand how you feel right now, but we need you, Gabby. I need you."

Gabby set Victoria's grimoire aside and sat up straight. "I love Regulus. I don't make excuses for it, and I will not talk to you about it. I won't entertain any negativity from you about him, so don't even mention his name around me."

"Understood."

"If you hadn't turned up, I would still be a small-town witch whose power could only light a candle. You've taught me so much just by consequence. I'm not the same witch anymore and I never will be. I'll probably be angry with you for a while yet, but we have a problem that needs fixing... for the greater good."

"That I can understand," Aya said wryly. "Truce?"

Gabby looked her up and down with a shake of her head. "No truce, Aya. We never needed one."

The hybrid smiled thinly at the witch and reached out for Victoria's grimoire. "Then let's get to work."

CHAPTER 17

Gabby read over the letter that Regulus had left her again like it was holding some secret message she'd been unable to find. All it'd contained was his wishes for her to inherit his assets and one word that meant everything to her. He'd signed it '*Your Love, Marcellus*'.

Love. That was the word she'd wanted all along.

She ran her fingers over his spidery handwriting with a sigh. He didn't want her to call him by his first name, but maybe he would've in time. Sliding the paper back into the envelope, she set it on the desk and turned back to Aya. The hybrid was sitting in one of the leather armchairs, a pile of grimoires beside her and another in her lap.

Aya had soon come to the same conclusion Gabby had. There were no answers in any of them and they were out of options. Well, save for one. She'd known it for days and had been trying to avoid mentioning it at all costs. She was from the ether and could walk both life and death if she chose. Gabby had done it once before with Aya, and now she could do it again on her own.

"Gabby?" Aya asked, looking up.

The hybrid knew she was struggling with something—she always did—so she just came out with it. "I have to go to the other side and find Katrin."

Aya frowned but didn't disagree.

"It's the only logical thing I can think of," she said. "Katrin is the only person who would know what to do next."

"She won't be very forthcoming."

"No, but what choice do we have?"

Aya sat up in the chair, putting the grimoire she'd been reading aside. "Do you want me to come with you?"

"No," she replied, shaking her head. "I have to do this on my own."

Turning back to the desk, Gabby ran her fingers over the envelope that held Regulus' letter. Picking it up, she held it in her hands and stared at it for a few minutes, trying to figure out if it was possible. She glanced at Aya, not sure if she had it in her to ask the question.

"Regulus died human and was reborn as a vampire. Where his soul has gone, you cannot follow," Aya said with a frown. "Katrin only died once and her soul was anchored. You should be able to contact her. You certainly have the strength to do it now."

Gabby tried to hide her disappointment. Of course, that's how it worked. Forever was a long time.

"I'm sorry, Gabby."

"I have to go now," she said with a sigh. "We're running out of time."

Aya nodded. "I'll be here if you need me. If you get lost... I can bring you back."

"A shock to the heart?" she asked with a slight laugh.

Aya held up a finger and gave her a lopsided grin. "Only a little one."

Sinking down into the chair she'd claimed as hers, Gabby closed her eyes, trying to fend off the weariness of the past few weeks. Finding the edge between life and death came easier this time. It was like turning the page of a book as her spirit brushed against the edges, a coldness seeping into her bones. Her physical body would remain back in the study with Aya looking over it, but she wouldn't be there. Not really.

The other side was an eerie representation of life. The entire world was shrouded in a pale grey mist, where physical features were mostly indistinguishable. She was here to find Katrin and so her intent was shaping the surrounding landscape, leading to where the witch resided in her incarceration.

Remembering back to when she'd severed the witch's anchor with Aya's help, Gabby knew the spirits of the other founding witches would've punished Katrin. Wherever she lived now was a prison.

Gabby's will was stronger than it'd ever been and she didn't quite understand it, but all she had to do was walk forwards and her destination would present itself.

She didn't know how long she'd been walking when she saw a shape emerge from the mist. Blurry at first, but as she approached, it became more solid. A tangible existence in an otherwise empty landscape.

Katrin was standing on a patch of colourless grass, the currents of death swirling around her platform, her hands folded in front of her. She wore a plain dress, faded like the colour of a sepia photograph that hadn't stood up to the test of time. Katrin's entire world was this spot—devoid and washed-out, lonely.

The witch looked up and her gaze met Gabby's. Recognition flashed there for a moment and her lips curled into a sneer.

"To what do I owe the honour?" Katrin drawled, turning away.

Gabby wasn't here for small talk, so she got right down to business. The founder's prison was already putting pressure on her already weary soul. "The Coven has awoken a Tuatha-hybrid."

The witch turned. "How do you know?"

"Regulus."

Katrin looked her over and snorted. "I can see he worked his wiles on you."

"It wasn't manipulation. He and I had a mutual agreement."

"A mutual agreement?" Katrin let out a laugh. "The only 'mutual' agreements Regulus had were one-sided."

Gabby's jaw tightened, but she wasn't about to let the greatest betrayer of her kind get under her skin.

"And if a hybrid is awake as you claim," Katrin went on, "then why hasn't he put it down?"

"Regulus is dead." Gabby's voice wavered as she spoke the last word, and the founding witch narrowed her eyes.

"Regulus is dead?"

"We faced the Tuatha and he was bitten."

"He faced it on his own? *The fool*," she hissed, turning away. "It was his own stupid fault, then."

"What do you know of the Tuatha?"

Katrin's shoulders rose and fell with a sigh. "As much as you, if Regulus told you everything he knew."

"He did."

"Then he told you about my heritage. The Coven."

"Yes, he did."

The witch shook her head and turned to glare. "If I'd known my secrets were being handed out like candy to children, I would've ended him myself."

Gabby held herself high and looked the founding witch right in the eyes. "What happened to Aoife and the original witch?"

"Isolde. Her name was Isolde."

"So, what happened?"

Katrin cast her gaze to the ground, the only sign that this made her uncomfortable. "Aoife sealed the hybrids away one by one. She then hunted the witch she'd created and tried to end her, but that didn't go so well."

"Isolde killed Aoife?"

"Yes, and so the original witch went on to found the Coven. They wanted to find where the Tuatha vampires were hidden and awaken them."

"But couldn't they glean that from Aoife's blood?"

"Once she died, her blood was useless. For that little trick to work, it needs to come from a live host. They had nothing and spent the next three thousand years searching."

"And they wanted you to infiltrate the last Celestines so you could find out?"

"That was one reason, but they didn't count on my betrayal. My chance for revenge."

"You wanted to destroy them." Regulus had already told her this. Born into the Coven without any power, Katrin had been forced to become one of the Five and had turned on everyone, creating a third side intent on destroying everything.

Katrin laughed, her eyes suddenly dark. "I might have embraced the dark, Gabby, but I would never side with the Tuatha. *The devourers of worlds*. The fact my family worked to revive the hybrids was their greatest folly. They could not bring an extinct race back to life.

A Tuatha made into a vampire? That is so much worse than turning humans. Aeriaya is a perfect example of that, and she's not an original. Imagine the horror she'd inflict on the world if she was."

"She'd be exactly like Aed. Human blood was the only thing that saved her from total insanity."

Katrin nodded. "In her full powers and those of a vampire amplified ten-fold? No remorse. No control. That is what your Tuatha is, and that's the only reason I am entertaining this little interrogation. My beloved Regulus is dead. You need your own original. Your Celestine-hybrid cannot help you this time."

"Our only option is to make another founder?"

"The only option."

Gabby paused, not knowing how to go on. They needed a human...

"I hope you have someone you can trust," Katrin said with a sneer.

"Who do you suggest?" Gabby asked, cocking her head to the side.

"Someone pure of heart," she scoffed. "Someone who understands control. Someone who has the stomach for a bloody fight. Anything less, and you'll have another monster on your hands."

Gabby swallowed hard, trying to keep her expression even. They didn't have anyone. "We don't even have the spell," she said carefully. Katrin had helped above and beyond what she'd expected from the witch, but this might be pushing it too far.

"You want me to give it to you," the witch said with a smirk. "How *original*."

"How else am I going to make another founder? I thought you wanted the Tuatha-hybrids gone forever. I'm here and I'm willing to do whatever it takes to put Aed down for good."

"Finally, we have a common enemy."

"And a little trust goes a long way." There was no way of knowing if Katrin still gave a crap about what happened on Earth, and there was no way of knowing the spell she might give her would be a trap. There was no other option but to trust the founding witch and Katrin knew it. "Besides, how often does the dead get help from the living to finish their life's work?"

Katrin narrowed her eyes. "For me to give you the spell, you need to find my grimoire in life."

"What happened to it?"

"When I died, it was before I was ready. I'd made preparations that would take effect once I set foot on the other side, but in the process, I lost my grimoire."

"Someone killed you?" Gabby asked, getting the witch's meaning.

"It didn't matter," she said, waving her hand. "It was already too late."

"Did you ever find your grimoire again?"

"No, but it was useless to me anyway. I wanted to pass it on to my daughter, but that never happened. She was lost to me in the process and my grimoire was never found, and I never bothered to look for it. It was a symbol of everything I'd suffered. Good riddance."

Gabby didn't like the sound of Katrin's story, but she wasn't about to ask for the gory details. The book was why she was here. Grimoires were basically indestructible. They had multiple spells woven through them to protect from all manner of harm. Katrin's would still exist; but after so much time, it could be anywhere, and anyone could be in possession of it.

Luckily for them, it took a certain amount of energy and skill to cast most spells and if Gabby was as right about the one that'd created the Roman founders, there was only one witch alive she knew of who could cast it.

"Tell me, Gabrielle," Katrin said with a smirk. "Have you ever made your own grimoire?"

Gabby frowned, wondering what she was getting at. Katrin's eyes sparkled and she stepped towards her.

That was the thing about spirits. Physical bodies didn't hamper them, and they could move fast if they wanted to. Before Gabby could step out of the way, Katrin's hands cupped her face and everything went dark.

"Katrin, my child."

As Gabby's vision cleared, she heard the voice beside her, and it brought her back into clarity.

"Yes, Mama."

Her voice didn't sound right, but she realised that she was in a child's body—Katrin's body. The founder had given her a vision and she was along for the ride, whether she wanted to be or not.

She felt herself meld with the young version of Katrin until she was the little girl. Blinking, she looked up at a woman with wild auburn hair and caramel eyes.

Her mama was called the matriarch, and all the other witches looked to her. Disobeying the matriarch was forbidden. Those who did went away and never came back. Those were the only witches she ever got to see outside of her mama's rooms. She said she was her secret shame and had to remain hidden. She wasn't a witch like them, but she should've been.

"You are going to make your own grimoire, child," she said, pointing to the bare book and the table full of witches tools, things she was forbidden to touch.

She looked with greedy eyes, hardly believing her mama would let her so close. She looked up into her mama's face and her eyes were kind, not like they usually were. She smiled, finally proud that she'd done something right. She wasn't sure what it was, but her mama wanted her to make her own spell book. Her heart swelled with pride.

"You are ten summers old, Katrin. You are my

daughter and have brought shame onto your coven. Do you know why?"

"I have no power, Mama. I'm not a witch."

A sharp slap echoed through the room and her cheek stung.

"I am your matriarch, Katrin. I am more than just your mother. If you lie, I can tell. Understand?"

"Yes, Mama."

"Tell me the truth, child."

"No, Mama, please," she pleaded, but she paid her no heed.

Her mama grabbed her wrist and held it over the bowl, her fingers digging painfully into her skin. Tears prickled in her eyes, but she tried to hold them in. If she cried, then she'd be beaten. Weakness was forbidden. They told her she had no power, that she wasn't worthy of being a witch, but she knew it was there. Tiny, hidden... *secret*. Mama knew. She was tied to her by blood.

She didn't dare struggle against her mama's grasp, but when she saw the glint of silver in the candlelight, her heart skipped a beat and her stomach felt sick.

Mama wouldn't hurt her.

"You've been telling lies, child," she said, her voice changing. Mama's voice always changed when she went away inside herself. The mama who she loved wasn't here anymore; she'd gone away and the bad one was here.

"Mama, please," she pleaded, but Mama wasn't coming back.

With an evil glint in her eye, Mama took the blade and sawed into her fingers. Screaming in pain, Katrin hardly felt it when the first finger plopped into the bowl on the bench.

"Please, Mama. No. It hurts, *please...*"

Blood dripped down into the bowl while her hand burned with white-hot pain, but Mama wouldn't let go of her wrist. She started speaking the words she used when she was casting, words she was forbidden to speak.

The knife cut again, a second finger joining the first. Katrin screamed, this time tears falling from her eyes. Why was her mama hurting her like this?

"Weakness is forbidden, child," her mama said, letting her go.

Clutching her hand against her chest, she sobbed at the pain, blood flowing freely from the wound, staining her dress. If this was what being a witch was, then she didn't want to be like them. She wanted to run away and find a new mama, one who wouldn't hurt her. She'd find a new family to love.

"Katrin, say the words with me." Her mama pulled her forwards, grasping her mutilated hand and forced her to hold it over the leather book. Her blood dripped all over the cover, seeping into the soft fabric, staining it red and brown.

If she didn't speak the forbidden words as her

mama bade, she didn't know what would happen to her. So, she spoke them and the ball of power she'd been hiding in her stomach flared into life. A little spark, but it seemed like it was enough. Mama smiled and for a moment, she thought the good one was back, but as she spoke the final words, Mama grabbed her maimed hand with a strange look in her eyes.

"I have a use for you, Katrin," she said, pinching her daughter's savaged flesh, making her cry harder. "You will become a witch, and you will help us find what we have lost."

"I'm going to be a witch?" she sobbed.

"Yes, you are."

Mama spoke witch words and the pain in her hand faded. She was going to be a witch? She'd made her own spell book with the tiny ball of power in her stomach. Her secret power, no smaller than a speck of dust. She was going to be like her mama.

As the witch words sunk into her hand, her eyes drooped. She wouldn't have to hide anymore. She wouldn't be locked away. She let her eyes close and her mama's spell take her.

As Gabby came back to herself, she realised she'd collapsed. Katrin looked down at her with a satisfied smirk and she realised she'd been clutching her hand. Looking down, she realised her fingers were intact and the phantom pain subsided. Katrin held up her hand and the air shimmered, revealing two missing fingers and ugly, puckered skin—a glamour.

"There is your affinity," Katrin said smugly. "Go back to your world and leave me be."

Glaring up at the founding witch, Gabby could only think one thing.

Being a mega bitch ran in the family.

CHAPTER 18

"Gabby?"

Gabby opened her eyes at the sound of her name, her entire body feeling sluggish. Aya's face slowly came into focus and relief washed over her. She was back.

"Are you okay?" the hybrid asked.

Nodding, she dropped her head into her hands. Her journey to the other side had taken more out of her than she thought it would, but then again, she hadn't slept properly in a while.

"Did you find her?" Zac asked, dropping a blanket around her shoulders.

She jumped at the sound of his voice. Everyone had come in while she'd been on the other side. Their concern and loyalty was a little bittersweet. Nye sat behind the desk, Tristan was by the fireplace, which was crackling away with a warm orange glow, and Zac was beside her, his hand in hers.

"Yes, I found her."

Aya glanced at the others uneasily. "Dare I ask…"

"She told me about her life, strangely enough," Gabby told them. "Apart from destroying her anchor, I never got to meet her before. Not on my own terms. She wasn't a nice person, but I don't know if that's because she was shaped like that by the Coven or if it was her true self."

"We could debate the level of good and evil in somebody for eternity and never agree," Tristan said.

"Did she advise you what we should do next?" Aya asked.

"She said we only had one option. We need to make a new vampire," Gabby said, glancing around the room. "An original."

"A founder?" Zac asked. "Who the hell do we know who would be willing to be turned?"

"No one," Tristan said with a sigh.

"What about the spell?" Zac continued. "I mean, I thought it was lost?"

Gabby shrugged, still feeling a little groggy from her trip to the other side. "Katrin told me how I can find her grimoire."

"Seriously?" Aya asked with a raised eyebrow.

"That seems like a long shot," Nye said, flipping open the laptop on the desk, "but has anyone tried this?" He began typing with a flourish.

"Did you just seriously Google how to kill a fairy?" Tristan asked, looking over the spy's shoulder.

"He is a fairy, right?" Nye asked, raising an eyebrow.

"I don't think Google is an entirely trustworthy source of information," Gabby told him.

The spy wasn't having it. "But you're not denying he's a fairy?"

"*Nye.*"

"Just getting all my facts straight, lovely."

"Technically, he's a hybrid... half and half."

"Ahh," he said thoughtfully, "a vampire fairy." He turned back to the laptop and typed it into the search engine.

"First things first," she said, disregarding the spy. "We need to find Katrin's grimoire. Then we'll worry about finding someone to turn. No use worrying about that bit until we have the spell."

"It could be anywhere," Aya said, rubbing her temples.

"Katrin gave me a memory. Not a very pleasant one, but one that would link me enough to the grimoire to scry for it. I need a map."

The hybrid glanced at her with a frown. Katrin's willingness to help them had unsettled her, but Gabby was on the same page. If the Tuatha tightened the Betrayer, then they were in for a wild ride.

"What kind of scale are we talking here?" Nye asked. He was still sitting at the desk, the laptop in front of him, fingers poised to type.

"Well, I think it'd still be in the UK, yes?" Tristan asked. "It was where she lived and died. The Coven didn't spread much farther, so it'd be here someplace. Historians are a funny lot. They don't like to see things leave the country."

"That's if someone actually kept it," Gabby countered. "It could be buried some place, in another country... Hell, another witch could have it and then we'd be screwed."

"We won't know until you scry," Aya said.

Gabby nodded and turned to Nye. "Print out a map of the UK and Ireland."

"Ah, taking a punt it's close to home. I like it." The spy winked and a moment later, the printer came to life, spitting out a black and white map.

"You don't have to scry now," Zac said. "You're worn out."

Gabby could hear the unspoken words in his voice. *Regulus has just died. Your heart is broken. You haven't slept for days. You just went into the land of death to speak with the greatest betrayer of witch-kind.* She couldn't hold it against him—or any of them—for trying to take care of her, but there would always be a part of her that felt like she didn't deserve it after the stunt she'd pulled faking the Roman's death.

"He's right, Gabby," Aya agreed. "You should get a good night's sleep, then I'll help you in the morning."

"Here you go," Nye chortled, handing the map to Gabby with a flourish.

"I'm doing it now," she told the vampires. "I won't rest easy until I have, so stop trying to wrap me in cotton wool. I won't break." That, she'd do behind closed doors. Continuing Regulus' work defeating the Tuatha was the only thing keeping her together. Once it was done, she would lay down and mourn her lost love. She'd made a promise, and this was one she didn't intend on breaking.

Ignoring the vampires, she got up from the chair by the fire and stretched out her aching muscles. Running her fingers along the bookshelf where the grimoires sat, she found the bowl of crystals at the end, propping up the ancient tomes like a bookend. Holding each in her palm, she knew that they had once belonged to a different witch. The rose-quartz that sat in her hand had a dull signature on it, a presence that was a telltale sign it'd been used before. Whoever she was, this witch's grimoire must be sitting on the shelf right in front of her.

What was Regulus doing with all these relics? Maybe they'd all been witches in his employ that'd died or been murdered. Maybe he'd had them killed? Shivering, she set the crystal down and plucked out a shard of citrine that'd been set into a silver clasp with a matching chain. Gabby held it close, the orange and white crystal feeling just right against her skin. Citrine symbolised good fortune, among other things, and it seemed fitting for their situation.

Turning back to the desk, she shooed Nye out of the chair and sat, laying out the map. Closing her eyes, she tried to clear the weariness out of her bones and focused on the memory Katrin had given her. It was difficult not to get caught up in it again and feel the pain the founding witch had felt.

Concentrating her thoughts onto the grimoire, she held up the crystal over the map and let it swing in a wide circle.

When she'd scried for Aya months ago, it'd been easy. She'd already had a personal connection with the hybrid, so getting a fix on her location was simple, but this was much more difficult. A grimoire, no matter how magical or special, was an inanimate object. It didn't have the same kind of presence as a living, breathing vampire or human. Her only saving grace was that it was made with a physical part of Katrin. Without the memory and without the knowledge, there was no hope of this working.

Gabby's eyes snapped open as the crystal dropped like it weighed a million tonnes.

"Where is it?" Nye asked like an excited child.

She waved him off and pulled the crystal aside. It was stuck to a point north-ish from London, but the map was too small to say exactly where. It looked like it was near Oxford, but there were so many smaller dots around it from neighbouring villages, towns, and suburbs, she wasn't sure. She didn't like it one bit, because she knew someone who lived there and that someone didn't need to be dragged into this mess.

Turning back to the laptop, Gabby printed out a

map of Oxford and set it on top of the desk, hoping with everything she had that she was wrong.

Focusing, she let the crystal swing in a circle. This time, it wasn't long until she felt the same pull and the tip of the crystal stuck to the page right over the spot she was dreading. Oxford University. There was probably a library vault full of ancient books, and the grimoire was most likely one of them.

"Oxford," Gabby said, an uneasy feeling rising in her gut.

"Why does that sound familiar?" Zac asked.

"Isobel," she said, reluctantly.

"Isobel?"

"Alex's sister."

Zac's expression fell. "Oh, shit."

"Yeah, shit. She's a student at Oxford University. I can feel a strong connection with the grimoire there."

"Convenient," Aya said. "Isobel could get us in. Give us information."

"But..." Gabby started, but she knew it as much as everyone else did. The last thing she wanted was to get Alex's sister involved in all of this, but the greater good and all of that.

"And she's human," the hybrid added.

"No," Gabby hissed, standing up. "I won't allow it."

"We might not have another option."

Gabby ignored Aya and scrolled through her email, an uneasy feeling in her stomach. She'd sent Isobel a couple of Christmas cards and letters over the years and was sure she still had her address saved somewhere.

When she finally found it, she felt sicker, her skin tingling. Alex would never forgive her, and he was definitely one person she didn't want added to the list of people she'd disappointed.

Isobel had been a few years ahead of her in school, so outside of hanging out with Liz and Alex, she didn't know her that well. And by the time she was old enough to have something in common with her, she'd gotten a scholarship to study overseas. Isobel was the kind of person who was just good at everything. It didn't surprise Gabby in the least that she was doing her master's degree in sociology and anthropology, and whatever else caught her interest.

But the bottom line was, Isobel knew nothing about vampires, witches, and especially not the Tuatha. There was no fancy degree in supernatural studies and turning up on her doorstep with crazy stories about magical immortal blood feuds... Hell, she'd think they were all on drugs. Dragging her into it more than that was out of the question. Isobel was their way into the university and nothing more.

"Okay, I have her address," she said with a sigh. "Let's get going if we're doing this."

"We can wait until mornin'," Tristan said.

"Yeah, it's only an hour or so away," Nye agreed.

"We're on the clock," Gabby replied, shaking her head at the vampire's inflated sense of time. "There's no time to rest with an insane hybrid on the loose. It's now or not at all."

Zac sat in the back of Nye's car, squashed between Aya and Tristan. If there were any more of them, they'd have to look into getting a minivan.

Gabby's sense of urgency had rattled them all and secretly, he agreed with her. Better to tackle this one now than wait any longer, especially since they didn't have a plan outside of the grimoire, and certainly no way of killing or incapacitating everyone's favourite psycho hybrid. If it meant waking up Alex's sister, Isobel, in the middle of the night with a crazy-ass story, then so be it. He certainly wasn't above compulsion and knowing Aya, she'd probably get to it way before he could.

Nye was driving and Gabby was beside him, staring out the window. Zac peered at her in the darkness, trying to understand why she kept pushing herself. She'd run herself almost into the ground, and it worried him. After everything she'd been through with Regulus and then Katrin… He was amazed at her drive, but that might be the only thing that was keeping her going.

The darkness slowly morphed into the orange glow of the city of Oxford. As they drove through the streets towards the address Gabby had given them for Isobel's apartment, the buildings grew older and the streets narrower. It was late, but there were still a lot of people hanging around. Christmas decorations hung across the streets and the remnants of a festive market were being packed away.

Nye pulled the car into a space in a back street and killed the engine. "Last stop," he said, opening his door.

The vampires piled out and Gabby pointed to the block that housed Isobel's apartment. "This is the building. We want number eight."

Looking up at the façade, Zac noticed a light illuminating one of the top windows. Someone was at home and still awake.

As they walked across the street, Zac tugged Gabby back into his side. "Are you sure you're okay?" he asked, glancing at the other vampires who'd kept going.

"I can't stop, Zac," she whispered into his ear. "I made a promise and I have to keep it."

"Not if it kills you. I don't think he would want to see you die because of this."

"Someone's gonna die, but it's not me."

He gave her a small smile and pushed her gently forwards. "Go on then, Glinda. I've got your back."

The entrance to the block of apartments was a tiny door set into the stone façade, leading into a dark foyer with a rickety staircase. There were two doors at the bottom, numbered one and two. Zac supposed they had to go right to the top. Aya went first, followed by Gabby, and then the three male vampires. They moved as silently as they could, not wanting to tip off anyone who might be inside that they were coming.

Gabby paused on the landing before the last flight of stairs, her brow furrowed. "I can sense Isobel, but... there's someone with her, but I can't sense them."

"There's a vampire in there," Aya declared, her lip curling in a snarl.

"Aed?" Tristan asked, his jaw hardening.

"No, it's not Aed," Gabby said.

"Then he's got a lackey," Nye declared. "Who else would want to suck a poor little university student into their web?"

"We'll hang back," Zac said, gesturing to Tristan and Nye. "We can't get in without an invitation, but we'll be here if they come out."

"I'll come with you," Aya said. "If things get ugly, I'll end it."

They climbed the last flight of stairs and he hung back with Tristan and Nye, waiting to see what'd happen.

Gabby stood at the door at the end of the hall and Aya stopped beside her, just out of direct view of whoever was inside. Raising her fist, the witch knocked. A moment later the door opened, and Zac caught a whiff of someone very human.

"Gabby?"

Zac gathered this must be Isobel, even though he

couldn't see her. Her accent was very American, with a little twinge of British, which gave away that she'd lived here for a few years.

"Hey, Izzy," Gabby replied. "Um, surprise?"

"What are you doing here? You're... You're in Oxford, I mean."

There was the sound of fast-moving air and Isobel let out a surprised scream. Gabby put out a hand to stop Aya from moving forwards, but the hybrid peered around the corner into the apartment.

"You know a witch?" a male voice asked, low and angry. "He said nothing about a witch."

Gabby still motioned for them to stay back, but Zac was having none of it. Stepping into the doorway, he saw what all the fuss was about. A man had his arms wrapped around a woman with the reddest hair he'd ever seen, a look of pure anger on his face. Anger at being interrupted, apparently. One look at the guy's changing eyes confirmed what he already knew. *Vampire.*

All Zac had to do was brush his finger against Aya's and she knew exactly what he wanted. Before anyone could react, she was inside, across the room, her hand on the vampire's head. She pushed him away from Isobel and he let out an annoyed roar, but it was cut short as she snapped his neck.

Isobel stared at Aya in shock before her gaze flickered down to the vampire who was lying on the floor, his neck at an odd angle.

Nye drew in a deep breath, spreading his arms out wide. "That, my friends, is the scent of victory! I like this being good thing. The good guys get to win more often. *I like it.*"

Isobel stumbled, and as her knees hit the edge of the sofa, she fell backwards onto it. "Y-you k-killed him," she stammered.

"I didn't kill him," Aya said with a sigh. "If he were dead, you'd need a bucket of bleach."

"Aya," Gabby hissed at the hybrid, who just shrugged. She stepped inside and sat next to Isobel, who didn't quite understand what was happening. "She's been compelled."

"Obviously," the hybrid said with a roll of her eyes.

"What's going on?" Isobel asked, glancing between the vampires. "Gabby, who are these people?"

"I'm sorry to show up like this, Izzy, but it's important. This is Aya," she said, pointing to the hybrid. "Those fools out there are Zac, Nye, and Tristan."

"Why are they standing in the door like that?"

"They need to be invited in."

"What?" Isobel looked at her like she was mad.

"You say, 'come in' and then we... come in," Nye said. "Easy-peasy."

"We're the good guys, Izzy," Gabby added.

"And who was he meant to be?" She pointed to the dead vampire. "He did some freaky thing with his eyes and... I just told him things. I couldn't stop it... Gabby, who is he? Who are you? He looked at you and was afraid."

"She is rather bitchy at times," Zac said from out in the hall, a little tired of being left out of the action.

"Ignore him," Gabby said. "That guy on your floor is a vampire. He's not dead, not really. He'll wake up soon enough."

Isobel looked at the vampire, then to Aya and back to Gabby. "A *vampire*? Are you on drugs?"

Aya let out a snort of laughter. "I wish I was on drugs right now. That's how well this conversation is going."

"Shit, Aya," Gabby hissed at her again, "I'm trying the gentle approach."

"Vampires?" Isobel asked again. "They're vampires?" She was pointing at the vampires out in the hall, and Zac gave her a little wave.

"Nice ones," Nye said, and Tristan kicked him in the shin. "*Ow.*"

"Can we come in yet? We're not going to eat her," Zac put in.

"I have to invite you in before you can come inside a human's home," Isobel said like she was working out a puzzle. After a minute, she looked up at Zac. "Show me."

"Show you what?" he asked, frowning at Gabby, who nodded.

"Show me that you can't get in."

With an exasperated sigh, he kicked the fresh air

that was the opening to the apartment and his foot hit right the threshold and stopped in mid-air.

"No way," Isobel said, her eyes wide. This time it wasn't shock, but curious surprise. "Do it again."

"No," Zac said. "Just invite us in so we can get this show on the road."

Isobel turned to Aya. "How did you get in? Did you do that crazy eye thing, too? You snapped that asshole's neck like butter."

Knowing the compulsion that'd been put on her by the guy on the floor had broken the moment she'd snapped his neck, Aya just shrugged. "I thought this one was going to be annoying for a while there," she said, grinning at Gabby. "I think I might like her."

"How do you do it?" Isobel asked again. "Are you the girl Alex has a crush on? You're *the* Aya, right?"

Aya might like her, but Zac was becoming very annoyed. "Uh, she's *mine*," he called out.

"Oh, come in already," Isobel said with a laugh, and the vampires came into the small apartment, Tristan closing the door behind them.

"You're taking this very well, Izzy," Gabby said. "Most people freak out."

"Um," she began, "I have a little confession."

Zac glanced at Gabby, starting to become a little concerned.

"Alex sent me an email, months ago now, asking about some crazy stuff regarding the vampire myth. There was one reference I gave him that was so obscure, I didn't think much of it. Not until I dug a little deeper."

Zac knew exactly what Isobel was talking about. He remembered it like it was yesterday. When he thought Aya was dead and Arturius came fishing around for Gabby, he'd called Aya by a strange name. Alex had mentioned it to Isobel hoping they might find a clue about Aya's heritage. Isobel had come back with an obscure reference, 'Aericura, the raven-haired star, her purity taken by devils'.

"I've been working on it for months," Isobel continued. "But I never thought any of it was real. I mean, this is bloody crazy."

"She swears a lot more than Alex," Aya said.

"Are you her?"

"Who's her?"

"Aericura."

Aya glanced at Zac.

"*You are*," Isobel said like it was the greatest discovery of her career.

"Listen, Izzy," Gabby interrupted, "we're not here for a research session. We came because we need your help."

She blinked. "My help? For what?"

"We're looking for a grimoire and we believe it's in your university," Aya said.

"I know it's there," Gabby said. "Without a doubt."

"A grimoire? You mean a witch's spell book?" Isobel asked, looking at Gabby.

She held up her hand and shrugged. "Witch."

"No way," she exclaimed. "What do you need it for? I'm guessing you're in some kind of supernatural trouble or something. Wait, if you're in deep shit and this guy shows up..." She pointed at the dead vampire. "Then someone else wants the same thing."

Gabby nodded. "We're hunting a three-thousand-year-old member of the Tuatha De Danann royal family, who was turned into a vampire."

"Basically, he's a vampire fairy crossbreed who's a few sandwiches short of a picnic," Nye said from his perch on the kitchen table.

"He was made with the blood of my people," Aya explained. "It should never have happened and it's too much for any mind to withstand."

"Your people?" Isobel asked. "You're not human?"

"Nope."

"Shit, we could be here all night," Zac said. "What I want to know is where this guy came from." He pointed to the comatose vampire.

"He probably knows we're looking for Katrin's grimoire and gleaned an association between us and Isobel," Aya said.

"Well, if that isn't the reason, then stuffed if I know," Nye added.

"I'll take him away someplace and get it out of him," Aya said. Before she scooped up the vampire, she turned back to Isobel. "I'm sorry we had to meet this way."

"Well, I guess it was memorable," she offered.

Aya laughed. "I guess so. Let us deal with the messy stuff; I'm sure Gabby will explain everything."

Tristan moved to pick up the dead vampire's feet. "Call us when you're ready to go for the grimoire."

Zac stood to go with them, but Gabby held out her hand. "Zac, Nye, can you guys stay? If someone comes looking—"

"We'll be here," Nye finished with a wink.

The spy sat next to Isobel and she looked him over before she asked, "What happened to your face?"

A cheeky grin spread across the spy's face. "Have I got a story to tell you."

CHAPTER 19

Z ac sat at the small table in Isobel's studio apartment, watching her make a pot of coffee.

She really did look a lot like Alex, except her hair was flaming red, whereas her brother's was more subdued. It made his thoughts go back home and he wondered how they were doing. Gabby had said Sam and Liz had moved to L.A. because Liz had gotten into a college there. Once upon a time, his little brother had been studying business so he could take over their family's plantation. Zac wondered if that's what he'd chosen to do, or maybe he was just there because Liz was. He wanted to call and ask, but that wouldn't help anyone.

Nye stood by the window, watching the street below through the curtains as dawn stretched its lazy wintery fingers across Oxford. It'd been a long night of explanations and wild stories, and everyone was a little tired. Gabby had finally fallen asleep on Isobel's bed as they waited to hear from Aya and Tristan. She, more than anyone, needed the rest.

Isobel sat across from Zac and hesitantly held out the coffeepot. "Do you drink coffee?"

"Not a fan," he said, his voice low.

"*Can* you drink it?" She tilted her head to the side, genuinely interested in the inner workings of his gut.

"Yes. Technically, I'm dead, but everything still works, you know."

"Got any booze?" Nye asked with a chuckle.

"Uh, no?" she replied, her expression betraying how out of her depth she was.

"What kind of student are you?" the spy asked. "I thought you all drank."

"The responsible kind," Isobel retorted, pouring herself a cup of coffee. She set the pot on a coaster before circling her hands around the porcelain for warmth.

"Do you have any idea why they targeted you?" Zac asked her.

"Obviously because I can get this book you want so bad."

"But how did they know you could?" Zac mused. "I mean, it's too much of a coincidence, what with the one degree of separation between us."

"Aya will get it out of that vampire," Nye said. "If she could torture your humanity back, I'm guessing she could torture anything out of anyone if she set her mind to it." The spy gave Isobel a wink when her eyes widened at the word 'torture'.

"You guys are weird," she said with a roll of her eyes.

"You haven't even scratched the surface," Zac said with a sigh.

Nye looked back out the window. "I'm going to check the street."

Zac nodded as the spy left, the door closing soundlessly behind him. He sat with Isobel in silence for a while, content to just let the time pass until Tristan called, because Aya still didn't like using a cell phone. Isobel was fidgeting across from him, sneaking glances when she thought he wasn't looking.

"So..." she began with a grimace. "Vampires, hey?"

"Have you heard from Alex recently?" he asked, putting her out of her misery.

Her shoulders sagged slightly. "No, not for a while. You guys are friends?"

"It depends. I'm not his most favourite person in the world."

"But you must care at least a little bit if you're asking."

"A little bit."

"Then you must know Liz, too. I wonder if she decided to go to college."

"She's at UCLA," he told her.

"Oh, really? That's great. Do you know what she's studying?"

"No."

She didn't seem to hear him. "Liz is the sweetest thing. Last I heard, she was dating this guy named Sam. Alex worked with him at the botanical gardens. Do you know him?"

Did Zac know him? Sam was his little brother after all, but it was probably safe not to mention it. Shit, he hadn't even told Nye.

"Yes, I know him." It came out a little too nonchalant.

Isobel eyed him suspiciously and took a sip of her coffee. "You lived in Ashburton? Why?"

"Long story."

"Give me the short version. Bullet points if you have to. Sitting here in silence is awkward as hell, especially since you're... *you know*."

He had to give it to Isobel. Her mind was wide open to their seedy underworld, but he guessed it had something to do with her field of study. It was in her nature to ask questions, and what was even more surprising was despite that, she wanted to understand.

"I was born there," he replied. "When you get to be as old as I am, reconnecting with your old life is a good thing. Supposedly."

"When did you..." She waved at him and he got that she wanted to know when he was turned.

"1865."

"Wow," she breathed. "You're like a walking, talking history book."

Zac grimaced. "Depends on what history you want."

"The Civil War?"

He nodded.

"Really?"

"Yes, really."

"Confederate, right? If you're from Louisiana."

"If I had understood a little better, I might've been Union."

She leaned back in her chair and shook her head.

"If you want to know about Medieval history, you should ask Nye. That's what you study, right?"

"Farther back than that, but sometimes."

"Then I'd have a sit down with Tristan."

"When was he born?" she asked with a hard swallow.

"Crusades, I think."

"1100s?" Isobel squeaked, but was interrupted as footsteps approached out in the hall.

They looked up as the door opened and Nye walked in. "All clear for now."

"When was he born?" Isobel asked, pointing at the vampire.

"1561," the spy said with a wink. "Want help with your history project? I'm great with collages, but I draw the line at glitter."

"You guys really know how to keep things to a dull roar," Gabby exclaimed. She shuffled to the table and took a mug from the bench, pouring herself a cup of coffee.

"Feel a little better?" Zac asked as she took a sip.

"Much. I didn't realise how tired I was until I crashed. Have you heard anything yet?"

"Not yet."

Gabby turned to Isobel and smiled. "I hope these boys have been behaving themselves."

"Mostly," she replied.

Downing the rest of her coffee, Gabby took out her cell and looked at the screen. "I'm going to meet Aya and Tristan and find out if they've learned anything."

"And I suppose we get to stay here and wait?" Nye asked.

"If you don't mind," Isobel chimed in. "I don't want to be alone if another bad guy shows up looking for me."

Zac's eye narrowed as he thought about another vampire hanging around. There'd be a second waiting in the wings and after they'd appeared... He glanced at Nye, who nodded. He knew exactly what he was thinking.

"Eyes open, Gabby," Zac said, and the witch smiled.

"Got it."

Gabby picked up her bag and went for the door. Standing, Zac caught her arm and whispered, "Where there's one, there's another."

The witch regarded him for a moment and nodded.

"I'll let you know what's happening as soon as I can." And then she was gone.

Zac sat back down with a sigh and noticed Isobel was staring at him again. He shouldn't have been so nice. Now he'd have to endure her barrage of questions.

"How do you become... you know?" She seemed to have trouble saying the word vampire.

He narrowed his eyes. "That's not for you to know."

"Have you ever turned anyone?"

He glared at her, offended. "*No.*"

"What about the vampire who turned you?"

"Never ask a vampire how they were turned," he snapped. "Not unless you're a vampire yourself."

She made a face. "I see Gabby was right about you."

Zac tilted his head and waited for the next stupid thing that was about to come out of her mouth.

"That right there." Isobel laughed. "You don't scare me, Zac."

"I haven't even begun trying to scare you," he spat, leaning closer to her, letting his eyes begin to change.

"Are you trying now?" She was trying to keep a straight face but wasn't succeeding. It irritated the hell out of him.

"I like this one," Nye said, winking at her. "I like her *a lot.*"

"Screw this, I'm going to check out the street." Zac stood abruptly, raising an eyebrow at the spy.

"What?" he asked with a wicked grin.

"Alex wouldn't appreciate it."

"Who's Alex again?"

"My very human brother," Isobel chimed in.

"Well, can't screw with the brother." Nye shrugged his shoulders and stood to follow Zac. When Isobel didn't move, he said, "Are you coming?"

"I thought a vampire was after me? Isn't the safest place here?"

"Doors will keep us out, but not the hybrid," Zac said from down the hall. "The safest place you can be is in between us. At least until we know exactly what he wants with you." What he didn't say was that if anyone was hanging around, they'd only show themselves if they laid eyes on Isobel. She was bait, but he wasn't about to tell her that.

Outside, the day was well underway, and the odd person walked by them on the street. Zac couldn't sense anything untoward, but that didn't mean they weren't being watched.

"How he was turned is a soft spot. Extra squishy," he heard Nye whisper to Isobel. "I suggest you don't ask again because he won't ever tell you. He's got a reputation, you know."

"Reputation?" Isobel squeaked, sinking into the bright green coat she'd pulled on before coming out.

Zac turned and glared at them. "I can hear you, you know, and I wouldn't believe everything you hear."

Isobel stared at him and he sighed. "Which way to the pub? I'm dying here."

She pointed the direction they'd been walking. "I don't think this is a good idea."

"C'mon, Isobel," he said. "I don't mean to scare you. I'm paying, after all."

"Well, there's a consolation prize," she retorted, her spunk coming back.

Nye took her arm with a flourish and they continued walking down the empty street, Zac out in front. They hadn't gone very far when he sensed eyes on them. If he stopped to listen, then whoever it was would know they'd been made. No, they had to flush them out before they could report back to Lord Nutcase himself.

Zac caught sight of a shadow on top of a building across the street. One moment it was there, the next it was gone. Then the same sensation of being watched from farther ahead. They were definitely being followed.

Glancing down a deserted lane that looked like it joined onto a main street, he glanced at Nye, who nodded. Time to flush their shadow out of hiding. Sooner rather than later, and all that.

"Where are you going?" Isobel asked.

"Shortcut," Zac muttered, one ear on her, the other listening for their friend.

Nye kept close to Isobel as they walked, the sound of their footsteps bouncing off the brickwork of the buildings on either side. Either the vampire was going to slip up or make a play for Isobel and when they did, Zac would be there to put an end to it.

They'd gotten about halfway down the lane when the sound of rushing air and boots on cobblestones made them all turn. A male vampire had landed in a crouch behind them. He rose to his feet slowly, eyes black and fangs bared.

So, he wanted a fight? Oh, he'd get one all right.

The vampire dashed forwards, pushing Nye out of the way, but before he could grab hold of Isobel, Zac had him by the scruff of the neck, hurling him against the wall. He collided with the brickwork with a loud bang and the masonry shuddered.

Isobel stumbled back with a scream, but Nye pulled her back into his chest, clamping a hand over her mouth. "Zac's got this," he said. "I've got you."

The vampire scrambled to his feet with a cry of rage, but Zac was already over him, eyes dark with the promise of blood. Grabbing the guy's head, he slammed it into the brickwork with all his strength. The sound of shattering bone was oddly satisfying. He paused a second, his hand still holding the vampire's head in place against the wall, and he shrugged. *Dead.*

Letting the body go, he turned back towards Isobel as the dead vampire slumped to the ground, blood trailing down the brickwork.

"Scared now?" he asked as his eyes faded back to normal.

Isobel cowered against the opposite wall, her heart racing and eyes plastered on the dead vampire. He took that as a yes.

Stalking over to her, he grasped her face, making her look him in the eye. "I am not your friend. I am not your project. The next time you make a smart-ass comment, remember what I just did. I am not human anymore, no matter how much you want me to be."

"Zac," Nye said, grabbing his arm, "leave off, mate."

Zac blinked hard and let Isobel go, taking a few steps back. Seemed like he still had work to do controlling his anger, but at least he was beginning to understand that blood was his trigger.

"Take her home," he said, turning away. "We got the guy. It's okay now."

"You knew this would happen?" Isobel asked with a horrified gasp. "You used me as bait?"

"Vampires are like mice," Nye explained. "Where there's one, there's always another."

"I can't believe you assholes!"

"Nothing would've happened to you, Isobel," the spy murmured. "Between the two of us, nothing would have gotten past."

"Except maybe that scary fairy guy everyone's so worried about."

Zac turned around, his anger flaring. "Take her home, Nye."

The spy nodded and threaded his arm through

Isobel's and began to lead her away. It was a dick move using her, but they couldn't move her anywhere while she was still being watched. That meant they couldn't make a play for the grimoire without Aed finding out about it.

He wondered what Aya and Tristan had gotten out of the other vampire. Depending on what he knew, that would determine how soon they needed to get the book. If Zac had his way, they'd go there right now and snatch the thing—in and out like ghosts.

Looking down at the dead vampire and the mess he'd made, Zac sighed. It was just another mess to clean up in a long history of messes. He'd thought that after a century, he would've learned how to be a little... neater.

Gabby looked up at the abandoned warehouse and sighed. What a cliché. She wondered when they'd have to stop lurking in shadow and hiding desiccated bodies. Probably never, which made it all that much harder to handle.

Winding her way through the warren of scaffolding and rubble, she found Tristan and Aya in a lonely corner, far from human ears.

The vampire they'd found in Isobel's apartment was chained to a concrete pylon and looked extremely pissed off. He was covered in blood and his own saliva, and his eyes were black with rage. Gabby didn't like it, but they had to get answers.

"Did you get it out of him?" she asked as all three vampires looked up at her approach.

"With a hell of a lot of compulsion," Aya replied. "Aed did a messy job on him."

"He's broken," Tristan said, crossing his arms over his chest. "His mind is total chaos."

"We managed to get a few things out of him, enough to piece it together at least."

"Let's hear it," Gabby said.

"It seems like Aed gleaned a lot more from Regulus' blood than just his sister's deaths."

"Katrin..." Gabby said with a groan. "He knows about her grimoire."

"Yes," Tristan said. "He wants to take out the spell before anyone can find it and use it against him. We gathered he could use his power to track it down somehow but needed some extra help to get his hands on it."

"He got this guy to do his legwork," Aya explained. "He didn't want to be seen, so he found a random human on the street, turned him, and compelled him to follow Isobel."

"He was tryin' to lure her out so they could snatch her and take her to Aed."

"We thought it was just so he could get into the vault," Aya added.

"But?" Gabby asked with a frown.

"There seems like there is another reason he's interested in her, but we're not sure. This guy didn't know why, but it was implied she was important for more than just her access to the university."

"I want to see," she said, approaching the vampire.

"Watch him," Tristan warned. "He's lost his humanity."

"Aed compelled him to revert to an animalistic state if he was compromised," Aya said. "He'll bite your fingers off if you're not careful."

Gabby nodded and reached out. For this to work, she needed physical contact. After witnessing Katrin's maiming so vividly, she wasn't keen on repeating it—especially not by having her fingers bitten off by a rabid vampire. She liked her hand just as it was.

The vampire snapped at her viciously and she drew back before biting the bullet and slapping her palm against his forehead. As soon as she made contact, she dove right into his foggy mind and his body slackened. Wasting no time, she sifted through his memories and it was just as Aya and Tristan had said. This vampire had been compelled to lure Isobel out of her apartment so Aed could snatch her.

Then she came across something she wasn't expecting. A loose thread leading to the impossible. In his haste, Aed had left a calling card, and a sloppy one at that. It stunk of inexperience because now she had a way into Aed's mind. Gabby knew she had to be quick or else he'd sense her presence.

Following the thread, she found herself standing in a courtyard, a centuries' old building around her. This must be inside the university grounds. The sky was overcast, and students walked back and forth, all bundled up in coats and scarves against the cold, books in their arms and bags slung over their shoulders. Something inside of her knew this was the last of the rabble for the semester. Exams were just starting, and Christmas holidays were on everyone's minds.

Glancing across the courtyard, she saw a woman in a bright green coat. She'd seen her before, and it was who she was counting on finding here. A shock of red hair peeked out from under a cream woollen hat and her heart stopped. She watched the woman as she exited the building on the right and crossed the courtyard into the library, just as she'd done every day that week.

Following her inside, she watched as the woman went into a room and came back out, but without her coat and bag.

"Hey, Izzy," a man called out as she passed a large desk. He sat behind a computer she supposed was a catalogue of some kind. He worked here as well.

"Hey, Matt," she answered. "Slaving away as per usual, I see."

"Slave to the wage," he said with a laugh. "You researching up in the vault today?"

"Yep." She seemed rather happy about it, bouncing on her heels.

"Lucky," Matt answered with a jealous sigh. "They don't let me touch anything in there, and I work here. So unfair."

Her vision started to blur, and Gabby jerked back, snatching her hand away from the vampire, the warehouse coming back into focus. That was close. Too close.

"Gabby?" Aya asked.

"He's trying to get into the vault," she said, peering at the vampire. "Izzy is his way in. He's been watching her for days."

"Then we have to get in before he does," Tristan said. "Can we get rid of this guy yet? He's givin' me the 'you know whats.'"

Gabby regarded the restrained vampire with sadness. He was gone, totally and utterly. The humane thing to do would be to put him out of his misery. Covering her face with her chilly hands, she nodded.

"I'll do it," Tristan said. "You can go back to Isobel's. I'll see you there."

"Thank you," Aya said and a moment later, Gabby felt the hybrid's arm around her waist.

"Let's take a walk," she said. "By the looks of you, you saw something a little more than what Tristan and I had compelled out of him, yes?"

As they walked through the abandoned warehouse

and back to the street, Gabby told Aya about the scene in the library with Isobel and the clerk named Matt. There'd been something else there, something she couldn't understand. "It was like he recognised her. How could he when he's been bound for three thousand years?"

"Well, he's not getting close to her again, so hopefully we never have to find out," Aya said.

"I hope not."

"I know you were worried about involving Isobel," the hybrid said kindly. "I know it's hard, but she would've been in more trouble if we hadn't intervened."

"There was no way of knowing..."

"No, there wasn't. Blaming yourself isn't going to help, Gabby. We need to find the grimoire and we need to find someone to turn. Isobel won't be safe until Aed is dead—none of us will. We keep fighting until it's over. There is no other choice."

Aya could be callous and inappropriate at times, but she was right on the money. They had a path forwards and they had to take it, no matter the consequences. If they didn't, then things would be a lot worse than they already were.

"Let's go back to Isobel's and work out a plan," she said to Aya. "We're going to get the grimoire tonight."

CHAPTER 20

Alex stood in the arrivals hall at Heathrow Airport and rubbed his tired eyes. What the hell had crossed his mind when he decided to get on that plane? He'd never been out of the country before, and now he was in the United Kingdom. Didn't they drive on the opposite side of the road here?

He pulled out his cell and turned it on, hoping it would find signal. He needed to call his sister. Last he'd heard, Isobel was still in Oxford. That was until he'd received a voicemail from her almost two days ago. Her frantic voice had terrified him.

"Alex, it's Izzy. Something's... happened. We need your help like yesterday. Please, bro, call me back as soon as you get this. Please, your friends are here. Gabby and some guy named Zac, and some scary woman. Call me back as —" The message had cut off along with his heartbeat. Izzy was in trouble, and if Gabby and Zac were there...

it could only mean trouble of the crazy kind. He assumed the 'scary woman' was Aya.

When Aya had disappeared and Zac had left with Regulus, he thought that was it. None of them were coming back. Then Sam and Liz had moved to L.A. and he was on his own. He'd been happy for a while, but it was only a mirage. And now here he was, standing in the airport in London in the early hours of the morning. What the hell was he thinking?

Twelve hours on a stuffy plane via a short stopover in New York saw him beat. It was an odd sensation, knowing he was standing in another country. The signs were different, the prices were all in pounds, people of all different nationalities walked around him... it was just strange, and he hadn't even left the airport yet. His worry for his sister hadn't abated, though. Spying an information desk, he walked up and smiled at the guy behind the counter.

"Excuse me. Can you tell me how I can get to Oxford?" he asked.

"Oxford?" The clerk scratched his head. "Well, you can go into London and get a train or a coach, or you can just rent a car. It's only a couple of hours from here."

"What's the quickest way?"

"This time of the morning? You'd be better off renting a car. Hardly any traffic on the motorways at this time. It'll take you less than an hour or so, by my guess."

"Thanks," he said, tapping the countertop and looking for a rental desk of some sort.

The clerk saw him looking and pointed along the concourse. "There's some desks that way."

Following the guy's directions, Alex found a bunch of kiosks ablaze with logos, pamphlets, and special pricing. Stopping at the first one, he startled a sleepy woman. Seemed Heathrow was a twenty-four-hour kind of place.

"Can I help you?" she asked, sitting up straight.

"I'd like to rent a car, please."

As the woman put through his details, he couldn't stop focusing on Isobel. He was worried, like mega-worried about her. When Gabby had left, he'd assumed she was going to travel. You know, do the whole backpacking thing, but it seemed like it was a lie on her behalf. She was obviously in cahoots with Zac and Aya about something and his bet was that it had something to do with those Roman vampires. What exactly, he couldn't say. It felt like too much hard work whenever he thought about it.

One thing was certain, though. When he got his hands on Zac, he'd throttle him, vampire or not.

"There's a courtesy bus out front that'll take you to the lot," the woman said, breaking him out of his thoughts. "This time of the morning, there should be one there waiting." She pointed to the automatic doors behind him. "Just out there and to your left."

Once Alex had finally located the car, he stared at

the right-hand drive and scratched his head. This was mental. Absolutely, one hundred percent, the stupidest thing he'd ever done.

He slid into the seat and fumbled with the GPS, then he had a mild heart attack when he saw how complicated the highways were around the airport.

Isobel better be in a shitload of trouble because he was blaming all of this on her.

When Alex finally arrived in Oxford, he killed the engine and looked up at Isobel's apartment. He'd never seen it before, so he took a moment to take in the place that his sister had called home for the past three years. He was quickly learning that everything in the UK was smaller and super old. The street he was on looked like something out of Medieval Britain with its cobblestoned road and bluestone buildings.

That's when he saw Isobel walking up the street with some guy he'd never seen before. He held her around the waist, almost possessively, but that's not what made his blood boil. The guy looked like a thug in his big black coat and boots and his face...

Without a second thought, Alex opened the car door, slammed it behind him, and strode down the street.

Isobel's gaze met his and for a moment, she said

nothing. She looked at him like he was some kind of mirage.

"Alex?" she finally gasped.

"This is your brother?" the guy with the scarred face asked.

"And who are you?" Alex asked, puffing out his chest. "I don't like the look of you. What are you doing here? What are you messed up in, Izzy?"

"The name's Nye," the guy said and then pointed to his face. "War hero. Thanks a lot."

Isobel pushed the guy away and grabbed her brother's hand. "You can't be here," she said, pulling him towards her building.

"You said you needed my help," he exclaimed.

"I said call me back, not get on a bloody plane!"

"Siblings," Nye said with a chuckle and shook his head.

"Vampires, Izzy? Really?" He rose an eyebrow at her.

"Wait? What?" Her mouth dropped open. "You know?"

"I know more than you think!"

"I can guarantee you it's not what you think," she retorted.

"It's not? Well then, please, enlighten me!"

"You might wanna go inside to have this conversation," Nye said, nodding at a passerby.

Isobel dragged Alex up the stairs and into her apartment. Normally he would've stopped to take in his sister's home, but today he was mad, and nobody was giving him any answers. Nye walked in behind them and he almost blew a fuse.

"You invited him in?" he almost yelled at his sister. "What the hell, Izzy?"

"He's a good guy, Alex. He might be a little rough around the edges, but he helped save me."

"Save you from what?" When neither of them answered, he yelled, "*Saved you from what?*"

Nye placed a hand on his arm. "Calm down, mate. Take a breath, okay?"

"Get your hands off me, and don't even think of trying that freaky eye shit."

Nye stood back, holding his hands out. "Suit yourself."

Turning at the sound of the door opening, Alex's gaze collided with Gabby.

"Alex?" Gabby exclaimed.

"Gabby," he said sharply, not even bothering with a hello. "You better give me some answers because I'm mad as all hell."

"What are you doing here?" This time, it was Aya who spoke, and he realised Zac was behind her and yet another guy he didn't recognise. How many vampires could fit in here?

"I called him," Isobel explained. "I didn't mean for him to come. I just wanted to talk to him."

"You called him?" Gabby exclaimed. "I wanted to keep him out of it!"

"He knows about this. What was I supposed to do? He's my brother," Isobel exclaimed.

"No, he doesn't know about this," Aya said, waving her hands around wildly. "I compelled him to forget."

"I know you're vampires," Alex said like they were all stupid. "I don't know what the hell you're doing with my sister, though. I'd appreciate it if you all pissed off and left her out of whatever crazy scheme you've cooked up."

Gabby glared at Aya. "You compelled him, too?"

"What do you mean *too*?" Alex asked.

"Oh, for heaven's sake," Aya exclaimed. "You asked me to, Alex. And I compelled Liz to forget about what I am. So what?"

"Maybe I wouldn't have a problem with it, but I sure as hell do now." He pointed at Isobel. "If she so much as gets hurt—"

"Oh, for crying out loud," Aya exclaimed and was across the room in a flash. Grasping Alex's face, she looked him right in the eye and said, "I asked you to forget some things. Now's the time to remember them." She let him go and sat back on the sofa like nothing had happened.

Alex blinked twice before shaking his head. "Hell, Aya, be nice about it."

"I fixed you, can we get the grimoire now?" she asked exasperated.

"Grimoire? Someone better explain to me what's going on because I'm going insane here."

Zac snorted, stifling a laugh. "You don't know how appropriate that comment is."

Alex ground his teeth together, trying to keep under control.

Gabby took his hand with a sigh and sat him at the table. "Let me explain this as simply as I can..."

The story she told him next seemed like a farfetched fairytale that actually involved fairies—though they weren't anything like the glittery flying things in picture books. Gabby told him everything from beginning to end. The truth behind the Romans, the Tuatha and their war with the Celestines, the Coven... Everything that'd happened in the last few months was laid out. When she was finally done, he slumped back in the chair and stared into space. An insane fairy vampire-hybrid was after his sister for a *book*?

"I can't let anything happen to Izzy," he said after a moment. "I'll do anything to help, just leave her out of it."

"You can't help with this, Alex," Zac said. "Aya won't let anything happen to her."

"Neither will I," Gabby added.

"You want to break into the university vault to get this grimoire?"

"Yes," Aya said.

"Where did that guy go?" He suddenly realised that that Nye guy was gone. He probably took off somewhere between the fairy and Aya's witch massacre.

"Nye's out with Maddox doing some reconnaissance on the security system," Zac answered.

"Who's Maddox?" Alex asked, glancing between the vampires.

"Another vampire who's helping."

"And where's Regulus?"

When nobody replied, he glanced between them all and caught the expression on Gabby's face.

"He's dead," Zac said, glancing at the witch.

"And you're sad about it?" Alex didn't understand. *Wasn't he the bad guy?*

"He was our only chance at killing the hybrid forever," Aya told him.

"That's why we need the grimoire. It was Katrin's," Gabby said with a sniff. "It has the spell that created the Romans. We need it to—"

"The only way..." Alex started to interrupt, but then fell silent.

"It's imperative we get our hands on Katrin's grimoire before Aed does," Aya stated.

"That's why you need the book," he said. "You need to make another vampire." Understanding suddenly dawned on him and he stood, anger boiling to the surface. "Keep your hands off her! No, Izzy. Is that what you're doing? No!"

"Alex," Gabby began. "We haven't even gotten the spell yet."

"I won't allow it," he hissed. "I'll do anything but *leave her out of it.*"

"It hasn't come to that yet."

"I'll do it," he said, thumping his fist on his chest. "Change me."

"You can't be serious," Isobel exclaimed.

Alex turned to face his big sister. "Oh, I'm dead serious. I'm not letting you ruin your life."

"And you'll ruin yours?" she shrieked at him.

"If I have my way," Gabby interrupted, "I'm not changing either of you."

"What other choice do you have?" Alex asked. "I may only be a small-town kinda guy, but I understand an impossible situation when I see one. You don't have any options. Just the one, and it's me."

Maybe he'd regret it once he cooled down, but maybe he wouldn't. The only thing he was certain of was that he'd protect his sister from all of this, no matter what it meant for him. Izzy might be older than he was, but she had such a bright future ahead of her. Alex? Well, he was just a gardener.

"Don't make any rash decisions, Alex," Gabby said, placing a hand on his arm. "One step at a time. We'll get the grimoire, then I'll need to decipher the spell. That could take time. Things can change in a blink of an eye."

"One step at a time," he echoed, looking around the room at the assembled vampires. Aya, who he'd had the biggest crush on. Zac, who he wanted to punch in the face. And that other guy with the curly hair must be Tristan. And then there was one of his oldest friends, Gabby, who turned out to be a witch. Out of all of them, he'd trust whatever his best friend had to say.

"One step at a time," she replied with a sad smile.

CHAPTER 21

"So, what's the plan?" Zac asked, cracking his knuckles. "I assume we're going for the grimoire tonight?"

"As soon as possible," Gabby replied. "Do you think Maddox and Nye can crack into the security now?"

"Apparently, Maddox is good at that kind of thing," he said with a shrug.

"Well, there's not much to it, I guess. Disable the cameras and alarms, compel the security guards to turn the other way, get into the vault, get the grimoire."

"Sounds easy when you say it like that," Isobel said. "The vault is locked with one of those fancy access panels. You need a code to unlock it."

"You've been in there heaps," Gabby said. "Haven't you ever seen someone put it in? Has someone given you a code?"

"No. I'm still a student. Only the staff who work in

there have codes. And besides, a lot of the books and manuscripts are locked inside as well.”

Zac groaned. “I don’t know if there’s a workaround for that.”

“Maybe the security guards know,” Aya offered, glancing at Gabby.

“You want me to prod around in their heads?” the witch asked. “You can compel it out of them.”

“Either way works.”

“I’ll give Nye a call and see where they’re at,” Zac said, taking his cell out.

“Who’s going in?” Tristan asked. “Not all of us, surely.”

“I have to go and Isobel, of course—” Gabby started.

“And me,” Aya interrupted. “I’ve got the skills necessary.”

“Why does Aya get to go?” Zac asked sullenly. “If it’s just compulsion, you need—”

“I can help determine which is the right grimoire,” she said, shooting him a look.

“You’ll still get to go,” Gabby said, elbowing the vampire. “You just have to wait outside.”

“Wait,” Isobel interrupted. “What about Alex? Can someone stay with him? What if that Aed guy comes looking here? Or another vampire?”

“I’ll stay,” Tristan offered. “Too many vampires spoil the... somethin’.” He shrugged.

“So, I’m getting babysat now?” Alex said from the

corner. He'd been sitting on the kitchen counter, listening to their planning in silence. He still looked a little overwhelmed after hearing their crazy story.

"Aed is unpredictable and strong," Tristan explained. "And he still has his power. I'm not enough to stop him on my own, but someone should still be here just in case."

"And give your sister peace of mind," Aya said with a smile.

"You're exhausted," Isobel said, wrapping her arms around him. "Get some sleep. We'll be back before you know it."

"How can I sleep?" he asked thinly.

"You close your eyes, then—"

"*Izzy.*"

"Alex, I love you, but I'm a grown woman. I can help your friends. I want to help them. You need to trust Gabby and Aya. They seem to know what they're doing."

"I do," Aya quipped.

"You should've seen her snap that vampire's neck. And Zac—" She stopped mid-sentence and clamped her mouth shut.

"Aw, shit," Nye groaned.

Alex turned on Zac, his eyes dark. "What did you do?"

"Nothing too... bad." But Zac's expression said otherwise.

Alex was too angry to listen and went to punch the

vampire right in the face. Before his fist could connect, Aya grasped his forearm.

"We're all here," Aya murmured. "We're all in one piece. This is a battle, Alex. We can't all get through this without having to fight a bad guy or ten. There'll always be an element of danger. I know you're angry, but you need to trust us. I will not let anything happen to Isobel. I will fight to the end. Do you understand?"

Her speech came across a little patronising, but he could tell from her tone she was serious. She cared. She understood. He didn't really have a choice, but he nodded and she let him go.

"Let's get ready," Gabby said, picking up her coat from the back of the chair she sat in.

"Then," Zac said, doing the same, "once we get the word from Nye and Maddox, we roll out."

It was close to one a.m. by the time they gathered together. A few streets over from the university, the air was swirling with a light misty rain, each drop illuminated with the orange glow from the streetlamps around them. Lingering in the darkness, they waited for Maddox and Nye to appear.

Gabby shivered and flipped her coat collar up. Isobel huddled in the doorway beside her, blowing on her hands, and the witch felt a pang of remorse. Izzy had agreed to help, but she hoped it didn't cost her or

Alex too much in doing so. The more she dwelt on it, the more she wished Regulus was here. He'd know what to do. The aching hole in her heart seemed to crack open a little further as she recalled the Roman's features. *It had only been five days…*

Zac leaned against the wall beside her and slid his hand into hers. He seemed to understand where her thoughts were, and she was grateful for the small gesture.

He straightened a moment later and nodded towards the end of the street. Two forms came into view and she recognised Nye, but the other man was a stranger to her. It must be Maddox.

She regarded him as they came closer and all she got was a bad feeling. She supposed he was meant to be a part of the Six with that kind of aura. He was a vampire's vampire—a thug, animalistic… ruthless. It was no wonder he'd sided with Regulus.

"Are we good?" Zac asked as the vampires stopped in front of them.

"The cameras are out," Maddox confirmed, looking over Isobel.

"Hands off, Maddox," Nye said, shoving the assassin.

"Just looking."

"Yeah, well, look someplace else."

"What about the security system?" Gabby asked, angling herself between Maddox and Isobel.

"Offline," Nye confirmed. "We also compelled all

the guards we could find."

"So, we can just walk in?" Aya snorted. "Just like that?"

"Are you doubting my skills?" Maddox asked with a sneer. "I might've been born in the Middle Ages, but it doesn't mean I'm still there."

"No one is doubting you," Zac told him. "If you say it's offline, then it's offline."

"The courtyard camera is out, but the ones around the street aren't linked to the university system," Maddox explained. "Those are linked to the citywide system. That's monitored by the bobbies."

"Bobbies?" Gabby asked with a frown.

"The police, love," Nye explained.

"We better go over then," Zac said.

"Over?" Isobel asked with a gulp.

"Across the roofs," he explained. "I can drop you off. Aya can take Gabby."

She looked a little alarmed, and Aya offered her a friendly smile. "Just a piggyback. It'll be over before you know it."

"C'mon," Zac said, gesturing for her to jump on his back. He stooped as she put her hands on his shoulders.

She took a deep breath. "You promise you won't drop me? I haven't forgotten this morning, you know."

"This morning?" Gabby asked.

"There was another vampire," Nye explained. "We needed to flush him out."

"You used her as bait?" Gabby exclaimed.

"She was safe with us," Zac said, then gestured at Isobel again. "You better hold on tight, Isobel. It's a fast ride."

With a grimace, she jumped onto the vampire's back and they were gone, and a small shriek signalled they were on the roof above. Aya turned and Gabby jumped up on her back and they followed close behind. The rise of air took her breath away and a few seconds later, they were outside the library doors, the same she'd seen in Aed's memory. It'd been full daylight then, but even in the dark, they were unmistakable.

Aya set her down by the door and she nodded to let the Celestine know she was okay.

Zac dropped Isobel and she held onto him for a moment to steady herself.

"Whoa," she said. "Talk about dizzy."

"Send me a text message when you're ready to be picked up," he said with a grin and was gone.

"I'll never get used to that," Isobel said, shaking her head.

Gabby smiled and turned to the door. It was locked, but a few words and a small burst of magic turned the mechanism and it popped open.

Casting her earth sense out, Gabby felt for signs life inside, but all she got was a couple of potted plants. Talk about sensitivity. She glanced at Aya and the Celestine nodded.

"It's clear," she confirmed. They entered the library, closing out the night and swirling rain behind them.

Walking down the hall, Isobel took the lead, and they entered the library proper, the open space stretching out in front of them. Aya halted and gestured for them to duck and Gabby realised a security guard was walking their way. They crouched behind the information desk at the front—the same one Gabby recognised from Aed's memory.

"Would he know the code?" Aya whispered to Isobel, nodding towards the man who was slowly approaching their position.

"He can't know what it is," she hissed.

"There's only one way to find out," Aya declared and stepped out of the shadows.

The guard instantly turned at the movement and startled when he laid eyes on the Celestine. "Hey," he exclaimed, fumbling for his gun. "You're not meant to be here. Hands where I can see them!"

But Aya was too impatient for that. She flew forwards, faster than Gabby's eyes could follow, and she pushed him back against the wall, a pale hand curling around his throat. The gun clattered to the floor and the guard's face slackened before he had a chance to call out.

"Hey, how you doing?" Aya asked, amused at his reaction.

"Fine," the guard replied in a monotone voice. "I

really don't want to be here, but I don't get paid otherwise."

With a laugh, Aya cocked her head to the side and asked, "I don't suppose you know the code to get into the library vault? You know the one with all the really old books?"

"The vault? Yes, I know it. It's my job to check it after hours."

"What is it?"

"Four, six, eight, five, seven."

"Thanks," she replied. "Now, forget everything that just happened from the moment you saw me. Once you've done that, go into a dark corner, count to... say, five thousand, six hundred and thirty-seven, then go home."

"Okay."

She let the guard go and he shook his head, looking totally bewildered, and then wandered off into the dark library.

"She did that freaky eye thing, huh?" Isobel whispered in Gabby's ear.

"Uh huh."

"Clock's ticking," Aya called out, gesturing for them to come out of their hiding place.

"Which way?" Gabby whispered, glancing across the library floor. All she could see were books and reading tables, and another level that looked much the same from down here.

"Follow me."

Isobel led them through the main reading room, between rows of tables with old-fashioned green and gold lamps, to a set of stairs at one side. Up on the second level, there were rows and rows of books that stretched into the darkness. This place was massive, bigger than any library Gabby had been in.

"The vault is through the doors at the end." Even though Isobel's voice was a whisper, it sounded loud in the silence and Gabby glanced around nervously.

Aya placed a hand on her shoulder. "We're alone."

"For now," the witch whispered, her heart feeling all fluttery in her chest.

"Wait," Isobel whispered. She disappeared into the stacks and appeared a moment later with a book in her hands. "This is the closest thing that I can remember that the spell books look like."

"A decoy," Aya said, her eyes twinkling. "I like it."

"With any luck, it won't be noticed for some time."

"And we'll be long gone," Gabby said.

"There's no way they'd link it back to us," Aya reassured them. "No fingerprints, no security footage."

"Maybe not for you," Gabby replied. "You never existed on record. I'll keep my gloves on, thanks."

With a smile, Aya cracked open the doors to where Isobel said the vault was located. The low hum of electricity greeted them as they entered the room, and Gabby scanned the door beyond that led into the vaulted area of the library.

"You know," the witch said, looking at the glass

windows and door, "I was expecting something a little more... I don't know, ominous."

"It's not a bank vault," Isobel said. "No gold ingots. Just a bunch of old, *irreplaceable*, books."

She stood before the keypad and punched in the number they'd gleaned from the security guard. Four, six, eight, five, seven. The light flashed green on the lock and a click signalled they were in.

"The vault is temperature-controlled," Isobel explained and as soon as Gabby walked through the door, she felt the sharp rise in temperature. "It's to keep the paper and ink from deteriorating."

"The grimoire won't dissolve," Aya said with an annoyed sigh. "That thing could survive the end of days without so much as a scratch."

"I think I know which book it is," Isobel said. "It's one that's been in the too hard basket for as long as I can remember."

"Please explain," Aya retorted.

"Well," she started, glaring at the hybrid, "there's about two dozen or so books that no one has been able to decipher. All have been carbon dated to different time periods. Mostly vague date ranges, because you can't really carbon date a book without destroying it, but the texts are in an unknown language. Most people think they're written in some kind of code, but nobody's broken it yet."

"Witch-speak," Gabby said, assuming they might be grimoires.

"You think they're all spell books?"

"It's the most likely explanation," she said with a shrug. "You know you can't tell anyone about this..."

"I know." Isobel sighed with what sounded like disappointment. "It just goes against my nature, you know. Solving a mystery, only to keep it to myself."

"If the truth got out about witches and vampires and everything else that exists in this world, can you imagine what the humans would do to us?" Aya asked.

Isobel grimaced. "You have a point."

The vault was set out into several rooms that split off one main area that was dominated by a special reading table. Isobel led them to the opposite side to another door that had a seal on it like a fridge. It let out a hiss as she pushed it open and Gabby followed with Aya close behind.

There were several sets of drawers lining the walls, some thin, some thick. It looked like the inside of a bank vault with dozens and dozens of safety deposit boxes.

"It has to be one of these," Isobel said, pointing to a row of drawers on the left-hand side. "But they're locked."

Gabby ran her gaze down the row of locks on each drawer. They were simple enough—small electronic keys slotted into the end, much like a keycard that they gave out in hotels, but much smaller than a credit card. They should be simple enough that she could short them out with her power. *Hopefully.*

Collecting herself, she pulled off her glove and pressed her palm against the first. Slowly, her power trickled forth, spilling into the lock and it spread to the entire row with ease. With a sharp jab, she heard the clicks as each one shorted, loosening the drawers one by one.

"Wow," Isobel breathed.

"Let's get this over with," she said, rubbing the metal with her glove. Definitely no fingerprints allowed.

Isobel slid open the first drawer. "This is one of them."

Gabby could instantly tell it was a grimoire. Magic seemed to radiate from it. It was a dull imprint, but it was there. Placing her hand on the brown leather cover, she shook her head. "Not this one."

Isobel closed the drawer and opened the next. They repeated it a few more times, all with the same result. The next drawer that opened, she felt something different. A familiarity, and even without touching it, she knew it was the one they were looking for.

It was smaller than the rest, worn and faded with use, not time. Whereas all the other grimoires Gabby had encountered all had brown leather covers, this one had a green embossed casing with a strange glyph etched on the front. It looked like an ancient Celtic symbol—a knot work design that looked similar to the modern sign witches used for flame.

As soon as Gabby put her hands on it, she knew it was Katrin's grimoire. The phantom pain she'd felt when the founder had given her the vision of its making sliced through her hand and she stumbled back with a hiss, holding her hand to her chest.

"Gabby?" Isobel asked, alarmed.

She drew in a sharp breath and shook her hand. "That's the one."

"I'll take it," Aya said, picking up the grimoire.

Isobel put in the decoy and slid the drawer shut. It wasn't a match, but it would throw the library staff off for a while.

"What just happened?" Isobel asked.

"Katrin gave me an affinity so I could locate the grimoire," Gabby explained. "It wasn't very nice."

"Explanations later," Aya said ushering them towards the door. "We've got what we came for and now we need to go. I don't want to linger longer than we have to."

Gabby gave one last look to the drawers that housed the grimoires and lamented leaving them there. They were no use to anyone else. If a witch had come across them, they'd know to keep quiet, but she longed to read them and find out what'd happened to the witches who owned them. If she could reunite them with their families—if they still had families alive today... Isobel closed the vault behind them and as the light flashed red on the lock, she sighed. Best to leave them.

They backtracked the way they'd come and to Gabby's relief, the library was still silent. She sent Zac a quick text to let him know they were on their way out and when they lingered by the exit, looking out into the courtyard, it was only a minute before the vampire rapped his knuckles on the door to let them know he was there.

Aya stepped out first and kissed him on the cheek. "Done and dusted."

"Any trouble?" Gabby asked as Zac gestured for Isobel to jump on his back.

"All quiet," he replied. "Too quiet if you ask me."

"Then let's get out of here while the going is good."

Aya knelt so the witch could jump on her back. Gabby's breath caught again as the vampires crossed the courtyard and jumped up onto the roof and into the night. It looked like they'd gotten away with it, but as soon as Aed realised they had Katrin's grimoire, he'd come looking. Gabby had to decipher the spell as soon as possible and that was the least of their problems.

The spell would be useless without the right kind of human. Gabby didn't want to acknowledge it, but Katrin had said they needed someone selfless and pure of heart. The only person who fit that bill was Alex.

Aya seemed to sense her worry and her grip tightened on her for a moment. Gabby hoped with all her heart it wouldn't have to come to that; that they would find someone else. Alex was going home human if it was the last thing she ever did.

CHAPTER 22

Alex tried to get some sleep. He closed his eyes, did his best to ignore the thousand-year-old vampire sitting in Izzy's cramped kitchen, but it just wasn't happening. He was overtired and over worried. What if they were caught? What if that Aed guy turned up?

"Would you like a drink?" Tristan asked, and Alex sat up with a groan. The perceptiveness of vampires was kinda freaky.

"Depends what you mean by drink."

"Booze," the knight said with a grin, reaching into his coat pocket. He pulled out a flask and waved it in his direction.

Alex took it and unscrewed the cap. "How long has it been?" he asked before downing a mouthful of whatever liquor was inside.

Tristan laughed when he handed back the flask

with a wheeze. "Steady, Alex. That's some powerful spirits in there."

"Don't you have taste buds? I think I just melted mine off."

The knight screwed the cap back on and set the flask on the table. "They've been gone a few hours. They should be due back any time now."

Alex glanced at the door with a frown. *A few hours? How long did something like this take?*

"I've known Arrow for a long time," Tristan said, catching his expression. "When she says she's goin' to do somethin', she follows through, no matter the cost."

"Why do you call her that?"

"Arrow? Well, it was the name she gave me when I first met her, and it stuck. I don't think I could get used to callin' her anythin' else."

Alex rubbed his eyes and stifled a yawn. Aya certainly had her secrets, there was no denying that.

"They're comin' now." Tristan nodded towards the door and a moment later, it opened and Isobel walked in.

"Izzy, thank goodness," Alex exclaimed, pulling his sister in for a hug.

"I told you it'd be fine," she said, pushing him back, "but I still need to breathe, you know."

Gabby and Zac followed and Aya came in last, bringing up the rear.

"You got the grimoire?" Tristan asked, rising to his feet.

Aya pulled out the little green book from the inside of her jacket and set it on the table.

"It's smaller than I thought it would be," Zac said, narrowing his eyes at it.

"It's different than any other grimoire I've seen before," Gabby said, peering at the book. "It's certainly changed from the vision Katrin gave me."

"It's likely she wanted to change it after she was made one of the Five," Aya said, sitting at the table. "If I were her, I would want to remove all attachments to the Coven, too."

"Alisandra's was full of awful things," Gabby said. "I'm a little scared of opening it."

"You can do it. You've gotten this far."

As Alex watched Gabby stare at the grimoire, he cracked his neck. This wasn't any place for him. What did he know about magic and vampires? Zero, zip, zilch, nada. He stood and everyone looked up at the movement.

"I'm taking you out," Alex said, pulling Isobel to her feet. He could see she was dying to see inside the book, but he wanted to spend time with her in a normal setting—preferably one with no mention of anything supernatural.

"I don't think that's a good idea," Zac said. "Lord Fairy Dust could be hiding around the corner."

"I can't sense him," Gabby said, frowning. "But—"

"Then it should be safe enough," Alex countered.

Zac didn't seem to like it. "Just because you can't

sense him, doesn't mean he's not hanging around, or has someone watching for him."

Aya sighed. "We already have the grimoire. He has no use for Isobel and certainly not Alex. I don't see the harm in them going out for an hour."

"See?" Alex said. "Just an hour. I'd like to spend some time with Izzy before... you know."

"I'm not turning you," Gabby exclaimed, her hands curling into tight fists. "I'm not, so just forget it already."

Alex exchanged a look with Aya. "Gabby, I—"

"Just let me decipher the grimoire. Can you do that?"

He nodded meekly. His friend was under so much pressure, it was unbelievable. How he hadn't seen it before. Gabby's strength was surprising, and it showed how much she'd grown in the last year.

"Okay, Izzy. Are you up for it?" he asked, drawing attention away from the witch.

"Just an hour. I'm kinda beat from a night of thievery." She gave him a wink and his worry eased a fraction. "We can bring back some takeout if you're hungry, Gabby?"

"Thanks," the witch replied. "That sounds great. It's easy to forget to eat when you're the only human in a bunch of vampires."

Alex pulled his jacket on and motioned for Isobel to follow. Before things got crazy and before something happened to ruin everything, he wanted to hang with his big sister. It might be the only chance he got while he was still human, and there wasn't anyone else he'd rather spend his last hours with. Who knew what would happen when he changed? If he'd still be the same person as he was now; if he'd still feel the same way about his family.

Alex's heart was well and truly set on sacrificing himself. Gabby was fighting against it, but he was the only one who was fit for the job and everyone knew it. It was time to say his goodbyes while he had the chance. Everything was fair game now.

***

If they weren't in such an awful place right now, Alex might've enjoyed seeing the place that Isobel called home. He would've liked to see the university where she studied, the places she hung out, met some of her friends, and gone sightseeing across the countryside. But they were stuck in the middle of an ancient war between two extinct magical races.

They wandered down the street together, Christmas decorations twinkling in every window, the promise of snow on the air. It should've felt festive and cheerful and all that, but all Alex could think about was his big sister and the looming threat of some psycho hybrid.

"Do you remember when we were little, and Dad

used to get up on the roof and decorate the house with Christmas lights?" Isobel asked.

Alex nodded, trying not to let it get to him. "Yeah, it was terrible."

"Half the lights were always broken."

"He tried so hard," he said with a laugh.

"We'd stand out the front in the dark and he'd make his speech and then the big show of plugging them in... and then only half the thing would light up."

"Didn't he blow the fuse box one year?"

"You remember that?" Isobel asked, threading her arm through his. "You were only about five or six."

"I remember it," he said, squeezing her arm. "How could I forget? Mrs. Landers called the fire department."

Isobel let out a loud laugh. "She thought he'd burn the entire street down."

They fell silent as they walked down the main street of Oxford, or what felt like the main street. Shops lined either side selling clothes, cellphones, jewellery, and a few of those souvenir places that had Oxford University sweaters and T-shirts hanging in the windows.

"Are you happy here?" Alex asked. "I mean, is it where you want to be?"

Isobel sighed. "Yeah. I like it here. The university is great. I like my apartment, even though it's a shoebox, but all the houses are here. I've made some friends... and made some great discoveries." She winked at him, biting her lip. "Even though I have to keep them to myself."

"Good. I'm glad."

"You don't sound very happy," she said. "What about your business? I thought you were starting your own building and gardening service?"

"I am... I was..."

"But?"

"But..." He hesitated, his heart feeling heavy with what he knew he had to do. "It's not meant to be."

Isobel instantly got his meaning. "Alex, you can't be serious. We may have different dreams, but yours are just as important as mine. Just because they need someone to, *you know*... doesn't mean it has to be you."

"And you'd rather it be you?" he asked a little too sharply.

"I'd do it," she said without blinking.

"No, Izzy," he cried, turning to face her, the light from an electronics store illuminating her face in the murky winter daylight. "I'm the only one who can do this, and you know it. I have the right mind, the right heart, and the right intent. Anyone else and it won't work." He'd seen the monster Arturius had become and he couldn't chance Isobel turning into that. He couldn't chance Isobel turning at all. It was completely out of the question.

"I don't want you to," she said, her voice quiet.

"Self-sacrifice has a lot to do with it," he replied. "I'd do it to save you. A million times over."

"It doesn't make it right."

"No, but it's what needs to be done."

A tear slipped down one cheek and she brushed it away furiously. "I can't. You're my little brother. I should be protecting *you*."

"Trust me, Izzy." He rubbed her shoulders and cast his gaze across the street, watching people pass them by. Ordinary people going about their business with their ordinary problems. How he wished they could be just like them.

That's when he saw a man standing across the street. He was dressed in a suit, no tie, and was just staring at them. Alex didn't know how he knew it, but something told him they needed to get out of there like yesterday. Was that guy the hybrid Aed? Alex wasn't going to stick around to find out.

Rather than alarm Isobel, he flung an arm over her shoulder and began leading her back towards the apartment, cursing the fact that he no longer had a cell number for Zac or even Tristan.

"Let's go back," he said in a low voice. "Wasn't there a takeaway place near your house? We can get Gabby some breakfast from there."

"I think it'd be more like lunch by now."

"Food's food, right?"

He looked over his shoulder and caught sight of the man in his peripheral vision, looming like some freaky sicko. They were definitely being followed, but he wasn't sure by who. It might be Aed, or it might be another of his vampire thugs keeping tabs. His only option was to keep walking like nothing was wrong. With any luck, they'd get back to Isobel's in one piece and the guy would keep his distance.

Worst case, he'd try something and there was nothing Alex could do about it. They were human and so it meant they'd already lost. Luck was the only way of getting out of this and luck was in short supply.

"Is there a shortcut?" he asked as they wandered back. "I'm freezing my ass off here."

"It's not like winter in Louisiana, huh?" Isobel said with a laugh. "I kinda miss that humid cesspool sometimes."

"Yeah, ice and snow... can't say I'm a fan."

"Okay, grumpy. There's a lane here we can cut through instead of going around the block." She pointed to a break in between some buildings ahead.

"I need a coffee, stat," he said cheerfully, hyperaware that their shadow hadn't dropped off.

They turned down the lane, their footsteps echoing around them, and he cursed when he saw how long it was. What was that thing about dark alleyways and horror movies? He lengthened his stride and Isobel almost had to jog to keep up.

"What's the rush?" she asked, but then her face fell.

"Just keep walking, Izzy."

"He's—"

"I don't know. We just have to make it back."

They'd gotten halfway down the lane before their

follower made his move. He landed in front of them with a thud, a hand on the cobblestones to steady himself before rising to his full height. Isobel gasped, clutching Alex's arm, and he pulled her into his side.

The man stepped towards them, his movements almost cat-like, but that's not what Alex was staring at. He'd seen some freaky eye shit with Zac and Aya, but this guy took the cake and ate the whole thing, too. His eyes were red. Not entirely red, but like some people had blue or brown irises. Red like a stoplight; red like blood.

His heart flip-flopped in his chest as he realised who was standing in front of them. *Aed.*

"Scared?" the hybrid drawled, his gaze fixing on the two humans. "You should be."

"Leave us alone," Alex said. "We can't help you. You've got nothing to gain by hurting us."

Aed smirked, his gaze falling onto Isobel. "I have everything to gain."

As he strode forwards, Alex pulled Isobel behind him, trying to shield her from whatever was going to happen. Fat lot of good that would do. The hybrid would just tear him into shreds before he could take a swing.

Another dark form dropped in between them and he instantly recognised Zac. Had he been following them this entire time? He was suddenly grateful the vampire was so sneaky.

"You?" Aed halted, glaring.

"Yes, me," Zac declared. "Just your friendly Celestine stinking, vampire watchdog here to put your plans of world domination into disarray."

"Do not get in my way," Aed hissed, "or I will rip you into little pieces."

"I cracked your head open once and I can do it again," Zac said. "If you want them, you'll have to go through me."

"It will be my pleasure."

Zac's shoulders squared and he ran towards Aed faster than Alex's eyes could follow. The vampire pushed the hybrid with a hard jab and he flew backwards, rolling to a stop towards the opposite end of the lane.

Pulling Isobel back into the safety of a doorway, he held her close. "It's going to be okay," he murmured, rubbing his hands up and down her arms. She was shaking like a leaf, her eyes wide with fear.

Peering around the doorway, he wondered if they could get away while Zac distracted Aed. The two vampires were in between them and the apartment, so they would have to go the long way around.

"We need to make a run for it," Alex said, cupping his sister's face. "I know you're scared—believe me, I'm shitting myself right now—but we have to get out of here."

Isobel nodded and they both looked at the vampires who were wrestling. He winced as Aed punched Zac square in the face, putting the vampire flat on his back, blood streaming from his nose and mouth. Their eyes connected for a split-second and all they said to Alex was, *run.*

Aed grabbed Zac's shoulders and pulled him to his feet with a roar. There was a sickening crack as the hybrid squeezed, shattering bone. The vampire let out a shocked gasp, the only indicator he felt any pain.

Zac's arms dangled uselessly beside him, and he let out an angry growl.

"Do you know what happens to fools who get in my way?" the hybrid asked.

Alex felt Isobel move beside him and he went to grab her arm, but she was too quick.

"Stop," she cried, standing in the middle of the lane. "*Leave him alone.*"

Aed's head flew up at the sound of her voice and he dropped Zac like a rock. In a flash, he was in front of her, hands on her waist. "Siobhan?"

Alex could see Isobel visibly shaking, giving away her terror. What was she doing?

"I know you are afraid of me, my love," Aed murmured.

My love?

"I know you are afraid," he continued. "I know you don't remember me, but I understand. In time you'll remember. I'll help you."

To everyone's shock, Aed cupped her face in his hands and pressed his lips to Isobel's forehead like he was her secret lover. She gasped at the contact, her entire body rigid.

Zac stumbled to his feet, his arms starting to move again, as the hybrid scooped up Isobel. She shrieked and beat her fists against his chest, but there was nothing any of them could've done. There was a whoosh of air and they were gone.

Alex stumbled out of the doorway and looked around wildly. "*Izzy*," he yelled, his voice echoing between the buildings.

"It's no use," Zac told him. "They're long gone."

"What—"

"Did you just see the same crazy shit I just did?" Zac groaned, massaging his shoulder.

"H-he t-took her..." Alex was stunned. This was shock, wasn't it? His limbs felt numb, his skin prickled with a thousand pins and needles, and he couldn't catch his breath.

"I knew the guy was mental, but that takes the cake."

"Who the hell is Siobhan?"

"Who knows what's going through that guy's head." Zac leaned against the wall with a grimace as his bones healed.

"We need to get her back," Alex said, desperation boiling to the surface.

"I know," the vampire replied. "We need Gabby. She can track him."

"She can do that now? I thought she could only sense him?"

"Regulus taught her before—" He stopped mid-sentence and shrugged. *Before he'd died.* Alex knew enough about it to understand.

Alex was just... He couldn't function properly and just stood there staring at the place where Isobel had been standing a moment before. She was in the hands of an insane vampire-hybrid. What if he turned her? His heart beat painfully in his chest as every worst-case scenario played itself out in his mind.

"Are you okay?" Zac placed a hand on his arm, bringing him back to the present.

"No," he said shaking his head. "Are you?"

"Yeah," he replied, flexing his muscles. "Bones heal, severed limbs not so much."

Alex frowned, casting his thoughts back to Isobel. There was only one option now and it wasn't going to be pleasant. Without a word, he strode down the street back towards the apartment with Zac trailing behind.

"Where are you going?" the vampire called out.

Not bothering to stop, he replied, "Where do you think?"

CHAPTER 23

Alex stormed into his sister's apartment, the door banging inwards against the wall. Gabby, Aya, and Tristan looked up and when they saw his expression, they shot to their feet.

"Alex, wait up a minute," Zac called out from behind.

"Gabby," he said, his determined gaze fixed on the witch.

"What's going on?" she asked and when she saw the blood all over Zac's face, her eyes widened.

"Aed turned up," the vampire said. "Smacked me in the face like a little girl."

"He took Izzy," Alex said, trying to hold everything in, but Aya was there winding a hand into his. She'd know, she'd always know.

Gabby drew in a sharp breath. "He what?"

"He snatched her," Alex said, but he couldn't formulate a proper explanation.

"He was probably looking for Aya and tracked me instead," Zac said. "I was following them at a distance to make sure they were okay, and when Alex changed course, I saw Aed follow them through the street. I hoped he'd keep his distance until we were all together, but he must have realised—"

"He tracked you?" Alex hissed, turning on Zac.

"He seems to think I smell like a Celestine—"

"I told him to follow you," Gabby interrupted. "I couldn't let you go without some kind of protection."

"He almost got me," Zac said, rolling his shoulders.

"He almost killed you?" Aya gasped and practically threw herself at the vampire.

"I'm fine," he murmured into her hair, holding her tight. "Thanks to Isobel."

"I got the feeling he recognised her," Gabby said like she'd been deep in thought.

"When?" Zac asked, looking thoroughly annoyed.

"When I sifted through his thoughts."

Zac turned. "You were in his head?"

"The vampire that was here, the one he compelled... He did a sloppy job and left a thread behind, a way into his thoughts."

"Gabby," Aya said, "he could've—"

"He didn't," she snapped.

"That's how you knew," the hybrid said, straightening. "I thought you'd gleaned it from the vampire, not Aed himself."

"You knew?" Alex asked, his jaw tight.

"He thinks she's his lost love," Zac said, putting a hand on Alex's shoulder. "He won't do anything to hurt her."

"You said it yourself, he's insane. Who knows what he'll see tomorrow?"

"We'll get her back," Gabby said, "I—"

Alex wasn't listening. Gabby was too preoccupied with not wanting to hurt anybody that she didn't quite grasp the fact there was no getting out of this without anyone suffering at least a little. "You need to change me. You need to change me, and we need to kill him. That's the only way I can keep her safe."

Gabby's eyes filled with tears, her calm exterior beginning to crack. "No. I won't. Not you."

"Change me, Gabby. You know there's no other option."

"Alex is right," Aya said.

"You really want this?" the witch asked him.

"I don't want it, but I have to do it. I know you want to spare me, but you can't. We've run out of time."

Gabby turned back to the grimoire and ran her fingers across the page she'd been reading. "Okay," she said meekly. "Okay."

"I'll call Nye and the Three," Zac said. "We need to get ready... and I need to wash my face." He gestured to the blood from his fight with Aed.

Gabby nodded like she wasn't able to do anything else.

"And I'll stay and help you with the spell," Aya said.

"I can't offer anything other than my presence without corrupting Alex."

"I know."

Zac stood to leave and Aya grabbed his hand. "Be careful. No more fighting Aed on your own."

"Believe me, I don't plan to." He leaned over and pressed his lips to hers, and a moment later, he was gone.

"I'm at your service," Tristan said with a grin. He'd been silent the entire time and Alex got that he was the reserved kind, but he'd been a knight, so honour and valour and all that was his game.

"It's up to Gabby," Aya said to the knight. "It's time to follow her lead."

"We need to find a quiet spot where no one will hear or see us," the witch said, opening Isobel's laptop. "Somewhere where I can be close to the Earth and that's free of distractions."

"Outside of town," Aya said. "A forest or a field…"

"There's a wooded area at the south end of town," Gabby said, pointing to the map she'd looked up on the laptop.

"Good," Aya declared. "Private enough for what we need to do."

"This is going to hurt, isn't it?" Alex asked with a grimace.

"I don't know what it was like for the Romans," Aya said with a shrug. "Turning on a good day isn't pleasant, so I would assume yes, it's going to hurt."

Alex paled and she placed a hand on his arm. "You'll be fine."

Tristan leaned over Gabby's shoulder and looked at the map. "I can drive you there and keep an eye out for trouble."

"I think Aed will be otherwise occupied," Aya said with a wave of her hand.

"No chances," Gabby said, glancing at Alex. "We can't take the risk of someone interrupting or finding out what we're doing."

"What happens if the spell is interrupted?" Alex asked, a little panicked.

"No idea, but I don't really want to find out."

"That's not reassuring me, you know."

Gabby smiled thinly. "Give me five minutes to get some stuff."

Alex fidgeted, watching as she went through the kitchen drawers and pulled out a sharp knife. His stomach instantly squirmed. What the hell had he gotten himself into? She flipped it over and inspected the edge in the light and seemed satisfied. Then she wrapped it in a tea towel and placed it on top of the grimoire. Ducking down, she rifled through the cupboards and pulled out a green plastic bowl. Alex wondered what she needed it all for. They were making him a vampire, not a salad.

"Okay," Gabby said. "That should do it. Let's go if we're doing this."

Alex stood, a little light-headed. In T-Minus an

hour or so, he'd be a vampire. Just like that. Gabby would cast the same spell that had created the Romans and that would be it. He'd be un-killable, powerful, fast, and all the above times ten. He didn't even want to think about the rest, at least not until it was all over.

Courage, Alex, he thought. *Courage.*

They drove out to the forest in silence, Alex's thoughts bouncing from Isobel back to what was about to happen to him. He didn't know which one he should be more worried about.

"Here's okay," Gabby said and a moment later, Tristan pulled the car over to the side of the road and killed the engine.

They piled out, the woods stretching into darkness around them, the dull glow of the city to their backs. Alex huddled into his coat and tried not to feel sick. Gabby and Aya set off into the tree line and he followed because there was no going back now. They had reached the point of no return the moment Aed snatched Isobel and took off with her.

Tristan sat on the hood of the car, watching as they disappeared into the forest. A moment later, the vampire and the road were both out of sight.

"You said you needed blood?" Alex asked as they walked. "Who's? I didn't think we could use either of yours..."

"We can't use pure Coven or Celestine blood," Gabby explained. "I'm neither, so mine is good."

"Does that mean I'll be linked to you like Katrin was to the others?"

"No, not unless I will it, and I wouldn't do that to you."

Alex wasn't sure if he should answer that and instead, he asked, "But Katrin was a part of the Coven. How could she make the Romans?"

"She had power before she was made one of the Five," Gabby explained. "But it was so small, it was negligible. For all intents and purposes, she was ninety-nine-point-nine percent human. Uncorrupted enough to be turned into a witch and to create the Romans."

"Katrin had power before?" Aya asked. "I never knew."

"The memory she showed me was of her mother forcing her to make her grimoire as a child."

Aya snorted. "I can imagine how that went."

They walked through the woods until they came across a clearing that seemed to be to Gabby's liking. It was large and open, but branches still hung over their heads, shielding them from the night sky.

"I need to cast a circle of flame," Gabby

explained. "Alex, you need to stand in the middle."

Aya looked at the grass and the surrounding forest. "Let me dig a circle out for you." They hybrid disappeared and returned just as fast with a branch and began to dig a haphazard trench. When she caught Alex frowning at her, she winked. "The last thing we need is a forest fire."

Gabby knelt, setting the bowl, knife, and grimoire at her feet. She flipped through the pages until she settled on one that must have been the spell she needed.

"It's ironic, you know," Alex said, watching Aya dig the shallow ditch around him. "I was the nerdy guy in school; nobody gave me a second look."

"You turned out to be a handsome, muscled gardener," Gabby said, looking up. "You were a hundred times better than the popular kids anyway. How many of them went on to do anything great?"

"How many of them turned out to be witches? Or immortal vampires?"

"It's no use dwelling on the past, Alex," Aya said, interrupting their little trip down memory lane. "It's gone and cannot be changed. The present and the future is all anyone has."

He groaned and ran an unsteady hand over his face. "I'm not sure what to say to that."

"Courage," the hybrid said. It was the same thing he'd told himself earlier.

Once Aya had completed her trench, she threw the branch aside and stood back to observe.

"Are you ready?" Gabby asked him.

"Ready as I'll ever be."

Gabby stood and raised her hands. There was a

sudden whoosh of scorching air and the night lit up with an orange glow. Alex looked around, eyes wide with awe as a circle of flame sprung to life in Aya's haphazard ditch, encircling the three of them. He'd never seen Gabby practice before, not like this, and it was something else.

"Give me your hand," she said, picking up the knife.

"My hand?"

She gestured for him to come forwards and he held out his hand, palm up. Without blinking, Gabby dragged the blade across his skin, opening up a long red gash. Hissing at the sudden pain, he curled his hand into a fist. Blood dripped into the plastic bowl and ironically, he thought, *no salad, then.*

Gabby drew the knife across her palm and together, they let their blood combine in the bowl until both their cuts had clotted.

"Okay, are you ready?" she asked. "I'm going to start the spell now."

All he could do was nod.

Offering him a reassuring smile, Gabby knelt to the ground and picked up the grimoire and started reading. The air tingled around them. He knew she was speaking the witch language, but to him it sounded alien. There was no hope of him understanding it.

For a few minutes nothing else happened and he wondered if the spell was working or if this was it. It was meant to hurt, so why wasn't it? As soon as the thought ran through his mind, a sharp, stabbing pain sliced through his heart.

"*Hell*," he hissed and fell to his knees. His chest felt like it was ripping apart, his heart felt like it swelled to a bursting point, and he panicked. Blood whooshed in his ears, stars prickled his vision, and it took all he had to hold on to reality.

"Don't fight it, Alex," he vaguely heard Aya say.

Of course, he was fighting it. He was dying, but that was the point, wasn't it? His humanity had to die in order for him to be reborn as a vampire. *He had to die.*

Clutching his head in his hands, he drew in sharp breaths, each slicing into his lungs like shards of hot metal. As his vision blurred to black around the edges, he could hear Gabby still speaking the words of the spell over and over until the strange language was all that he knew. Letting it overwhelm him, he trusted Aya's advice and stopped fighting.

Alex breathed out and he swore he felt the moment his heart stopped beating. There was a second of nothing but oblivion, and he thought he could see forever... and then there was silence.

That's the thing about being knocked out, or falling asleep for that matter, because when he finally came to, it always felt like a second had passed. Alex felt all his senses come back long before his eyesight joined the party. Even before he started breathing again, which was a strange sensation. He fought against the current that was weighing him down, searching for the light.

"How long until he comes back?" he heard Aya ask through the fog.

"I'm not sure," Gabby replied. "It could be a minute; it could be an hour. There's no time limit on this."

Fixing on their voices, he willed his eyes to open and when they did, he sat up sharply, gasping for air. As his heart started to beat again, he clutched his chest as the first thud echoed in his ears. How the hell did he even hear that?

"There's your answer," Aya said with a shrug.

"Alex," Gabby knelt forwards, a palm on his forehead, "are you okay?"

"No," he croaked. "That was messed up." He felt like he'd been beaten within an inch of his life, and he could remember a few times he'd been beaten up. The most recent being in the gardens back in Ashburton. It'd been one of Katrin's vampires who pummelled him, and he'd been the bait to lure out his friends. That was also the night he found out about... well, vampires and witches and every other supernatural mumbo-jumbo creature that was living within five yards of his house.

"Is that it?" he asked, wiping his brow.

"Not quite." Gabby held out the bowl that contained their blood and nodded. "Drink. It'll complete the change."

He'd forgotten about that part. The bit with the blood.

Looking at the contents, he felt like throwing up, but as soon as it swirled around in the green plastic bow, a scent washed over him. Grabbing it from her hands, he drank greedily, like he was parched after a day of hard labour in the gardens.

He felt it slide down into his stomach and the moment it hit, he choked as a sharp pain spread through his abdomen. Dropping the bowl, he doubled over and wrapped his arms around himself.

They didn't tell him about this part.

As the pain spread through his body, it felt like he was ripping apart, burning from the inside out—he'd never felt anything so horrible in his entire life. *Better him than Isobel.*

Aya suddenly appeared next to him, cradling his head in her lap, her hand stroking through his hair. "It's going to be okay," she crooned. "It'll pass soon."

He gasped as another spasm ripped through his chest. "Is it supposed to feel like this?"

"You're being reborn," she told him. "Your entire body is changing how it works. It's going to hurt until it's done."

"Let the pain take you, Alex," Gabby said. "Let it take you and it'll feel so much better."

He trusted Gabby with his life and letting his fear

go, he let the pain wash over him as he made the final transition into a founding vampire.

Even as his consciousness stared to fade, he thought about his sister. He had to focus on why he was doing this; why he had sacrificed himself to become the thing he never wanted to be.

Hang on, Izzy, he thought. *I'm coming for you.*

Alex's eyes opened slowly—darkness to the bright light of the night around him. Curling his fingers in the grass on which he laid, he stared up at the sky and wondered why it was so bright.

A thousand, million, trillion stars shone down at him through the canopy of trees above and he wondered if they'd really been there all this time. A slight breeze ruffled the leaves above him and drew his focus a little closer to Earth. Sound pulled his attention in every direction and he couldn't decide which to listen to first. The scurrying of some night dwelling creature, the far-off sounds of cars and trucks on the highway, or a thump-thump sound he couldn't quite place.

After a while, he realised he was hearing a heartbeat. Focusing on the sound, he heard three distinct patterns all intertwined, beating out a complex rhythm. He sat up slowly and squinted as his eyes focused.

"Alex?" He heard a voice call out to him and it was familiar somehow. An image of an olive-skinned woman with wild brown hair came to mind and he turned to find her watching him, concern in her hazel eyes. No, hazel wasn't right. Caramel?

He sighed. "Gabby."

Gabby glanced past him, her shoulders sagging in relief, and he turned to find another woman beside him. Her eyes were so blue, they could be called cold, but he only saw warmth there.

"How do you feel?" Aya asked.

"Overwhelmed." Everything was beating down on him, demanding to be heard, seen, tasted, touched—a high-definition assault.

Aya smiled and rose to her feet, holding out a hand to him. "Let me help you."

Grasping her hand, he stood and marvelled at how fluid it felt.

"We should go back to Isobel's and prepare," Gabby said.

At the mention of Isobel, Alex felt anger sear through him, and the intensity took his breath away. He'd seen Sam and Zac change into their vampire modes on several occasions, but when he felt his teeth start to move, he slapped a hand over his mouth.

"Shit," he hissed, feeling slightly embarrassed.

"Deep breaths," Aya said, holding his shoulders. She understood; of course, she understood. She had issues with controlling this kind of thing, didn't she?

Alex suddenly understood how she felt. It had happened so easily, so fast... One brief mention of his sister's name and his anger almost took him some place he wasn't sure he ever wanted to go.

As he breathed in the crisp air, he felt everything go back to as it should. His teeth seemed to settle and his vision wasn't quite as sharp.

"Okay?" the hybrid asked, and he nodded. "It'll take time, but we're here to help you."

"I know."

Aya wound an arm around his back and helped him walk through the forest back to where Tristan was waiting with the car. He looked around, not quite believing what he was seeing. Reaching out, he brushed his fingers along the trunk of a tree, felt the breeze against his face, and breathed in the earthy scent that hung all around them.

Alex sighed and looked up at the sky again. How had all of this been here and he hadn't noticed it before? All this... *life*.

Aya looked up at him and smiled, her eyes shining bright with laughter. "You're like a baby seeing the world for the first time."

Smiling back, he replied, "That's because I am."

CHAPTER 24

Zac stood with Alex in the lane behind Isobel's apartment, the night slowly giving way to the dawn. He promised he'd help Alex adjust to his new life and now was the only time they had.

He'd been through it with Sam, but it was a whole different game this time. Alex was vastly different than his little brother. They both had kind hearts, but Alex was innocent. Gabby had told him once that Alex was the underdog at school. He was the one that bullies had picked on, and still, he went out of his way to help people after they'd pushed him down. Either that was stupid or incredibly brave. Right now, Zac would bet his last dollar on the fact that those bullies would run the other way. Alex was kind of bad ass.

"I don't feel cold," Alex said, his voice full of disbelief.

"That's normal."

"I'm just so..." He shrugged.

"C'mon." Zac pointed to the roof. "Have a go."

"What, just jump?"

"Yeah, just jump. I'd aim, though."

"I don't..."

"Don't worry about looking stupid," Zac said. "There are worse things than missing. Besides, this is the fun part."

Alex looked up at the roof, three stories above, and his jaw tensed.

"Do you want me to go first?" Zac asked with a laugh. "I can catch you."

"No. I've gotta grow a pair."

Zac stood back and watched as Alex stared up at the roof and a moment later, he jumped. A crack signalled his arrival on the roof and what sounded like a couple of broken tiles. With a laugh, he jumped and landed beside Alex. "Nice, huh?"

"That's incredible. I had no idea. I mean, I knew you guys were fast, but it's something else actually doing it."

"We'll go for a run one day. I like to call it the ten second mile."

"That'd screw the Olympics right up."

"Try passing the drug test."

Alex sat on the topmost part of the roof and Zac perched beside him. For a while they just stared out over the city, keeping their thoughts to themselves. What a screwed-up world that it had to come to this to save everyone. Zac had done a lot of stupid things since moving home—and treating Alex like an annoying ant was one of them. He guessed he owed him one hell of an apology.

"I'm sorry, Alex," he said wryly.

"What for? There's a lot of stuff, so you have to be more specific."

He let out a laugh. "Yeah, well, all of it, I suppose. I was an ass to you for no reason. I got you messed up in all of this. I got your sister messed up in it. And now you're a vampire. Can't get any shittier than that."

"Nope."

"Remember when you ran over a vampire with my car?"

"Shit, do I," Alex said, running his hand through his hair.

"Shattered the windscreen."

"As if that's a comparison for all of this."

"You know, I never got around to getting it fixed."

They fell silent for a while until Alex waved at the city. "Everything feels... sharp, like the world's suddenly in HD."

"Get used to it."

"I don't remember all these stars being here before," he murmured, looking up at the sky.

"Everything is multiplied ten times now. Sight, smell, sound, even your emotions."

"I feel like I could run for days and not even get tired."

"You're faster and stronger. You'll have to compensate until you get used to it."

"Is this burning normal?" Alex waved at his throat and swallowed hard, like he was trying to get rid of a bad taste.

"Yep. Alcohol helps with that."

"So that's why you're such a boozehound."

"What can I say? I had issues."

"*Had*?"

"I'm dealing."

"Does the burning go away?"

"It gets better with time," Zac replied. "It's like when you were human and your stomach rumbles to tell you you're hungry."

"Great. I think I'd rather the rumbling stomach. This feels like acid reflux."

"It's the thing that some vampires struggle with in the beginning. It's like an itch you can't scratch and until it's sated, it drives you mad. Some never get their heads around it. I had a lot of trouble with it and still do sometimes."

"Does everyone go through it?"

"No." He shook his head. "Sam didn't. I guess because he had someone there to help him."

"You."

Zac grunted. "I won't leave you in the lurch, Alex. I've got your back for however long you want me around."

"However long..." he whispered. "That sounds like

such a weird notion. I've got loads of time now, unless Aed bites me, right?"

"Or you get into a fight with Aya."

"Remind me never to piss her off."

"I don't think you could, even if you tried. She thinks the sun shines out your ass."

"Really?"

"You were the first one of us to give a crap about her for the kind of person she is. I wanted her for what she could do for me, and it took a long time to realise that your approach is a better way of going about things."

"I guess we can learn a lot from each other, right?" Alex asked with a grin.

"Ah, don't get too cocky," Zac said with a laugh and slapped his friend on the back. "You're taking this surprisingly well, you know. I thought this would be a lot harder."

"I guess I'm not the traditional candidate for vampirism, hey?" he asked wryly.

Zac frowned. "We'll be there for you, don't worry about that. You've got a load of support to draw on, and there's no way in hell any of us will let anything happen to you. If we have our way, you'll live a billion years along with the rest of us."

Alex grunted. "I don't want to think about a billion years. Talk to me in a hundred, and I'll give you a status update."

"Vampires have an inflated sense of time. We've got

a lot, so urgency is not high on the agenda. You've got to know when to strike and when to hold back."

"And now is one of those times to strike," Alex said morosely.

"That it is."

Alex glanced at him, wanting to ask something. After a moment of hesitation, he came out with it. "What do I do? I mean, for blood?"

"Find a human, bite, drink."

"I don't like the idea of sucking on some random's neck."

"It gets easier."

"But there's got to be another option, right? Sam and Liz feed on animals..."

"That's all well and good, but feeding on a fluffy bunny rabbit isn't going to keep your strength up in the long run. Listen, feeding straight from humans isn't nice, but it keeps you strong, and we need you strong right now. I'm sorry, it's just the way things are."

"What if I can't stop? What if... what if I hurt somebody?"

"I'll be there to stop you," Zac said. "But you gotta know that being turned by a spell makes you very different from me. You're a lot stronger physically, for one."

"So, you mightn't be able to stop me if I lose it?"

"There's always the chance, but I don't believe it'll be an issue for you. You still care. Sometimes turning can take that away. I've been through it a few times—

the not caring part—and I don't recommend it, but when Aya left me and I went with Regulus... I saw her with Tristan, and I just couldn't take it anymore."

"What did you do?" Alex asked, looking alarmed.

"I just turned it off." He shrugged and looked away. "Once your ability to care is gone, it takes your humanity away."

"But you've come back."

"Yes, but it takes a lot to want to," he explained. "If you don't have anything or anyone to care about, then some vampires never come back. They never have control. They never stop."

"Then how did you? Was it because of Sam?"

"Yes, because of Sam the first few times."

"This time?"

"Aya forced me. She jumped me from behind, snapped my neck, locked me in a dungeon, and tortured me into coming back." Alex stared at him with wide eyes. "It doesn't mean any of that will happen to you. I truly believe it won't."

"It doesn't make me feel any better, though. It's against my nature and believe me, I know how ironic that sounds."

"Don't worry about hurting anyone," Zac told him. "You can compel them to be still so you can feed, heal the wound, and make them forget it all happened."

"Then after all of this is over, I can find some baby kittens."

"That's the spirit," Zac said with a laugh. "There's

always pinching a few bags of blood from a hospital. Done that before. Or get yourself a vampire girlfriend."

"Um, that sounds... kinky?"

Zac snorted. "Doesn't satisfy your hunger a hundred percent, but it sure is satisfying in other ways."

"Too much information, Zac."

"Blood sharing is probably the most intimate you can get with another vampire. Humans have marriage, we have a more screwed-up means of commitment."

"What does it taste like? Blood?"

"It's hard to describe," Zac replied. "Everyone tastes different."

"What do you mean?"

"It's like you can taste the kind of person they are— sweet or sour; good or bad. I guess it's something you have to experience for yourself. You'll like it. It's how you are now."

"How I am now," Alex echoed, dropping his head into his hands, stifling a sob. "What have I done?"

"Hey," Zac said. "It's messed up, I know, but think about Isobel. Think about her, because right now, you're her only hope. You can spend all your time agonising over the fact your life has changed, or you can spend that energy on the task at hand. There's plenty of time for moping after she's safe and sound. Anyway, I won't let you be a mopey bastard."

Alex sniffed. "What the hell happened to you? Did Gabby replace your brain or something?"

"I got a reality check," Zac told him honestly. "I've been through my fair share of woe. If any good can come of it by sharing with you, then so be it."

"I'm just worried about Izzy. Aed seemed to think she was his lost love. What if he's turned her into a vampire? What if he's hurt her? I'm suddenly this powerful founding vampire and I'm just sitting here."

"You have to have hope, Alex. That's the only thing that gets you through. I was the master of diving in headfirst and asking questions later. Take it from me when I say we need to plan this. The only way we're going to get one up on Aed is with a solid, airtight strategy. Besides, did you see the way he looked at her? I don't think he'd hurt a hair on her head. He said he wanted her to remember. Whoever this Siobhan is, he loved her and cared enough to give her time."

"I hope so. I really do. I don't think I could ever forgive myself if we were too late."

"It's not your fault. Gabby told you about it. Isobel would've been in a lot more trouble if we didn't show up when we did. We all would have."

"It doesn't make it any better."

Zac sighed, worried about him. If his state of mind was slipping, then it could mean trouble. Alex was the perfect candidate and their only one. If he faltered at the last minute, it could mean everything was over for real. "When the Three get here in a few hours, we'll meet up at the warehouse that Aya and Tristan found.

There's no use worrying about it until then. You're just working yourself up."

Alex sighed sharply, rubbing his eyes. "Then tell me a story to take my mind off it. You've probably seen a lot of stuff. Tell me something."

"Nye's got some zingers," Zac said. "He's lived a lot longer. Aya still doesn't like to talk about her past, so don't even ask. I'm sure their stories are a lot nicer than mine."

"What about Tristan? Do you guys still hate each other?"

"No," Zac said, shaking his head. "We've got a shaky alliance these days."

"I want to hear one of yours. I've known you for a while now, but I don't really know you, if you get my meaning. Sam mentioned once that you enlisted in the army?"

Zac grimaced at the memory. "I died in the Civil War and for a long time, I thought killing was the only thing I was good at... it was the only thing I knew. I spent most of my vampire life enlisting in wars. In part because of that belief, and because I couldn't curb my bloodlust. I used it as an excuse. If I was fighting and killing the bad guys, then it was okay. It wasn't, it never will be."

"What made you stop?"

"The last time I enlisted, I went to Vietnam. I thought I'd seen all the brutality that humans were capable of, but I was wrong." He shifted on the rooftop, glancing at Alex. "Are you sure you want to hear this? It's not exactly award-winning stuff here."

"I guess it helps me understand you better. You're a complex guy."

Zac smiled wryly. That was an apt description if he ever heard one. "Napalm," he said, casting his gaze away.

"Napalm?"

"Some people called it sticky fire. Once it was lit and adhered to something like buildings, forests... people, it was almost impossible to stop. When I saw it used against the enemy and innocents, I just threw my gun down and walked away."

"Right there?" Alex's eyes were wide. With fear, horror, admiration... who the hell knew.

"Right in the middle of a mission. I just turned around and never looked back. Their suffering was horrendous and even with all my strength and speed, there was nothing I could do to stop it. That was the day I decided to start trying again."

"I had no idea."

"*Be the change you want to see in the world...*" Zac said, remembering something Sam had told him once. He was sure his little brother had gotten that nugget of wisdom from someone a little more prolific. "It's the simplest thing in the world, and it took me another forty years to understand it."

"I think I get it," Alex murmured. "Right now, I feel this sadness... I don't know how to explain it, but it's deeper than anything I've ever felt. It's almost overwhelming."

"And that's what it's like to be a vampire holding on to your humanity. It's a constant struggle."

"I'm sorry," he blurted.

"What for?"

"I never understood how hard you had it. How much you must have struggled every day. I'm sorry I was so quick to brand you as an asshole."

Zac shook his head, surprised that Alex felt the need to apologise at all. "I *was* an asshole."

"I'm still sorry." And that was why Alex made the perfect founding vampire.

"If you ever need anything, Alex, put me on speed dial, okay?"

Alex smiled and thumped him on the back. "You've got yourself a deal."

CHAPTER 25

Aya watched Zac and Alex on the rooftop and smiled.

They really made an odd couple, but if anyone was equipped to help Alex with his change, it was Zac. After everything he'd been through in the last one hundred and seventy years, he had a lot of wisdom to share. All the highs and lows a vampire could experience.

Since day one, Alex had been the most selfless one of them all. Innocent in every aspect, he was the perfect founding vampire... and the perfect human. It was ironic that with all the combined power that was assembling in Oxford tonight, that Alex was the one who was going to save them all.

She couldn't help but smile when she saw him jump from the roof and land across the street. He had a great landing for his first try. He turned and saw her watching him and shrugged.

"Hey," she called out.

"Hey."

Crossing the street, she said, "Nice landing."

"Thanks, I think. It'll take some getting used to."

She didn't want to ask, considering it would be the one everyone asked him for a while, so she cocked her head to the side.

"I'm fine," he said with a thin smile. "I'm going inside to see Gabby. Zac's still on the roof."

"Thanks." Before Alex could leave, she grabbed his arm and pulled him back. To his surprise, she circled her arms around his waist and leaned her head against his chest. She gave him a squeeze before letting him go. "We'll be in soon."

Nodding, Alex stepped back and disappeared inside the apartment block. On the outside he seemed to be taking things really well, but since Aya had the unfortunate ability to sense emotions, she knew under the surface was another story. With a frown, she jumped to the roof, curious to see what Zac thought about it.

He looked up as she landed, a little more delicately than Alex had done before, and she felt at least a little guilty that she'd spied on their training session.

"How is he?" she asked, sitting beside him.

"As well as can be expected," Zac said, winding an arm around her back.

"His emotions are all over the place," she mused, burying into his side.

"They always are in the beginning, and he has a lot of pressure to deal with at the moment."

Aya sighed, curling her fingers through Zac's. He always had this knack for calming her down just when she needed it, and she needed it now.

"You're worried about him?"

"I'm worried he will hesitate at the last moment," she said. "He's too kind, too compassionate. I'm afraid he won't do what he needs to."

"We'll be there to help him."

"I know."

They sat in silence for a while, pondering what was about to come. She'd just gotten Zac back and had almost lost him again yesterday. He wasn't as indestructible as Aya, no matter what he seemed to think. She'd spent so much time and effort pushing him away in the beginning, but now he was here, and there was nothing she wouldn't do to save him. Without even asking, she knew he felt the same and wasn't that what love was? Trust, selflessness, compassion?

She looked up at him. "I'm worried about you too, you know."

"You don't need to be," he said, glancing at her in the greying light.

"You said it yourself, Aed almost had you if not for Isobel. I can't lose you, Zac. Not now, not ever."

"Hey," he murmured, sliding a hand over her cheek. "I'm not going anywhere without a fight."

"It took me a long time to find you. I'm not willing to take any chances."

He tilted her chin up and pressed his lips to hers. With a small moan, she kissed him back, her hands curling into the lapels of his coat. It was too easy to get lost in this and it was too easy for it all to be taken away. She'd lost him once and never wanted to go through that again.

"Aya," Zac murmured, pulling away. "We'll always have worry in our lives, but with each other, we can do anything."

"Anything?" she asked, tilting her head to the side.

His lips curved into a sly grin and he brushed a thumb over her lips. "Pretty much."

"I intend to take you up on that offer once this is all over."

"I intend to allow you."

"I'm going to take you places you've never been, Zac Degaud."

"Shit," he hissed. "I knew you were bad, but never wicked."

With a smile, she pressed her lips to his again and when they parted, they were breathless.

"Faith, Aya," he whispered. "We'll get through this. All of us."

"I hope you're right."

"C'mon," he said, rising to his feet. "It's time to rock 'n' roll."

A sense of dread settled in her heart and as Aya

took Zac's hand, she hoped it wasn't a premonition. She had the curse of living on while everything around her withered and died—and she would even outlive the immortal if she chose to. But despite all of that, she knew she would do whatever it took to protect Gabby, Tristan, Zac, and Alex from Aed. They'd become her family when she was sure she'd never get to have one again. Forever and always, they were the people she'd die her true death for.

Gabby looked up at the warehouse that sat on the outskirts of Oxford for the second time in as many days.

Had it really been yesterday she'd stood here, gleaning information out of Aed's compelled vampire? Looking at the time on her cellphone, she supposed it was actually three days ago now. It was well past midnight and she yawned despite herself. It would be a while yet before she could get some sleep. It was a sad feeling to know she was the only human left among her friends, except for Isobel.

Tristan appeared beside her and she smiled as he offered her his arm. She regretted that she hadn't had the chance to get to know him a little better, especially since Aya seemed to hold him in such high regard.

As they weaved their way through the dark warehouse, four figures slowly came into focus through the shadows. She recognised Nye immediately —he had that kind of presence about him—and she'd met Maddox the day before when they'd gone to get Katrin's grimoire. The other two men she supposed were the other members of the Three, Pyke and Rix. Dropping Tristan's arm, she glanced at Alex, who grimaced in return. He didn't need to say anything. She felt exactly the same way.

"How's your face?" Nye asked with a laugh, slapping Zac on the shoulder.

"Flawless, thanks for asking," the vampire replied, and the air seemed a little less heavy.

They really were a sight. The newborn founder Alex, and the Celestine hybrid Aya, stood beside her. Then there was Zac, Tristan, and Nye, otherwise known as the good guys. And finally, there were the Three—a.k.a the bad guys—Maddox, Pyke, and Rix. Add her to the mix, and there was an entry for the history books.

"What's the plan?" Nye asked. "I assume you've got something cooked up?" He glanced at Gabby.

They were all looking at her and the gravity of the situation laying on her shoulders was crushing.

Straightening up, she said, "The only way we're getting close is if Aed is weak."

"How do you suppose we're going to do that?" Maddox asked, the petulant lit in his voice was annoying the hell out of her. If he thought her ideas were stupid before she'd even voiced them, then why didn't he offer his own? Oh, that's right, *he didn't have any*.

"We can't rely on my power or strength," Aya said, narrowing her eyes at the assassin in warning. "We need another way."

"Celestine blood weakens him," Zac said, taking her hand. "When he took a bite out of me, he threw it up like I'd poisoned him."

"Then we find a way to get some into him," Gabby said. "Fill syringes and shove it down his throat if we have to. With the glyphs I learned from Alisandra's grimoire, it should be enough to bring him down to our level."

"I hope so," Aya said with a grimace.

"And what does he do?" Maddox asked, pointing at Alex.

Gabby scowled at the assassin. "He rips out Aed's heart."

"I— Wait, *what*?" Alex exclaimed.

"Was that a good idea?" the assassin asked with a roll of his eyes. "Making *him* a founder?"

"It was the *only* choice." Gabby stood to face the vampire; the warning clear in her stance. They couldn't afford trouble and Maddox was the worst kind.

"Maddox, leave it be, mate," Nye said, putting a hand on the assassin's shoulder.

"It may be that we all have to hold him down to subdue him," Tristan said.

"A pile of vampires?" Nye asked with a laugh. "Stacks on."

Gabby shook her head at the latest joke from the spy. "Regulus said there was a reason there were six founders."

"We don't have six founders," Rix said, finally speaking up.

"We have as many as we're getting," Aya told him. "There's no way in hell we're creating more founders, and we don't have the time anyway. We have a chance at doing this right and we're taking it."

"Isobel is counting on it," Alex said thinly.

"Right, the human girl," Maddox sighed dramatically.

"She's my sister, asshole," Alex hissed and before anyone could stop him, he was across the room, pushing the assassin against the wall, breathing hard through his teeth.

"Hey, settle down," Maddox exclaimed, holding both his hands out like he was trying to calm a wild beast.

"Alex." Aya was beside him, her long fingers prying his away from where they were fisted in Maddox's shirt. "You need to calm down. I know it's hard, but you have to hold on, okay?"

"See?" Maddox exclaimed, shoving Alex back. "He can't even control himself."

"I can do it," Alex said, ignoring everyone else, his eyes fixed on Gabby's.

"I know you can," she replied.

"Okay, so we find out where he is hiding, then we figure out how to get to him," Zac said, changing things back to the task at hand. "It's all well and good planning his demise, but we have to get our hands on him first."

"Zac's right," Gabby agreed. "I'll track Aed first, then we can work out the bit in between."

"So, what happens once we come face to face with him?" Pyke asked. "What do we do?"

"Rix, you'll cover Alex," Zac said, taking point. "You were a bodyguard in a past life. Once Aed realises Alex has turned, he'll go straight for him."

The vampire nodded. "Aye."

"He's our one ace and doesn't have the experience we do." Zac glanced at Alex. "You need a little protection, no offence."

Alex shrugged. "None taken."

Zac nodded. "The rest of us will keep him busy until Gabby can cast her glyphs."

"And we'll try to stick him with some Celestine blood," Nye said with a twinkle in his eye.

"How do the glyphs work?" Aya asked.

"I need four glyphs around him," Gabby explained. "The fifth I need to cast on his body. That'd be the part where you hold him down."

"Once you've done that, that's when I... rip his heart out?" Alex asked with a frown.

"Yes." She caught Aya's frown out the corner of her

eye and hoped Alex didn't notice. The hybrid was worried, and that made her hesitate. "Aed needs to be dismembered and burned to ash, just to be sure."

"I can do that part," Maddox said with a wicked smirk.

Gabby bet he would take great pleasure in it and couldn't wait until she could see the back of him.

"Right, if we're done for the moment, I need to get a bite to eat," Rix said, elbowing Pyke.

"I think we all should," Tristan added.

"I'll take you to feed," Zac said to Alex. "You'll need it more than the rest of us."

"We meet back here in one hour," Aya said and glared at the Three. "Don't be late, or I'm reserving the right to kill you myself."

"I'm good," Nye said, nodding towards Gabby. "I'll hang here."

Gabby watched the vampires depart and wrapped her arms around herself with a shiver. Nye offered her a lopsided smile as she sat on a crumbling brick wall. Closing her eyes, she cleared her mind best she could and reached out into the void, searching for the one man she didn't want to find.

CHAPTER 26

Aed had found a perfect house in the middle of the English countryside. A stately manor with a skeleton household staff who were employed to keep the property in order over the winter until its owner's return in the summer.

A home fit for a prince and a home fit for his one true love... until they could find something more suitable for his plans. He'd slaughtered the staff and made them his own, and the grounds were now protected as well as he could manage.

He knew it was a sign the moment he'd seen Siobhan at the university library a week ago. The blood of the founder, Regulus, had compelled him to come for the grimoire that held the key to his demise, and it was her he'd seen entering the vault where it was kept. It was fate. He would go back to Oxford and get the grimoire, but for today, he would watch over

Siobhan and see her rested. A day was nothing in the shadow of three thousand years.

His thoughts went back to the day before, when he'd followed Siobhan on the street. The human man who'd been with her had called her Isobel. *What a curious name.* He longed to taste her blood, to read into her human life, but he found himself reluctant. He didn't want to hurt her, despite her humanity, which he found so insulting.

Now she was asleep in the best room of the house, resting from her ordeal.

Aed sat on the edge of the bed and let his gaze wander across Siobhan's features, taking her in. She had died a long time ago and to add to the madness of this world, his love had been reborn human. It wasn't like there was another option for nature to take. Their kind were extinct, and the life they were destined to live was a mere fabrication. He would not rule the Tuatha and he would not have Siobhan stand at his side as his queen. He would not rule as he was supposed to, but he would still rule another kingdom—the human one.

Siobhan stirred, her eyelids fluttering, and he resisted the temptation to reach out and run his fingertips across the soft skin of her cheek. He regretted having to compel her, but there was no other way to calm her down. The poor girl had been terrified of him, but it was no wonder. Aoife had turned him into a monster with red eyes that lusted after blood, and Siobhan did not remember him... but she would in time. He'd help her remember, even if it took forever, even if it forced him to make her like him.

Siobhan's eyes eased open as she slowly woke from her slumber and he looked down at her with a smile. She was just as beautiful as he remembered. Her long, flowing red hair, the colour of a flaming sunset, her hazel eyes, her perfect pink lips. He remembered what she could do with those.

She licked her lips and peered up at him and he knew she still didn't remember.

"Are you thirsty?" he asked with a frown.

She nodded, her eyes wide, but they never left him.

"You," he said, clicking his fingers at a slack-jawed man who was standing in the corner. "Fetch some water for your mistress and be quick about it."

The man shuffled from the room, closing the door behind him.

"I'm sorry I scared you," he murmured. "But I had to take you when I had the chance."

Siobhan just stared at him, the terror he'd seen yesterday still in her eyes. She opened her mouth to speak, but no words came forth.

"I know you have a lot of questions and I am willing to answer as many as I am able, but you first have to ask them."

"Who are you?" she rasped.

"I am Aed," he said, trying not to let his disappointment show. "We were to be married once."

"M-married?"

"Yes. You were to be my princess and one day, my queen."

The door opened and the man came back in and her eyes jerked away from his.

"Who is that?" she asked, flinching as the butler set a jug of water on the bedside table.

"He's the help," Aed said. "Reanimated, of course. I can't have an inferior race in here doing whatever that want."

"But..." she began but halted as if she was going to say something she didn't want him to hear.

"But what, my love?" She clutched the blankets around her like they were some kind of shield. "You don't have to be frightened of me. You can tell me what you're thinking."

"But can't you compel him? Did you have to kill him?" she whispered. Her entire body tensed as if she was readying herself for a blow.

"He is human, and I cannot allow him in my home."

"But I'm human."

Aed sighed, his eyes searching Siobhan's. "You are, aren't you?" She stared up at him like a frightened animal, like a baby fawn in the forest, innocent and naïve. "You don't need to be frightened of me." He reached out and pried her fingers from the blankets and pulled her into his lap. She cried out and tried to push away, but he was far too strong for her.

He cradled her in his arms, breathing in her alien scent, relishing the feel of her against his chest. Her hair smelled like some kind of flower he didn't recognise, the sweetness already ingrained into his memory. Aed supposed he would have to make fresh ones now.

"What do you want from me?" Siobhan asked, her voice muffled against his neck.

"I want your love," he replied and pressed his lips against the top of her head. "I want your love and when I have it, we will rule this world together. We will have our revenge, and the world with run red with our triumph."

There was no denying it. Aed was bat-shit crazy.

He held her in his arms like a lover, like he knew every intimate part of her body, and it scared her to death. Gabby and the others had warned her that he was unstable, but this was another level.

"Please get dressed, Siobhan," Aed murmured. "I have instructed some breakfast be prepared for you. I know you must be famished."

"Breakfast?" she asked, a little worried as to what that might entail.

"Yes. I understand that you need to eat real food, my love."

He set her down on the edge of the bed and rose,

his stature a little dominating for her tastes. Leaning down, he caressed her cheek with a powerful hand before tucking a strand of hair behind her ear.

"Breakfast will be served downstairs in the dining room shortly," he said. "Don't be late." Then, in the span of a blink, he was gone.

Isobel looked around the room, but she was alone. Her clothes were folded on top of the dresser and she cringed a little at the nightgown she wore, wondering who'd put it on her. The last thing she remembered was being in the hybrid's arms, flying over rooftops, trying to fight him, the *terror*... Then he'd set her down in the woods and...

He'd obviously done that freaky eye thing to put her to sleep. There was nothing she could do. If she fought him again, he'd just make her stop.

Not wanting to push Aed any further, she quickly dressed and cracked open the bedroom door, peering out into the hallway. A set of eyes peered right back, and she let out a yelp of surprise and stumbled back. The door eased open revealing the zombie-butler staring at her with dead eyes.

"Hell," she hissed at him. "Do you have to be so creepy?"

He just continued to stare. She wasn't sure if he could still speak, let alone understand her question, but he'd followed Aed's order. Maybe it had to do with his weird fairy power?

Isobel shivered and her skin prickled with

revulsion as she edged past the butler. It wasn't the poor guy's fault he was dead, but it still freaked her out. He followed her down the hallway with a lumbering gait and when she got to the bottom of the stairs, she turned to watch him. Surprisingly, he was pretty sure on his feet for a dead man.

When he reached the bottom, Isobel felt her curiosity spike and she reached out and poked him in the chest. Nothing happened, of course. He just stared at her, waiting for her to continue to the dining room.

"Siobhan," Aed called out, "leave the help alone."

Startled, she looked around and found Aed standing in the foyer and she grimaced. "Sorry?"

"Come." He offered her his arm and reluctantly, she took it.

He led her through the house, and she studied the eighteenth-century décor as they went by. The entire house was a thing of the past, full of antique paintings and furniture, and the only modern fixtures were the electric lights and heating that'd been wired through every room. Whoever the actual owner was, they were filthy rich.

The dining room was just as lavish at the rest of the house, with a long table made from mahogany and a crystal chandelier hanging from the high celling. The walls were lined with English countryside landscapes and at one end, an enormous portrait of a black stallion took up most of the space.

Aed sat her down at the head of the table at a place

setting for one, with what looked like to be the best silver and crystal in the house. He sat beside her, his graceful motions almost cat-like. He was a predator in every sense of the word—a dangerous, unpredictable predator.

It was a woman this time who shuffled into the room, her black dress and white apron marking her as the maid, but that's not what made her stare. Her apron was speckled with drops of dried blood and her face was pale to the point it was almost blue. *Another corpse reanimated by Aed's creepy Fae power, then.* The zombie-maid set a plate of food in front of her and to her surprise, it actually looked edible. Glancing up at Aed, he gestured for her to eat.

"It's quite edible," he confirmed. "She might be what you call a zombie, but she is still quite capable of cooking a meal."

Tentatively, she poked at the plate of bacon and scrambled eggs. A plate of toast and a glass of orange juice appeared, and she almost dropped her fork when she caught sight of the maid's sickly bluish-grey hands. How could she eat anything that was prepared by a walking corpse? *Gross.*

Aed leaned back in his chair and folded his arms across his chest, watching her every movement like she was some kind of toy. Waiting for her to slip up or for her to give in and remember some past life she was sure didn't exist. His red eyes freaked her out and the longer he stared, the more her stomach churned.

"Eat," he said a little too forcefully when she didn't move.

Isobel jumped at his sharp tone, picked up her fork, and stuffed a mouthful of eggs into her mouth. If she had to choose between suffering Aed's wrath or eating eggs made by a dead woman, she'd take the eggs every single time.

All Isobel could do was play along with Aed's whims and hope Gabby, Alex, and the others would find her before it was too late. She knew her brother, and he would've made Gabby turn him by now. They'd be plotting Aed's death. *They had to be.*

There was no hope of escape on her own and if she tried and failed, she'd either die or he'd lose interest and turn her. And if he turned her into a vampire, then what kind of monster would she become with his blood in her veins? Somehow, she knew she'd rather die before letting that happen.

Shivering, she cast her gaze down and ate her breakfast and prayed Alex would hear her prayers. He was her only hope.

CHAPTER 27

Gabby stood on the side of a lonely back road, looking out across England. A thick mist had settled over the countryside, trees and fences looming out of the whiteness like ghostly figures. The Cotswolds were the country getaway spot for the rich and richer, full of stately manor homes, both new and historical. It seemed fitting that Aed had found himself a place to live here. He was royalty, after all.

She thought of Regulus and wondered if he would be proud of her, standing on the cusp of completing his life's work. She wondered if she listened hard enough, if she could feel him watching over her. Casting her hearing out, all she got was the overwhelming presence of Aed. Gabby missed Regulus terribly, more than she ever thought possible.

She stood on the rise of the hill, the group of miss-matched vampires around her, looking at the roof of the manor house that peeked through the mist.

Manicured hedges framed frost-tinged lawns and a long, gravel driveway led up to the entrance where a granite fountain sat—any water that'd once flown through it, silent. It looked like something out of a Jane Austen field adaption, though there was no Mr. Darcy in sight.

"Bastard sure knows how to live it up," Nye said with a scowl.

"Do you suppose it was empty before he came along?" Gabby asked, her voice muffled in the heavy air.

"Maybe, maybe not," Aya said. "As far as I can tell, nothing lives down there, but that doesn't mean anything. Perhaps someone is inside."

"Better check if we can get in first," Tristan said. "Hate to get to the door and be denied."

"I'll wait and see before I cast the glyphs," Gabby offered.

"You said you needed four of them," Zac said, appearing at her side.

"Yes. One at each corner of the house on the outside should be enough."

"I'll come with you," he told her. "I've got a strange feeling something is waiting for us down there."

"You mean other than Aed?" Nye asked.

Aya glanced at Zac, understanding flashing through her features. "He may have resurrected a few friends to protect the house."

"Oh great," Nye exclaimed. "Zombies? Are you kidding me?"

"No, I am not kidding you," the hybrid drawled.

"Does everyone know the plan?" Zac asked. "If there's any questions, now's the time to ask. We've only got one shot at this."

Everyone was silent and Gabby took that as a yes. They'd been over and over it, and it was simple enough but mistakes were totally out of the question.

As they moved out, she grabbed Alex's hand and pulled him back. "Good luck," she whispered, tears welling in her eyes.

He threw his arms around her and hugged her tightly. "Thanks. You, too."

Instead of approaching from the driveway, they took the scenic route through the field and over the fence onto the manor grounds.

"I don't like this," Tristan said. "It's too quiet."

"Yeah," Maddox said with a hint of sarcasm, "I thought there'd be a little resistance. A chance to get my hands dirty."

"You'll get it soon enough," Zac told him.

"Eyes open for zombies," Nye said, putting in his two cents. "Stay here and I'll check the threshold."

They lingered behind a box hedge as the spy dashed across the open drive and past the fountain. He twisted the doorknob and glanced back at Gabby, who was peeking through the bottom of the hedge. The door creaked open ever so slightly and the spy peered through before testing the threshold. His hand went through without any problems and he gave everyone a thumbs up.

Gabby didn't wait to see if everyone got inside. She led Zac to the far corner of the manor, weaving through the garden. As they reached the house, they ducked underneath windows.

It was oddly quiet for the home of an insane Tuatha prince. The air was thick with mist, but it was also thick with the cliché of foreboding.

Reaching the first corner, she placed her hand on the bluestone and started casting the first glyph, tendrils of power seeping through her skin into the masonry. When it was done, she nodded at Zac before they continued to the next corner.

The mists were lifting as the morning progressed and the sun was shining through. It would be clear skies today, the first since she'd arrived. As more of the grounds were revealed, the emptier they looked. Surely, it couldn't be that easy? Rather than look a gift horse in the mouth, she cast the second glyph. When she pulled her hand away, she glanced at Zac. He was starring off into the distance, his face contorted into a scowl.

"What is it?" she asked.

"I can't tell for sure, but I think we have company."

There was a loud crash from inside the house and they both looked at each other, knowing their friends were counting on them.

"Let's go," she said and ran towards the far corner of the house. Before she could get to the end, a figure launched itself from the hedges around the rear garden, arms outstretched. Gabby skidded to a halt as the man tried to grab her, but Zac was there, shoving him away.

"Guess we know what happened to the groundskeeper," he said wryly as the man stumbled backwards.

The man seemed to lack any semblance of dexterity, so it took him a while to steady himself and when he did, he lumbered forwards again. Zac grabbed the zombie's head and in one fluid motion, smashed it against the wall of the house.

"Go," he said to her. "I've got your back."

Zac was beside her as they went for the third corner and as she slapped her hand against the wall, three more zombies lurched towards them. Her heart sped up and the glyph melted away in her hands.

Damn. She couldn't let fear get the best of her, not now.

Closing her eyes, she tuned out the sound of the vampire struggling with the three undead men and casted the glyph into the fabric of the house. The power pulled away from her skin and it was done.

Her eyes snapped open and she looked frantically for Zac, but he was standing beside her, his hands covered in blood.

"Next," he said with a shrug.

The fourth glyph was easier and closer to their location. She nodded at Zac once it was complete.

He took her hand, the blood tacky against his skin, and squeezed. "For Regulus."

Gabby was a little taken aback but smiled anyway. "Let's get the bastard."

Aya watched as Zac and Gabby disappeared into the mist, a pang of worry stabbing into her heart.

"They'll be okay," Tristan murmured in her ear.

"I know, but I still worry."

"C'mon," he said, coaxing her forwards, "let's end this once and for all."

Aya lifted a hand and caressed her friend's cheek. "Let's go."

As soon as they walked into the foyer, the air shifted and Aed appeared at the end of the hall. Suits of armour gleamed in the half light, like they were ready to come alive at the hybrid's call. Luckily for them, they were empty.

"I thought I smelled you, Celestine," he drawled. Isobel appeared behind him and Aed grabbed her, holding her small body against his chest. "You're not going to take her away from me again. I will fight to the end to keep her."

"She's not your long-lost lover, Aed," Aya said. "Let her go."

With an annoyed roar, Aed pushed Isobel aside and lunged for Aya, but his hand smacked into thin air as she let her power flare, lighting the room with a blue hue, before it faded away just as quickly.

"We cancel each other out, remember?" she leered. "Your power is useless in this fight."

Isobel cowered against the wall, her eyes wide with fear. When they latched onto Alex, Aya caught the sudden wave of hope that washed over her.

"Who is this?" Aed asked, tilting his head to the side, his gaze firmly on Alex.

Rix's shoulders squared and he moved in front of the founder.

"Oh, I see," the hybrid declared, turning to look at Isobel. "You found the grimoire."

"Time's up," Aya said stalling, knowing Gabby needed to be here before they restrained him. "Any last words?"

"Last words?" Aed scoffed. "You're the one who needs last words, Celestine *scum*."

"You can't kill me, but I'd like to see you try."

"No, I cannot kill you," he said, eyeing her, "but I can kill *him*."

Aed's eyes misted over red as he lunged for Alex, but Rix was in the way, steeled for this exact thing. It was his duty to protect their last chance at ending the Tuatha, but he wasn't fast enough. He would never be fast enough.

Aed's hand punctured Rix's chest and he flung the

vampire across the room like he was nothing but a rag doll. As Rix rolled to a stop, his eyes glazed over, blood pooling beneath his body. Maddox roared in pure anger as his friend desiccated and turned on the hybrid.

"You'll pay for that," the assassin roared, and he threw himself at Aed, fangs bared, looking for the kill. He wasn't going to get it, but there was no stopping him. Aed ducked, ramming his shoulder into the vampire's gut and sent him flying. Maddox landed over the staircase bannister and there was a loud crack as his spine snapped in two. He half-slid, half-rolled down the stairs, and when he reached the bottom, he was out for the count.

Nye nodded at Tristan. "Stick him."

Tristan flew across the foyer and stabbed the needle into Aed's arm. They hybrid pushed him away, but it was too late. Aya's blood merged with his and he stumbled, looking bewildered.

"*Poison*," he hissed, pulling the syringe from his arm and casting it aside.

Nye appeared behind him and rammed another into his neck. "Tasty, huh?"

"*Fools*," Aed roared, shoving Nye aside. His gaze fixed on Alex and he advanced.

"It's done," Gabby said, stepping into the room.

"*You*." Aed stopped mid-stride and snarled at the witch.

"Yes, *me*, and this time, you won't be so lucky."

Aed stepped towards her, but Gabby's appearance was their signal. It was time to get down to business.

Tristan and Nye grasped Aed's arms from behind, and Zac and Pyke used their strength to push him down onto his back. Aed landed with a thud, a vampire holding each limb, and Aya straddled him, curling her hands around his throat. The moment she touched him, all his malice slammed into her with enough force to take her breath away.

Aed struggled against them, his anger seething through his skin right into her heart. Her eyes changed as she struggled to keep her control and Gabby was in front of her. The witch slapped a hand on Aed's forehead and began to cast the fifth glyph.

"*Bitch*," Aed hissed, baring his fangs. "I will rip you to shreds, little girl."

"You'll have to get your hands on her first," Aya snapped, her fangs beginning to lengthen as the hybrid's anger infected her senses.

Gabby snatched her hand away and scrambled backwards. "It's done."

"Alex," Aya called, looking up at him. She knew she was a terrible sight to behold, but when she saw the blind terror on his face, her anger swelled even more. "Alex. *Do it now.*"

He hesitated and she felt like throttling him as well. Her Celestine power simmered in response and the air charged around her.

"*Alex*," she shrieked.

Aya's cry was enough to snap Alex into action.

Stepping forwards, he looked down at Aed, who was struggling with all his strength. He was just meant to rip his heart out... Just like that? He'd never hurt anyone in his life...

He went to kneel, but with a roar, Aed pushed against his captors with all his remaining energy and his arms came free. Aya fell backwards with enough force to take Zac and Pyke with her and Aed was loose.

He turned on Alex with blazing red eyes and hissed at him. Instead of going in for the kill, the hybrid grasped the front of his shirt and threw him across the room. The entire thing happened in a handful of seconds, even before his friends could stumble to their feet.

Alex expected to hit the wall and fall to the ground, but a sharp pain ripped through his stomach and his body fell limply, feet dangling in the air. A long blade protruded from his gut and for a sickening second, nothing happened. Then blood poured from the wound and dripped onto the floor below.

Swatting numbly at the blade, Alex realised he'd been impaled on one of the halberds that were being held by a suit of armour against the wall.

His gaze met Isobel's and she was white. It must be bad. It didn't feel bad. Not yet, anyway. Did vampires feel shock?

A figure stepped into his line of vision, obscuring his sister, and he focused on Aed. The hybrid looked up at him with a sick look of satisfaction on his face. This was the end, right? He couldn't get down, he couldn't function... This was the part where he died for real this time.

Aed's muscles seemed to coil as he readied himself for the kill, but just as suddenly as he'd broken free, his face fell into shock. A long silver blade protruded through his stomach and he spluttered in surprise, blood spraying from his mouth and running down his chin.

The entire room fell silent as all eyes fell onto Isobel. She stood behind the hybrid, a look of crazy determination on her face, her small hands wrapped around the hilt of the sword.

Aed swung around with a grunt, the sword well and truly lodged in place, his eyes betraying his surprise to find Isobel behind him.

"Siobhan?" he gasped, blood bubbling in his mouth. "*Why?*"

"Why?" she hissed at him. "Because I'm not your girlfriend, you crazy asshole."

Aed fell to his knees, disbelief etched onto his features. He swatted helplessly at the sword, too weak from the glyphs Gabby had cast to pull it out. A pool of blood formed around him as he gasped for air.

Alex looked up as Aya and Zac appeared beside him and nodded. They had to get him down and he supposed it would hurt more taking the halberd out than putting it in. Nye was behind them, bracing the shaft of the weapon as the two vampires heaved.

Gasping in pain, Alex would've fallen to his knees if it wasn't for Aya and Zac. Just as suddenly, the pain started to fade as his body began the healing process. Talk about an itch he couldn't scratch.

"Do it, Alex," Aya said. "It's your last chance."

"Siobhan, please..." Blood dribbled down Aed's chin, his eyes full of tears. "I love you, *please...*"

Alex clutched his stomach, trying not to focus on the weird feeling of his organs and muscles knitting back together. Aed looked up at him, his eyes swirling red and he was a pitiful sight. He believed his lover scorned him, his entire family was dead, he'd lost three thousand years, and his entire race. It was time to put the hybrid out of his misery once and for all.

Alex placed a hand on Aed's shoulder and took a deep breath. Collecting his strength, he pushed his outstretched fingers into the hybrid's chest, the sensation of his hand travelling through flesh and bone making him feel sick. Then he held the hybrid's beating heart in his palm and he gasped. It pumped against his skin and the weight of his responsibility sunk onto his shoulders with a crash.

This was his first kill as a vampire—his first kill *ever*—and what a kill it was.

With a grunt, he grasped Aed's heart in his fingers and pulled. It came free with an awful sucking sound and as soon as it hit air, it dried and crumbled into ash that fell through his fingers like sand. The hybrid fell limply to the floor, eyes open and unseeing, the sword clattering against the floorboards.

Alex hoped he didn't have to do that ever again.

"Alex," Isobel shrieked, throwing herself into his arms. "I knew you'd come. I knew it!"

Embracing his sister, he glanced at Aya, who simply nodded. He took that as confirmation that it was done.

"Maddox," he heard Zac say and a flurry of movement whirled around him, but he was only worried about Isobel.

"Izzy," he breathed. "You stabbed him in the gut with a sword."

"That's nothing," she told him. "You ripped his heart out."

"I didn't enjoy it, you know."

Isobel frowned. "You... you turned."

Alex nodded. "To save you and everyone I care about." After a minute, he choked out, "I'm so proud of you."

"Thank you, Alex," she whispered. "Thank you for everything."

With a sad smile, Alex took Isobel into another room while the others took care of Aed and their fallen friend Rix. Gabby said they needed to hack the hybrid into pieces, which was something he didn't want his sister to see, even though she'd had the guts to impale the guy with a sword.

Alex watched Nye, Zac, and Aya through the window as they built a pyre of wood in the manicured garden and when they stood around waiting, he looked down at Isobel.

"You wanna go outside? You don't have to, you know."

"I want to stay," she replied. "I want to make sure he isn't going to come back and kidnap me again."

With a smile, Alex took her hand and led her out into the garden.

The blue sky the mist had promised was beginning to cloud over. It was England, after all. It wouldn't be right if the sky wasn't grey with a side of drizzle.

Tristan stepped forwards and tipped a can of kerosene over Aed's remains and Rix's wrapped body. They were silent as the knight flicked a lit match into the pile and a whoosh of flames cast heat against their faces.

The vampires and their human and witch friend stood in the yard, bloodied, beaten, and bruised as the flames from the pyre reached into the air.

Looking up, Alex saw the first flakes of snow fall before anyone else noticed. Drawing Isobel closer, he smiled down at her. They were safe and he would protect her and his family forever. This was the last heartache they would ever have to face.

That was his eternity.

CHAPTER 28

Zac sat on the roof over Isobel's apartment. Oxford was well and truly alive, the streets full of people Christmas shopping, spending time with their loved ones, and walking through the multitude of festive markets. It was that time of year and despite how drawn he was, it was infectious.

Aya appeared beside him in that invisible way of hers and he leaned over, burying his face into the crook of her neck. "Hello," he murmured, pressing his lips against her jugular.

"Hello," she replied, breathing in deeply. "You do smell like flowers, you know."

Pulling away, he took in her familiar features—her pale skin that seemed to shimmer in the moonlight, her clear blue eyes, her long black hair. He'd never tire of looking at her.

"Why do you like sitting on the roof so much?" she asked, pressing against him.

He kissed her cheek. "It's quiet up here."

"I know what you mean." She looked up at the sky and frowned. "It's closer to the stars here, but something should be done about those clouds."

Zac laughed, shaking his head.

"What?"

"Are you saying you can move the earth *and* the sky now?"

Aya's eyes crinkled with laughter. "No, not this Celestine."

"Good, you had me worried there."

"Worried?"

"My manly pride couldn't handle it if my girlfriend was *all*-powerful."

Aya shoved him playfully with her shoulder. "Too much responsibility."

"How's everyone?" he asked. He hadn't been around much, and he felt a little guilty, but Gabby needed to rest and Alex needed to spend time with Isobel. Distance and time to recuperate were first on the agenda.

"As well as can be expected," Aya replied. "Nye took Gabby to a hotel and he's looking out for her for the moment. Tristan is watching over Alex and Isobel. Time is what they all need now to process everything, especially Alex."

"I have faith in him."

"Everyone has their own decisions to make as to what happens next."

"And there's no rushing them, either," Zac finished. He understood now more than ever the need for making choices with a clear head.

"What happened to Maddox and Pyke?"

After they'd dispersed from the pyre in the manor grounds, the Two, as he supposed they were now called, disappeared. Both of their promises to help with Aed's demise had been fulfilled, and they were free to go in whatever direction they chose.

"I don't know," Zac replied. "Hopefully, they find whatever it is they're looking for."

"Took them long enough."

"At least they have the chance," he said morosely. "That's all anyone can hope for."

Aya smiled up at him and ran a hand through his hair. "You realise we're free too, right?"

"As free as we'll ever be."

"I still have a promise to keep," she said. "To the witches."

"Of course. I would never ask you to abandon them."

"Would you go with me if I needed to?" Her voice was full of doubt.

"I'll consider it on a case by case basis," he said with amusement.

Aya slapped him on the arm. "Stop it."

"Of course, I'll come with you. I'm never letting you out of my sight again. You're well and truly stuck with me now."

"How unfortunate," she said with a laugh.

"I love you forever and always, Aeriaya."

"I love it when you use my true name, but only in private, okay?"

He wiggled his eyebrows up and down. "Does it turn you on?"

"It takes me places I've never been," she retorted, and Zac laughed at the memory of their conversation on the very same rooftop a few nights ago.

"Where do you want to go first?" Aya asked, tilting her head to the side and his eyebrows rose. They could go anywhere, but there was only one place he wanted to go.

"Let's go to L.A.."

"Let's," Aya echoed, pressing her lips to his.

Zac kissed her back, pulling her as close as he could.

Oxford bustled below and the stars shone beneath their wintery blanket overhead, and he knew he'd made it. The old Zac Degaud was finally gone and the new one was ready to live.

It was time to go home.

Gabby sat at the small table in her hotel room in the middle of Oxford as Nye helped himself to the minibar.

"I hope you're paying for that," she grumbled as he lined up all the little bottles of alcohol.

"You're loaded now, lovely. Why am I paying?" he said with a chuckle.

She'd slept for three days straight and had woken to the spy reading the newspaper in the corner. Seemed he'd stuck around to keep an eye on things after he'd dropped her off. To say she was relieved was an understatement considering the last few months.

Now things were settled, she had the time to properly mourn Regulus and sort through his estate. He'd left her his wealth and what with all the Tuatha hunting, she hadn't processed it at all. She had to go back to London, and she had to convince Nye to come with her. If there was anyone she or Regulus would choose to take over, it'd be him.

"Have you given any thought to my proposal?" she asked, knowing he'd get what she was asking.

The spy looked up at her and winked. "I know your game, lovely."

"Don't you want to play?"

Nye laughed and unscrewed the top off a bottle of vodka. "You're getting wickeder by the day."

"You know you're the only candidate."

"King of the thugs? Me? A lowly spy who got conned by a street urchin?"

The last reference went straight over her head. "You know you want to, Nye. You've wanted recognition your whole life."

"Witches are just bloody trouble if you ask me."

"Times... oh, about a billion." She laughed, kicking him under the table.

He leaned forwards, his eyes on hers. "And you'd support my claim?"

"Yes, and I believe if he were here, Regulus would, too."

"Well," he said, downing the vodka, "when you put it like that... I'll come to jolly old London town with you and I'll think about it on the way."

"*Nye.*"

"Oh, all right. You twisted my arm."

"I did no such thing."

With a lopsided grin, he opened the next bottle and handed it to her. "Cheers, lovely. Long live the king of the thugs." He clinked a little bottle of scotch against hers and they downed the liquor. It burned a trail right down into her stomach, making her cough.

"Lightweight," the spy teased.

Before she could retort, there was a knock at the door. Nye got up and looked through the peephole and his face split into a grin. Flinging the door open, he cast his arms out and chortled, "Zac, my old buddy, my old pal. And the ever lovely Aya with the sharp tongue. Come on in."

"Hey," Zac said, shoving him aside. Aya was close behind and smiled when she laid eyes on the witch.

"How are you feeling?" the Celestine asked, sitting

at the table. Her gaze fell onto the little bottles of alcohol and her eyebrow rose.

"I'm much better since Nye's paying," she explained with a laugh.

"Oh, a toast," Aya said, unscrewing the cap off a little bottle of whisky. "Here's to Nye's money!"

"Hey," Nye exclaimed as she downed the liquor.

"Have you spoken to Sam yet?" Gabby asked Zac, shaking her head at the vampires.

"Who's Sam?" the spy asked.

"He's my brother," Zac explained.

"You have a brother? Like a human one?" Nye cried.

"A human one who was turned shortly after I was."

"Why didn't you tell me?"

"He was also turned by Victoria, and you could imagine what would've happened to him if it became common knowledge that he also had Celestine blood."

"You need to tell him about that, by the way," Aya chipped in.

"Are you going to L.A.?" Gabby asked, her eyes brightening.

"Yes," Zac said with a grin. "On the next flight we can manage."

"Well, you know I have to meet this fellow," Nye said sullenly.

"You're always welcome to visit," Zac said, thumping his friend on the shoulder. "Once you get your kingdom in order."

"I'll be there to rain on your parade, don't you worry, mate."

Zac threw his arms around Nye and thumped him on the back and to everyone's surprise, when they parted, the spy pulled Aya in for a hug, too. Before Gabby could make a smart comment about it, Zac had her in his arms.

"You'll be okay?" he whispered into her ear.

"I'll be fine."

"Nye'll look out for you, you know. And I'm only a phone call away."

"Zac, you don't have to worry about me anymore," she said, pulling back. "Things can only go up from here, right?"

"Sure."

"I'll miss you."

"I'll miss you more than you'll ever know."

"Oh, I think I already know," she said, choking up with tears. "Why does this feel like goodbye?"

"It's not goodbye," Zac said. "It's see you later."

"Damn you, Degaud," she said, wiping away her tears.

"You're crying over me?" he asked, feigning surprise. "Glinda the good witch?"

Gabby slapped him on the arm. "I told you, I prefer Tabitha from Bewitched."

Aya stepped forwards and embraced her. "We'll see each other soon," she said. "After all, you are my sister."

"You're all part of my family now," Gabby said and when Nye rolled his eyes, she laughed. "That means you too, Nye."

"Great," he said with amusement. "It's like I always say—"

"Witches are bloody trouble," they all chorused and fell into fits of laughter.

———

Aya walked hand in hand with Zac down the main street of Oxford, weaving through Christmas-themed market stalls, the scent of mulled wine and roasted chestnuts thick in the air. Her heart swelled with pride and happiness that their long struggle was finally over.

"Are you ready to go?" Zac asked, stopping to buy her a mug of wine. "We can get a flight in the morning."

"I just have one thing I need to do," Aya said, taking the cup from the attendant.

"Get drunk?" Zac asked with a laugh.

"No," she said with a groan. "I need to see Tristan."

Zac said nothing, he just watched her sip the warm liquid.

"I need to make sure he'll be okay. He spent hundreds of years looking for me and now that everything is wrapped up into a neat little package, I just…"

"I know," he replied. "Let's go over to Isobel's then."

As they walked, Aya couldn't help but wonder what Tristan would do now. He'd spent so much time with her in the beginning and when they'd parted, he'd tried to forge a life for himself but his need to find her had overwhelmed everything. It'd resulted in him joining Regulus, the enemy, hoping to find her. She hoped he'd finally find some kind of peace on his own. Whatever he needed, she would help. If Aya had her way, she'd never lose contact with the knight again. This entire experience had taught her that life was fleeting, even for the immortal.

When they reached the apartment, they found Alex and Isobel coming down the stairs.

"Hey," Isobel said brightly.

"Hey yourself," Aya replied, throwing a grin Alex's way. She looked much better; her eyes sparkled and her cheeks were flushed.

"Tristan's upstairs," Alex said. "We're going out for a little while."

"I'll come with for a bit, if you don't mind," Zac said.

"Sure," Isobel declared. Aya knew she'd forgiven him for using her as bait, especially after everything that'd happened at the manor. She'd be the best protected human in history for the rest of her life, and that was just regarding her brother.

Zac kissed her on the cheek and they disappeared outside as she continued up to the apartment. When she opened the door, Tristan looked up and smiled.

"Arrow," he said, standing. "I thought you'd be gone by now."

"How can I leave without saying goodbye to my oldest and dearest friend?"

"You're too good for me," he said with a laugh.

"I think you mean, you're too good for me."

"Never."

Aya sat at the table and leafed through a newspaper that had been left out.

"Are you going back to America with Zac?" Tristan asked, sitting opposite.

"Of course. He and I are one now. What I want to know is what you're going to do?"

"I'm going to stay and help Nye," he said. "He needs it and I have experience."

"You're too good for it, Tristan."

"Arrow, it's a chance to make this place a little less... brutish. Regulus ran things a certain way, with fear and violence, but maybe I can help change that. Now that things are well, I need to find my own place in this world. You have Zac and the witches, but I need somethin' else."

"If you say so."

"I know so."

"Good," she declared. "As long as you're happy."

"I'm not sure about happy, but I'm workin' on it." He stood and pulled her in for a hug.

"Oh," she said as he let her go. "Before I forget, I have one of these now." She pulled out the smartphone

Zac'd bought her that afternoon. She still didn't understand how it worked, but she could no longer deny the thing was useful.

"You have a *phone*?" Tristan asked in surprise.

"Yeah, don't get cocky about it," she said with a laugh. "Zac's teaching me, but I know I'm going to have trouble with this auto-correct thing."

Tristan took the cell phone from her and punched in his number. A moment later, his began to ring. "Now I have your number and you have mine."

It was so normal, exchanging numbers like the friends they were, it made her smile brightly. "You'll really be okay?"

"I'll be perfectly fine," the knight replied. "I've got plenty to keep me busy. You know how much of a handful Nye is."

"That he is. But if you ever need me..."

"I have your number."

"You better use it, even if you don't need me."

"You can count on it, Lady Arrow."

Alex wandered down the street with Isobel at his side. Zac leaned against the outside of the building and nodded for them to keep going.

"Don't let me intrude," the vampire said. "I'm waiting for Aya."

Alex shot him a grateful smile. "Thanks."

"Don't forget to call if you need anything."

"You're on speed dial." He raised a hand in farewell and Zac disappeared into the night. They rounded the corner into the laneway that'd seen so much trouble in the past week, taking the shortcut into the main part of town. They were going to the Christmas market for some sense of normalcy, *and* he wanted to buy Izzy a present.

"Remember the time when a crazy fairy kidnapped me from this very spot?" Isobel asked with a laugh.

Alex groaned. "Don't remind me."

"I'm sorry you had to... you know."

"Turn into a founding vampire?"

"Yeah, that."

"Don't be sorry. No regrets." Alex had been thinking about it for a few days and it was time to tell his sister about his plans. He had to move forwards and most importantly, Isobel had to go on living the life she wanted. He wouldn't allow her to drop everything for him. Her life was more important to him than his own, he'd already made that crystal-clear. "I want you to have my house and my things."

"No, I can't," Isobel cried. "What about you?"

"That life has ended and now I have to start a new one."

"But—"

"You'll stay here and finish your masters," Alex interrupted. "Don't feel obligated to drop everything because of me. I want all of your dreams to come true and getting your masters is your dream, Izzy. It always has been. You're the next Indiana Jones, the female one, at least."

His joke fell on deaf ears. "What about your dreams, Alex?"

"My dreams have changed and I'm okay with it. I really am."

Isobel let out a shaky sigh like she was holding back tears.

"Izzy," he said, holding her shoulders so she'd look at him. "This won't be the last time you see me. I didn't die or anything; I was reborn into something else. I intend to stick around for a very long time. I hope one day I will see you get married and have children. I hope I get to see them grow up and have their own. Times that by like a billion, and you have my life's purpose. I will protect this family with my immortality and strength until the day the world comes to an end. I swear it on my life."

Isobel couldn't hold her tears in anymore and they spilled down her cheeks. "I love you, Alex. *Always.*"

He pulled his big sister into his arms and held her tight. "For eternity."

EPILOGUE

Zac shielded his eyes against the warm L.A. sun and scanned the lawn in front of him.

It seemed to be semester break in this part of the world and only a few students hung around the campus of UCLA, maybe because they were from here or didn't have much to go back to. After so long in the dead of winter in the UK, the temperature change seemed like a time warp.

His gaze fell onto a familiar sight and a smile pulled at his lips. Leaning against a tree, he watched his little brother Sam and the ever-adorable Liz, across the lawn and wondered how long it would take for his presence to be noticed. They were sitting in the grass, Liz surrounded with books while Sam tried to distract her with a long piece of grass in his fingers. He ticked her cheek with it every so often, making her laugh and swat him away.

They looked happy... *carefree*. Just as he'd hoped.

When Sam finally looked up, he knew his brother had sensed someone was watching them. He frowned as he looked around, his gaze finally settling on the shadowy form of his big brother. He shot to his feet, Liz scolding him when the books scattered.

Zac grinned lopsidedly and walked across the lawn towards them. As Sam came to meet him, he threw his arms around his little brother and thumped him on the back.

"Zac." He sounded relieved.

"Little brother."

Sam drew back and looked him over. "I didn't know if I'd ever see you again. At least, not in this decade. How are you?"

Zac knew exactly what he meant and grinned. "Better than ever."

"Aya?"

He gestured behind him where the Celestine sat on a bench watching their reunion, sticking out like a sore thumb in her black clothes and combat boots. She raised a hand in greeting and Sam shook his head.

"You guys finally worked it out?" he asked.

"Not without some melodrama." He threw an arm around Sam's shoulder and they walked towards Liz, laughing.

"There's always melodrama with you. Where have you been?"

"Brother," Zac said, shaking his head, "have I got a story to tell you."

"You've got a story? Wait until you hear about what Liz and I have been doing."

Liz was in Zac's arms a moment later. "Never do that again," she cried.

"Do what?" he asked, stifling a grin.

She slapped him on the arm. "Disappear and never call."

"I knew you had a thing for me."

"Zac!" she shrieked.

"You're making me jealous," Aya said, appearing at Zac's side.

"I've only got eyes for you," he said, pulling the hybrid close and sunk down onto the grass.

Aya was at his side and his brother and sister before him, and after all this time, Zac realised it was the thing he'd been searching for all along. His family had always been here waiting for him... he just had to have the courage to find them.

Zac was twenty-three when he died.

But he was one hundred and seventy before he started living.

YOUNG BLOOD
A Witch Hunter Saga Novella

The day **Liz Evans** went for a run in the forest, she didn't expect to die.

She didn't expect to turn into a vampire, either.

Her world is turned upside down in an instant, and her dreams of college and falling in love have gone right out of the window. Now all she can think about is blood.

But with a little help from her vampire boyfriend Sam and his brother Zac—the guy she's definitely not meant to have feelings for—her life is able to go back to normal. Well, as normal as being a vampire can be.

When Liz can finally cope with her new reality, she wants answers, knowing she may never find them.

Until she does.

Young Blood *is a* **Witch Hunter Saga** *story that is part prequel, part companion novella.*

Spoiler alert *for the first three books of the series!*

Young Blood is OUT NOW!

chaos...*without losing everything to a bunch of blood-thirsty witches.*

The Unhallowed is OUT NOW!

OTHER BOOKS IN

THE WITCH HUNTER SAGA

series is complete!

Enter a world full of supernatural creatures, ancient curses and love that stretches over hundreds and thousands of years. You've never seen vampires and witches like this before...

The Witch Hunter #1

The Return #2

The Shadow's Son #3

The Awakening #4

Young Blood #4.5

The Unhallowed #5

The Keeping Place #6

ABOUT NICOLE

Nicole R. Taylor is an Australian Urban Fantasy author.

She lives in the western suburbs of Melbourne dreaming up nail biting stories featuring sassy witches, duplicitous vampires, hunky shapeshifters, and devious monsters.

She likes chocolate, cat memes, and video games.

When she's not writing, she likes to think of what she's writing next.

Follow Nicole Online:

Website: www.nicolertaylorwrites.com
Facebook: facebook.com/nrtaylorwrites
Newsletter: www.nicolertaylorwrites.com/newsletter
Email: nicole.this.is@gmail.com

THE CELESTINES AND THE FIVE FOUNDING WITCHES

The five founding witches were gifted their powers from the last five Celestine adults. The last children were Aeriaya and her brother, Aydrenn (finally named in *The Awakening*).

Aya's parents gifted the element of ether and the element of earth.

The remaining Celestines gifted air, fire, and water onto three other humans before passing to the other side.

The Celestine Syriah gifted the essence of fire unto the witch Katrin.

The Celestine Cerydrn gifted the essence of air unto the witch Lizbeth.

The Celestine Firaya gifted the essence of water

unto the witch Yolande.

The Celestine Dydrenn gifted the essence of earth unto the witch Jorgen.

The Celestine Ayasti gifted the essence of ether unto the witch Ismena.

AYA

When Aya went back to her home in the field of white flowers, it was her mother's power that allowed a fragment of their souls to remain to farewell her.

Ayasti had an affinity with the ether, the other side, and was able to do this as a gift to show her daughter that it wasn't her fault for being taken.

When it came to her power, Aya took after her father. She had the ability to move the earth (as displayed in *The Shadow's Son*).

When she was imprisoned by Katrin and the Romans, her family never came to free her because, after granting their power to the Five, they didn't have the strength. If they had faced Katrin, they would've lost everything. Aya never understood this and never got the chance to find out, but she forgave them anyway.

MORGAN

After Zac left Morgan at the docks in Calais in 1944, she returned to complete her work with the French

Resistance. She was responsible for saving hundreds of lives during WWII.

When she turned up in Ashburton, Louisiana, looking for Zac in *The Return*, she was telling the truth. She did hear rumours about a massacred werewolf pack and that's what piqued her curiosity. She'd come to America with thoughts of the soldier she found in a ditch by the side of a dark road outside of Paris in the nineteen forties (Zac), otherwise known as 'the one who got away'.

Her code name in the Resistance, which she never told him or anyone else, was Banshee.

THE SIX

In *The Awakening*, we heard everyone's stories—Nye, Rix, Maddox, and Pyke. But we never heard from Rob or Holly, who weren't around very long anyway.

Rob was a new vampire who replaced an earlier member, Will, who was cut in half with a scythe by a rouge vampire. He wasn't the same Will who accidentally turned Morgan (as told in *The Return*). Rob was a cage fighter who Maddox met at the underground ring mentioned in *The Awakening*.

Holly was a prostitute in eighteenth century London. One of her clients was a vampire who wanted to possess her, so he turned her. It wasn't until a hundred years later that she joined the Six on Regulus' bequest. Much of her life before is a mystery, as she never spoke of it to anyone.

AOIFE

Aoife was born in the stars and was given the Celestine name Anorel.

She was the daughter of one of the most powerful Celestines who came to Earth, and during the end days of the war with the Tuatha Fae, she was offered as a bride to the Tuatha king, Lir, as a peace offering. The terms were agreed to and the pair married soon after. She was given the Tuatha name, Aoife, as a part of the ceremony.

Aoife's fate is ultimately unknown, but it is thought that either Lir exacted his revenge after he realised her betrayal or Isolde killed her when the Celestine tried to end her insane hybrid creations. Katrin the Betrayer claimed it was the latter, but no one knows for sure which of the two really happened.

TRISTAN NA TRI TOR

Tristan (his name is old Irish for Tristan of the Three Towers), was the son of a lowly Irish Lord. He was sent to London at a young age to squire for a knight who later went in to found the Knights Templar in the mid to late 1100s.

There, Tristan took a wife (Rose) and had a

daughter (Rhiannon) with her. Unknown to him, his wife died while he was away fighting the Fourth Crusade (where he was when he was turned underneath the city of Constantinople—what is now known as Istanbul, Turkey). His daughter lived and married into a merchant family and lived a long life believing her father had died a hero.

The castle outside of Dublin that Regulus took Gabby to in *The Awakening* was Tristan's ancestral home.

THE ORIGINAL WITCH - ISOLDE

In *The Awakening*, Aed spoke briefly about the witch who created him and his sisters. Her name was Isolde.

Isolde was Aoife's human handmaiden given to her by the Tuatha. They developed a strong relationship and thus, the Celestine trusted her enough to conspire, and together, they created the first human witch. But Aoife didn't understand the magic she was using, and as a result, Isolde was driven mad from the potent Celestine blood used in the ritual.

Isolde created the Tuatha-hybrids as instructed by Aoife, but they realised too late that her instability had been passed to them.

After hunting down and binding the Children of Lir, Aoife attempted to kill Isolde, to correct her terrible mistake, but the witch escaped, never to be seen again... until she founded the Coven.